dark seduction

BOOK TWO

VAMPIRE ROYALS OF NEW YORK

CHAPTER ONE

Dorian Redthorne was on fire.

His blood.

His bones.

His fucking soul.

The woman's betrayal burned through all of it, carving a path of devastation that left him hollow and raw, no matter how hard he tried to outrun it.

Manhattan quickly blurred into Harlem, into the Bronx, into the northern suburbs, finally giving way to the lush autumn woods along the Hudson River.

Still, Dorian didn't stop.

If he stopped, he would remember. And if he remembered, the flames inside him would abate, and the darkness —so near he could feel its cold breath on the back of his neck—would swallow him whole.

So, Dorian ran, a pale streak against the black night,

until he was so far removed from civilization, no human would cross his path or taste the pain of his vengeance.

As far as he was concerned, only *one* human deserved that now, and he had no intention of seeing her again. Not tonight. Not ever.

The flames burned hotter inside.

Dorian pushed harder, desperate to leave his reckless mistakes behind.

Vampires weren't meant to blur such great distances over a short time, but tonight, he had energy to spare. Aside from the fact that his heart had nearly been liquified—first, by Duchanes and his demon pet, and later, by the traitor formerly known as Charlotte—Dorian had never felt better. The magical tattoos on his forearms, so faint they'd all but vanished, now shone a deep, inky black, just as they had when he'd received them centuries ago.

It was the blood.

The *traitor's* blood, he reminded himself. It fueled his body as effectively as her lies fueled his rage, and by the time he'd burned through enough of both to tire out, he found himself upstate, deep in the lonely woods beyond Ravenswood Manor.

Certain he'd left humanity behind, Dorian finally stopped to take stock, leaning against a birch tree for support as the world came back into focus. It left him unsettled, his stomach rolling, his head throbbing. When he took a deep breath of mountain air, his lungs burned.

He hated that he could still taste her blood.

Hated that he still wanted more.

Hated that he still wanted *her*.

It hit him again, all at once.

Lies. All of it. Every word out of her mouth. Her smile, her laughter, her breathy moans, the way she'd cried out for him as he fucked her into beautiful oblivion. It was all part of her carefully constructed web, meant to ensnare him from the very start, all in service to her master plan.

And what *was* the plan, he wondered? Liquidate his art estate? Was it that simple?

Or was she after a bigger prize?

Tucked into his waistband, the notes and floor plans he'd found under her bed burned into his skin. Not for the first time, he wondered if she was working for his enemies. Duchanes, Chernikov, any number of foes seeking information that could weaken the Redthornes' royal standing... There were almost too many to count.

Was *this* what she'd tried to apologize for? Weak and fading in his arms, sputtering out her final confession before death claimed her?

If you find... Forgive me... I didn't...

Her words floated through his mind, twisting him up inside. He'd drained her to within an inch of her life, yet *she* was the one apologizing...

No. Guilt clawed at the doors of his heart, but Dorian refused to grant it entry. Never mind his vow to protect her. To keep her from harm.

Her treachery negated all of it.

How could he have been so blind? So willfully ignorant?

He glared down at his cock as if the damn thing might

have a ready explanation, but that only served to deepen his depression.

Last night, that cock had been buried between her thighs, in her hands, in her soft, wet mouth. And for those brief moments, when all else faded away and there was only Dorian and the passionate, beautiful, insatiable woman in his bed, he'd almost felt…

Bloody hell.

He squeezed his eyes shut as the searing pain scored his chest anew. It didn't matter what he'd felt. Didn't matter that he'd wanted to die when Duchanes put his filthy hands upon her. Didn't matter that she'd saved his life, risking her own by offering the vein. Didn't matter that the taste of her blood had left him drunk and euphoric, the memory stirring his cock to life again even now.

Dizzy with rage and ruin, hands trembling with the sudden itch to rend some poor living creature in two, Dorian fell to the ground like a beast. Frantically, he tore at the earth, fingers plowing through the mud and the stone and the brittle bones of the dead, as if he could somehow dig his own grave and bury his miserable heart.

He dug until he hit water, until his back ached, until his fingers bled.

Still, the pain did not abate.

A scream of fury boiled up inside him, but when he opened his mouth to curse her very name, he couldn't bring himself to say the words.

Charlotte D'Amico…

The taste of it so close to his lips brought her beautiful

face to his mind, and deep in the dark cavern of his soul, the devil rattled his chains.

It wanted out.

It wanted to destroy.

It wanted to consume.

And for the first time in forty-nine years, one month, and twenty-four days, Dorian was ready to set that monster free.

He rose to his feet, blood dripping from his fingertips, panting like a ghoul as he scented the air for prey.

Fuck. Kill. Feed.

The mantra hammered through his skull in time with his heartbeat.

Fuck. Kill. Feed.

Some dim, faraway part of him knew it was wrong, knew he had to fight it, knew he couldn't lose control.

Fuck. Kill. Feed.

But that part of him—the human part—cowered in the shadows as the devil gathered strength.

Fuck. Kill. Feed. Fuck kill feed fuck kill feed fuck kill fe—

The snap of a twig, the whisper of the night breeze through the pines, and a new scent reached his awareness, wild and musky. Dorian spun on his heel, hackles raised.

Wolves.

The shadows came alive with them—nearly a dozen. They surrounded him, growling and snapping, closing ranks until they'd penned him in completely.

He tried to blur out, but his movements were slow and uncoordinated, the long-distance travel and emotional turmoil finally catching up with him. He stumbled and swayed, and the wolves descended, knocking him onto his back.

Dorian landed a good kick to a soft snout, but the favor was returned with a sharp bite around his ankle, another piercing his shoulder. Pain sizzled through his skin, burning up his leg and down his arm, finally unleashing the desperate howl he'd been holding back all night.

Dorian tried to kick again, but he had nothing left. No fight. No wits. He was a shell with a blackened heart, his final words a hoarse scream.

The wolves clamped down harder, sending twin bursts of agony through his limbs.

He was about to close his eyes and welcome his end when a man crept out from the dark woods, his nude flesh streaked with mud, leaves and sticks tangled in his matted hair.

"Ease off, boys," the man said. "He ain't one of 'em."

The wolves retreated—all but the one clamped around his ankle. A pup, Dorian realized. Warm blood leaked from the fresh wound in his shoulder, soaking the earth.

"Long way from the city, nightwalker." The man crouched down beside Dorian's prone form and extended a hand, unperturbed by his own nudity on the chilly autumn night. "Thought you old-ass vamps knew better than to provoke a wolf on his home turf."

Dorian took the offered hand and let the man haul him to his feet. He swayed again, and the wolf attached to his ankle bit down harder.

"And I thought you stopped taking in stray dogs in the eighties," Dorian said. "Yet here we are."

A collective growl rumbled through the pack, but the man fisted Dorian's hair and gave his head a playful shake, a grin splitting his mud-streaked face. "God *damn*, it's good to see you, Red."

Through the pain, the rage, the sheer exhaustion, Dorian smiled, his chest filling with an old, familiar warmth.

"You as well, Cole. Now, if it's not too much trouble…" He gestured at the ferocious little mutt still attached to his ankle. "Would you kindly remove this *fucking* beast from my person? Or would you rather I tear his head off and feed it to the others while you watch?"

CHAPTER TWO

"Rogue vampires?" Dorian asked. "In *these* woods?"

"Been trackin' the fuckers all week." Cole handed him a mason jar filled with something he'd poured from a dusty brown jug. "They keep slippin' the traps."

Sitting at a dingy linoleum table in Cole's backwoods kitchen, an icepack on his shoulder and the wounded ankle bandaged and propped up on a chair, Dorian sipped the moonshine. He was fairly certain it would eat through his stomach lining—the stuff could probably strip the paint from his cars—but at least the burn distracted him from the blistering pain of his wounds.

Contrary to popular myth, the wolf bites wouldn't kill him. But they *would* take a few days to heal, leaving him to suffer through every excruciating moment.

Dorian glanced out the kitchen window, searching for the wolf who'd bit him. A few patrolled the perimeter, the rest of them still scouring the woods for the rogues. The sight of so many wolves in one place was beyond unusual these days, especially at Cole's place.

He'd always preferred his own company to the complex, often violent dynamics of pack life. It was something he and Dorian had in common.

"And your new friends?" Dorian asked. "How did they get involved in your little hunt?"

Cole took the chair across from him and set the jug of moonshine on the table, pushing aside a pile of junk—pizza boxes, a palette sticky with acrylic paints, an ashtray overflowing with cigarette butts, half-spent joint balanced on the rim.

Dorian tried to recall the last time he'd seen the man—five years ago, maybe six. There was a time—after everything had gone to shit and Dorian's brothers had left New York—when they'd hike the woods together almost every weekend, often with Aiden in tow. But Cole had become even more reclusive than Dorian in recent years, often losing himself in his next masterpiece for weeks or months at a time.

Dorian had missed him, he realized now. Cole's land truly was a favorite place, just like he'd told Charlotte. Like so many things in his life, it reminded him of simpler times.

Perhaps that's why he kept returning, long after his old friend had retreated.

Perhaps he was searching for that elusive connection to brighter memories, just as Charlotte sought her father through their shared love of art.

Charlotte…

Dorian took another sip of his drink, obliterating thoughts of the traitor before they sank their claws in any deeper.

"Called in a few favors," Cole said now. "They're helping me with the search. Last thing I need is a bunch of rogue killers making themselves at home on my property."

"How many are you tracking?"

"A dozen, give or take. Hard to tell with all the mud." Cole took a long pull from his drink, then shook his head. "All month, things ain't been right. I could feel it, Red. The woods, the air... I'd go out there to paint, and I'd get them chills on the back of my neck, like someone was watching me."

Dorian shifted in his chair, holding back a shiver that had nothing to do with the ice on his shoulder.

"Few days back," Cole said, "the animal carcasses started turning up. Four deer so far, and two black bear cubs, along with a shit ton of raccoons and rodents. One look, and I knew exactly what we were dealin' with."

"How so?"

"Too brutal to be a natural predator, but too..." He stared into his glass, searching for the word. "Too *specific* to be human hunters."

"Specific?"

"Throats torn clear out. Blood drained. No signs of struggle though, thank fuck. I doubt those animals suffered —it happened too fast."

Dorian took a deep breath of cigarette-and-marijuana-tinged air, his mind churning. He couldn't imagine why any vampire would do such a thing. Animal blood didn't sustain them, and most vampires with a taste for mutilation preferred human victims.

"It doesn't add up," Dorian said. "If not for the blood, I'd say we were dealing with something else."

"Ain't just the blood." Cole fished something from the pocket of his flannel and tossed it on the table.

Fangs. They scattered between them like dice, jagged and broken, stained with blood and rot.

Dread pooled in Dorian's stomach. Vampires didn't lose their fangs.

But the wraiths did—those vile, inhuman creatures without access to human blood, bound to misery in the dark, dank places of the world.

Dorian selected one of the sharp, yellowed bones from the table, turning it over against his palm. "There haven't been any reported sightings of the grays in decades."

Grays. A mildly pleasant euphemism for monsters that were anything but.

"Near as I can tell, they're coming from up north. Probably a cluster of 'em holed up somewhere in the Adirondacks." Cole scratched his scruffy beard, his brow creasing. "Any idea what would bring 'em down our way? Can't imagine they're here to pay respects to the late king."

"Nor to swear fealty to the new one."

"I'm bettin' not, your *highness*." Cole grinned, a moment of levity that brightened the dark night. "Gotta admit, I didn't think the ol' man would *ever* kick off."

"No one was more surprised than I, believe me."

"I'd say sorry, but I know how you felt about him."

Dorian appreciated the man's honesty. "The world is certainly a better place without Augustus Redthorne."

"Can't imagine it's easy though, all your brothers being back." Cole dug through the junk on the table for a lighter, then plucked the half-spent joint from the ashtray, sparking it up and taking a deep drag. "How you holdin' up?"

Dorian laughed. "I see your self-imposed isolation hasn't prevented you from keeping up on the latest vampire gossip."

"Matter of survival. Gotta know who the players are." He offered the joint, but Dorian declined, and Cole took another hit, the pungent smoke quickly overtaking the tiny kitchen. "Besides, if this bullshit with the rogues proves anything? Ain't no place secluded enough to outrun fate. Not for us."

"You think being stalked by grays is our fate?"

"I'm just sayin'... The human world? That's exactly what it is. The *human* world. We can play in their sandbox, Red, but it won't ever be ours. *Our* world is..." He shook his head and scooped up the teeth, fisting them tight. "Blood and death, brother. Blood and death."

Cole had always been prone to philosophical tangents when he smoked, but tonight's declaration felt particularly ominous.

Blood and death, brother. Blood and death.

He was right. That *was* their world. And Dorian, in the blind, selfish pursuit of his own desires, had dragged an innocent woman right into the thick of it, putting her directly in the path of Renault Duchanes and his demon mercenaries...

She's not bloody innocent, you knob.

"Anyway," Cole said, "I figure something must've changed up north, right? Something messed with their home environment. Either that, or someone led them here on purpose. But who the fuck would do *that*?"

"Renault Duchanes." The name was out of Dorian's mouth before he could even think it through, but the moment he said it out loud, he knew it was true. "House Duchanes is plotting against the crown. I turned down their alliance after my father's death, and after that, everything just... fell apart."

Dorian told him the story—the spurned offers for the Duchanes witch and the blood donors, the attacks on Charlotte, the string of threats in Dorian's penthouse. So much had happened, it was hard to believe it'd only been a few hours since he'd left Charlotte's bedside.

Since he'd nearly drained her dry.

Since she'd nearly died in his arms.

Since he'd discovered her betrayal.

"I heard some of the vamps got pretty riled up after your old man died," Cole said, "but I had no idea shit hit the fan so hard. So Duchanes has demons in his back pocket, and now you're saying the grays are his too?"

"Duchanes is desperate for power, Cole. I put nothing past him, no matter how dangerous or despicable."

"That's what worries me." Cole stamped out the last of his joint and refilled their mason jars. "We don't even know how many we're dealing with here, Red. If these fuckers get out of the woods, they'll—"

Dorian held up a hand to silence him. *That* was one picture Cole *didn't* have to paint—it shone in vivid, technicolor detail in Dorian's mind.

It was hard enough for so-called "civilized" vampires to control their urges. The grays had *zero* control—they operated purely on instinct, and that instinct pushed them to consume. It was just as he'd told Charlotte: they could hunt, they could fuck, and they could feed, and that's exactly what they did, until they burned up in the sunlight or rotted from starvation.

If they escaped the woods and reached a populated area, no one would be safe. The creatures would destroy everyone in their path, leaving no witnesses alive. And if by chance a single human escaped to tell the tale, no one would believe him anyway—it was too outlandish, even for the most open-minded among them.

By the time humans realized what they were dealing with, scores of innocents would be dead.

It was a terrible, brutal bit of chaos—and the perfect way to slaughter humans without getting one's hands dirty.

Duchanes' name was written all over it in blazing neon letters. For all Dorian knew, the pathetic vampire had a safe house nearby and was presently holed up inside with whatever sycophants he'd gathered, licking his wounds from the earlier confrontation and plotting his next attack.

"So tell me about the woman," Cole said. "I assume

she's the reason the boys found you vampin' out in my woods tonight."

Dorian's silence confirmed it.

"Do I need to stage an intervention?" Cole asked. "Thought you were done with that psycho vampire shit."

"I was. I *am*." Dorian swirled the moonshine in his glass, his chest burning with a mix of leftover rage at Charlotte, the shame of nearly losing control tonight, and the swill he'd been drinking for the last hour. "I was just… blowing off a little steam."

"Right. And this little steam… She got a name?"

When Dorian didn't answer, Cole said, "She's the one you brought out here the other day, right?"

Heat rose in Dorian's chest at the memory. Charlotte, twirling like a fallen leaf in the wind. Gasping at the beauty of the landscape. Peppering him with lightning-round questions on vampire origins. Laughing as she tested the limits of his Ferrari as well as his patience.

"I wasn't aware you'd been watching us," he said.

"Peepin' Tom ain't my style." Cole laughed. "But the scent? No hiding that, my friend. Wolves have an even stronger sense of smell than bloodsuckers. I'm surprised you two didn't bang right there on my rocks."

"The thought *had* crossed my mind."

"Just a thought, huh?"

Dorian shook his head, intending to steer Cole onto some other topic—*any* other topic. But when Cole rolled a fresh joint and offered Dorian the first hit, something inside him broke loose. This time, he took Cole up on the offer, sucking in a deep drag, letting the pungent smoke work its way into his system.

And then, the dam burst.

Before Dorian could shut himself up, the whole story spilled out. How he and Charlotte had met, the instant chemistry between them, the intrigue, the way her devious smile had shone a light on the darkest places inside him.

And the shameful admission that he still bloody *yearned* for her, even now.

"A beautiful woman plotting against a ruthless, blood-thirsty vampire king?" Cole said when Dorian had finally reached the end of the story. "Sounds like the start to a bad soap opera."

Dorian rolled his eyes. "Yes, my reputation precedes me."

"And she's still alive because...?"

He tightened his grip on the drink and met Cole's gaze through the smoke, attempting to channel some of that inner ruthlessness. "Because I've yet to decide the precise manner in which I'll stamp the light from her eyes."

Cole scratched his beard, trying not quite hard enough to hide a smirk. "I see."

"You see *nothing*," Dorian snapped.

"If you say so, Red."

"Charlotte D'Amico is a liar and a thief, and that's putting it kindly." Dorian lifted a hand, counting down on his fingers. "She's been playing me from the start. She's got connections to at least one powerful demon crime syndicate —which, by the way, she refuses to discuss. She's oddly fixated on two pieces of art from my collection—which, by the way, she *also* refuses to discuss. She's manipulative, self-ish, infuriating, and… and bloody hell, Cole. I wish I'd never met her."

"Yeah, I can see that."

"Sarcasm? Really? I bear my soul, and that's the sage advice you have to offer?"

"Sage advice?" Cole shook his head, still smirking. "Okay, here's the thing. Wolves? We mate for life. Takes a long time to find the one, but when we do, we fucking *know* it. And there's nothing we won't do for our mate, no matter how badly she fucks up. I mean *nothing*, brother."

"I'm not a wolf."

"And I'm still single, but that's not the point."

"Have you not heard a word I've said? She's after my art, Cole. Left to her own devices, the woman would probably steal the very silverware from the dinner table. In fact, I should check my collection. For all I know, she pocketed her fork after brunch the other day."

Cole laughed, his eyes like half-moons in the smoky haze. "If you think this is about your art—or your damn silverware, for that matter—you're even blinder than you are stoned."

"She's connected to Alexei Rogozin, for fuck's sake!"

"Connected how, exactly?"

Dorian didn't have an answer for that—not for lack of trying. Charlotte had completely shut down at the mention of the demon's name. Before they could revisit the conversation, Duchanes attacked, and they'd nearly died.

Dorian, because of Duchanes and the demon.

Charlotte, because of Dorian.

A surge of guilt rose inside him, but he chased it away with another swig of moonshine.

"I know you nightwalkers don't like to be tied down," Cole continued. "I get it. Keep your options open for the long, immortal slog. But I'll tell you what, Red. That look in your eyes?" He tilted his glass in Dorian's direction. "That's not the look of a man out for a few quick fucks. That's the look of a man who—"

"Whatever you're about to presume about my present state of affairs, about what I feel, about whom and how frequently I choose to *fuck*, allow me to disabuse you of—"

Dorian's cell buzzed, cutting him off.

Aiden.

Keeping his eyes locked on Cole's irritating, know-it-all smirk, he took the call, hoping his friend had some good news about Charlotte's sister Sasha.

"Aiden. Have you—"

"Where the bloody hell *are* you?" Aiden demanded. "For fuck's sake, Dori. Your brothers said you took off without even—"

"I'm upstate. Have you found the girl?"

"What are you doing up—"

"*Sasha*," Dorian said. "Is she with you?"

"Not yet. I've been to every club and coffee shop and dreadful hipster bar in Brooklyn too—no trace."

"Keep looking. She's not safe with Duchanes on the loose."

"And what of Charlotte?"

Across the table, Cole snickered.

"*Charlotte*," Dorian bit out, tossing one of the broken fangs at Cole, "is a grown woman. She can look after herself —believe me."

"Against an unhinged vampire like Duchanes? And a band of merry demon dickheads we've got no idea how to track? Have you gone bloody mad?"

"Yes, Aiden. As a matter of fact, I *have* gone bloody mad. So, unless you're hungry for a taste of my wrath, I suggest you... you simply... *fuck*." Dorian's words tangled, the marijuana slowing his thoughts, turning his tongue heavy and thick. He let out a deep sigh, scrubbing a hand over his face. "I'm... sorry. You're right. The situation is... less than ideal."

It was a long moment before Aiden spoke again.

"What happened?" he finally asked Dorian. "Why did you leave Manhattan? I thought she was under your protection."

"She... is," Dorian said, realizing it was still true.

Fucking hell, woman. What have you done to me?

"Has there been any change in her condition?" Dorian asked softly.

"According to Colin, she's resting comfortably, on the road to a full recovery. They sent Marlys home."

Dorian let out a breath of relief, but the feeling didn't last long.

In all his personal suffering over Charlotte, he'd almost forgotten about the damn demons. He had no idea which clan Duchanes' minion belonged to, nor the rabble he'd scented en route before he leaped out of that window with Charlotte.

He imagined his Tribeca penthouse was thoroughly trashed.

Fresh worry tightened his chest, cutting through the numbing haze of the marijuana. Had tonight's attack truly been an attempted payback for the slights against House Duchanes? Or were the overly ambitious vampire and his demon fuckwits searching for something else?

And why the fuck had the mention of Rogozin's name sent Charlotte into such a cold, impenetrable state of fear?

The sting of her betrayal tore through him anew, but Cole was right—it wasn't about the artwork or the silver. Dorian didn't know what she was really after, but something told him it went far beyond his collection.

Artwork could be bought and sold, stolen, auctioned off to the highest bidder... But so could secrets.

And in Dorian's experience, secrets were *far* more valuable.

There were secrets lurking in the crypts of Ravenswood —secrets that could destroy not just the Redthorne line, but every member of every supernatural race in existence.

There were secrets Dorian's father had shared with Nikolai Chernikov—secrets the demon lord had not-so-subtly wielded as threats.

There were secrets Charlotte had locked away—secrets Dorian suspected tied back to his enemies, whether Charlotte herself realized it or not.

Dorian closed his eyes, trying to slow the progression of his thoughts.

It didn't matter that he never wanted to see her treacherous, beautiful face again.

She was a loose end—one the vampire king could not allow to unravel.

"Keep looking for the girl," Dorian finally said. "I want Colin back at Ravenswood. I'll have Malcolm and Gabriel keep an eye on Charlotte's building."

"And the demons?"

"I'll take care of it."

"Are you certain?"

"Not in the slightest."

Aiden sighed, his concern weighing heavy on Dorian's conscience. "You're exhausted, Dori. You need to rest."

"And I will. In my next life."

With a promise to return to Ravenswood soon, he disconnected from Aiden, then met Cole's gaze again. Outside, the mournful call of a lone wolf echoed across the forest, raising the hairs on Dorian's arms. In perfect succession, the other wolves joined in.

They'd found something.

An eerie quiet settled into the kitchen—the calm before the storm.

"We're in some shit now, ain't we," Cole said softly. It wasn't a question.

"It's not your fight."

"No, I reckon it ain't." He folded his arms across his chest and leaned back in his chair, a smile breaking across his face. "But it *is* my woods, my cabin, my hooch, and my weed. What's one more IOU between friends?"

Dorian gave a slight bow of his head, more grateful to the wolf shifter than he could express. Thumbing through the contacts on his phone, he said, "There's an idiom in the human sandbox, Cole. Something about hornets' nests and kicking them?"

"Then we best get you some boots, brother. Wouldn't want you to scuff up those thousand-dollar, pretty-boy Italian shoes."

Dorian laughed—the last one, he imagined, for a long while.

Then he hit the call button and brought the phone to his ear, the last remnants of a pretty nice buzz leaving him.

"Commissioner? Dorian Redthorne here. I'm sorry to disturb you at this hour, but it's come to my attention that a nightclub on St. Mark's Place is conducting illegal activities in our fair city. Drugs, human trafficking, underage drinking—quite terrible, really. I'm certain you'll find a *thoroughly* invasive investigation and an extended shutdown warranted. Bloodbath—yes, that's the one. Thanks so much. My best to Gina and the kids."

Cole shook his head and grinned. "You slippery sonofabitch."

"It pays to have friends in high places."

Cole glanced at the phone, eyeing the name of the next contact Dorian pulled up. "And low ones, I see."

"I like to keep a full spectrum on hand." At that, Dorian hit the call button, knowing the man on the other end wouldn't be quite as accommodating as his friend in law enforcement.

As expected, the call went straight to voicemail.

"Meet me at Luna del Mar at sunrise," he demanded, skipping the pleasantries. "And *comrade*? Don't be late."

CHAPTER THREE

"Dorian, look out!"

Charley struggled against the nightmare's deadly grip, tossing herself clear out of bed. The impact jolted her awake, scattering the last of the dream-monsters from view.

Tangled in her sheets, she sat up on the floor and leaned back against the nightstand, waiting for the room to stop spinning. Her head pounded, her mouth was full of cotton, and the very act of running her fingers through her hair left her weak and trembling.

What the hell did I get into last night?

She closed her eyes and forced herself to focus, fishing for the memories until—one by one—they finally bobbed to the surface.

Dorian's penthouse. Midnight Marauder. A night of mind-blowing passion. Later, discussing Dorian's art contacts. Vincent Estas, the dealer. Alexei Rogozin, demonic kingpin—a man her father and Rudy had encountered when Charley was just a girl.

Charley's head spun as the rest of the memories rushed in—Duchanes yanking her from Dorian's bed and tying her to the chair, naked and vulnerable. Slicing her wrist as a taunt, knowing her screams and the scent of her blood would bring Dorian running.

The look on her vampire's face when he'd finally found her... She'd never seen anyone so terrified. Despite his own pain in the face of the demon attack, he'd fought for her.

And then, when he had nothing left to give, she fought for *him*.

She wrapped her fingers around her bandaged wrist, welcoming the memories of the bite. The pain had been tremendous, but also deeply erotic, the pleasure of his lips on her skin spreading languidly up her arm and across her chest, making her hot and wet even as the blood loss weakened her muscles.

Sharing that with him... God. Charley had never experienced anything so intimate before. At one point, with Dorian's head in her lap and her wrist pressed to his mouth, he'd glanced up and caught her gaze, his eyes full of something so raw and beautiful, Charley was almost afraid to remember it now—afraid that looking at it too closely would make it disappear.

But then it'd faded, replaced with her vampire's desperate, primal hunger, his eyes turning red as his desire for her blood demolished the last of his control.

He'd taken too much, and Charley eventually lost consciousness.

Everything that happened after that was a blur, faces and voices and scents mixing together in a thick haze: Men arguing in the other room—Dorian's brothers? The doctor with the dimples and kind eyes. An older woman cleaning Charley up, dressing her in pajamas, poking her with a needle. And then, chanting something that sounded like a spell. Dorian shouting at them from the hallway, ordering them to heal her.

And later, sweet and tender words whispered over her bedside, a kiss as soft as a prayer alighting on her skin.

Charley opened her eyes, and the images faded away.

A wave of nausea rolled through her stomach, and she scrambled to her feet, barely making it to the bathroom before she retched. She was faint and dizzy, the headache making every movement an act of self-torture. As she washed her face and rinsed out her mouth, the reflection staring back from the mirror looked haunted and ill, her eyes ringed with dark circles, her hair wild.

Her wrist throbbed, but even the deep, erotic bite from her vampire felt like a memory now. She pulled off the bandage; her skin was unmarred.

Had she imagined the whole damn thing?

She needed to talk to Dorian. Why wasn't he there?

Worry tugged on her heart as another memory surfaced —Dorian, begging her not to die. Blaming himself for drinking too much blood, his eyes full of anguish and fear.

A woman imploring him in the hallway. *You've done enough, Dorian Redthorne...*

No. Charley needed to talk to him. Now.

With slow, awkward movements, she searched her bedroom for the phone, but it wasn't there. It was probably still at Dorian's place in Tribeca. For all she knew, it'd fallen into the hands of Duchanes and the demon.

Without her phone, she couldn't get in touch with Dorian. She couldn't even check on her sister. Sasha had planned to stay at Darcy's all weekend, but what if she had an emergency? What if Duchanes had somehow tracked her down?

What if Duchanes had come back for Dorian or his brothers?

The tug of worry on her heart turned into full-blown panic.

Ignoring her throbbing head, Charley slipped into her bathrobe, then put one shaky foot in front of the other and exited the bedroom.

Almost immediately, she sensed it—something was off.

The roses, she realized. The smell had been so sweet and overpowering, yet now, she could barely detect them. All she could smell now was bacon. *Burned* bacon.

Someone was in the kitchen. Not Dorian, as she'd foolishly hoped. Someone graceless and crass, cursing up a storm as he rifled through the cupboards, silverware and dishes clanging, breakfast burning on the stove.

As she reached the end of the hallway, her heart dropped into her stomach.

The roses were gone. Every last one of them, erased as if they'd never even been there at all.

And there, standing at the stove with a towel draped over his shoulder, scraping charred bacon from the cast iron skillet, was the man responsible for ruining her day before it'd even begun.

"Uncle Rudy?" Charley's voice cracked, her throat raw.

Rudy glanced at her over his shoulder and grinned—a warm, welcoming smile for his favorite niece.

Right.

Charley didn't miss the warning flickering behind it.

"Good morning," he said, taking in her disheveled appearance. "You look… hungry."

"What happened to my roses?"

"I had the doorman remove them." He clucked his tongue. "Honestly, Charlotte. They were starting to rot."

Tears stung her eyes, the headache behind them roaring into five-alarm migraine territory.

"What are you doing here?" she asked, willing the tears not to fall. Rudy would never understand how much those flowers had meant to her. In his eyes, they were just one more beautiful thing he saw fit to ruin—one more way to drain the color from her life.

"Take a seat," he said, ignoring her question as well as her obvious distress. "Breakfast is almost ready."

Breakfast with him? *Like hell.*

"I'll just grab a coffee. I'm not feeling—"

"Sit *down,* Charlotte." He turned to face her, abandoning the bacon on the stove.

28

Now, instead of the spatula, he held a gun.

"Holy shit!" She backed up against the wall, holding up her hands in surrender. For all his bullshit, Rudy had *never* pulled his gun on her. "What the hell are you *doing*?"

"You and I? We're going to eat breakfast together, like a real family. We're going to have a serious conversation about the way things need to change around here. And Charlotte?" He crept toward her, his eyes sparkling with cold, hard malice. "You're going to drop that *fucking* attitude, or the next time a man sends roses, it will be for your funeral."

CHAPTER FOUR

It was unwise to confront Chernikov without the proper protections, but Marlys was unreachable and Dorian couldn't locate a backup witch on such short notice. Cole thought he should wait it out, but every minute that passed was another in which Duchanes could recover his strength and stage another gruesome attack.

Dorian had no idea what the vampire was planning—only that it likely ended with the Redthornes in a pile of smoldering ash, the city's supernatural factions suffering under the reign of a vicious moron, and Duchanes vampires running roughshod over the entire human population.

As for Charlotte…

Dorian sighed. He could only imagine what would become of the woman if Duchanes got his way. She'd survived not only the attack by his sirelings at Ravenswood, but Duchanes' own ambush last night.

With those near misses on the books, there was no way

Duchanes would let her slip away unscathed a third time. Without Dorian to protect her, she'd likely end up...

No. He refused to entertain the thoughts. Charlotte D'Amico was no longer his responsibility. She was merely a regrettable distraction—an indulgence he could no longer afford.

"This the place?" Cole asked, slowing his ancient pickup truck in front of the turnoff for Luna del Mar.

Dorian nodded and directed him to a spot at the back of the parking lot, out of sight from the main road.

The sun was just peeking up over the horizon, struggling to break through a thick blanket of clouds. The day hadn't even begun, but Dorian could already tell it was going to be wet and gray.

He should've welcomed the relief from the sun's incessant assault on his eyes, but this morning, the damp, chilly weather only darkened his mood.

Cole killed the engine and retrieved a pack of cigarettes from his shirt pocket, peering through the windshield at the café's back entrance. "I don't like dealin' with demons, Red. Smokey little fuckers always leave a bad taste in my mouth."

"I'm surprised you can taste anything at all, what with that unfortunate tobacco habit." Dorian popped open the glovebox and retrieved Cole's lighter. "Anyway, you *don't* have to deal with them—not today. Wait for me here. If I'm not out in thirty—"

"What, no dogs allowed? I put on my best flannel."

"Yes, and don't think I don't appreciate the effort."

Dorian wrenched open the door and slid out from the cab, gesturing for Cole to stay put.

When it'd become clear that Dorian was heading to the meeting with or without a witch, Cole insisted on accompanying him, leaving his wolves to deal with the two grays they'd trapped in the woods. Dorian was more than glad for the company, but he wouldn't let the man put himself directly in harm's way.

If things went south with Chernikov, he didn't want the wolf anywhere near it.

"The terms of the Accords forbid me from bringing backup without advanced warning," he explained.

"Thought they prohibited meeting without a witch too, but here you are, charging in like the bloodsuckin' Lone Ranger."

"Such is the burden of a vampire king." With a wry grin, Dorian tossed his phone to Cole. "If I don't return, someone will need to phone Aiden and my brothers with the news of my untimely demise and make arrangements for my priceless collection of scotch."

"Well, shit, brother. If I'd known you were putting me in the will, I would've come outta hiding months ago." Cole lit his cigarette and sucked in a deep drag, then exhaled a plume of smoke in Dorian's direction. "But seriously, asshole. We just got the band back together. Try not to get yourself killed."

~

"Dorian Redthorne, my old friend." Chernikov beamed at him, holding court at the same private-room table they'd shared last time, his usual array of vodka bottles lined up like little soldiers. "My sources tell me you have demon problem."

"*We* have a demon problem, Nikolai." Dorian sat down across from him, taking in the demon's appearance. Mornings didn't agree with him; his hair was unkempt, his suit wrinkled. Beneath a thin sheen of sweat, the snake tattoo around his neck looked particularly unpleasant.

"No hocus pocus today?" Chernikov glanced toward the doorway as if he expected Marlys to appear, toting her box of tricks.

"I'm trusting we can both remain civilized this morning. Do *not* make me regret that decision."

"I don't attack my friends, Dorian Redthorne. Do not make *me* regret decision, either. Coffee?" Chernikov snapped his fingers for the waitress.

Still buzzing from the inescapable rush of Charlotte's blood, Dorian wasn't interested in a caffeine hit, but he nodded anyway, figuring the mug would give him something to do with his hands. He'd only been in the demon's presence a few moments, and already the need to choke him was making his fingers twitch.

The waitress returned quickly, delivering two fresh coffees with nothing more than a smile. When she disappeared back into the main area of the café, Chernikov lowered his voice and said, "You are right. Demon problem is mutual."

Dorian gripped the mug. "I presume you heard about the attack at my residence last night?"

"They were not my guys."

"Then how did you learn of it so quickly?"

"Demon and vampire attack king. More demons follow. Gray vampires run loose upstate." He glanced at Dorian's shoulder, where a spot of blood from the earlier wolf attack soaked through his shirt. "Wolves make error in judgment."

Dorian continued to glare, but Chernikov only shrugged.

"News travels fast in this city, vampire king." He grabbed a nearly-spent bottle of vodka and dumped a healthy splash into his coffee, then offered the last of it to Dorian.

Dorian slid his mug closer, accepting the shot. "If the demons taking orders from Renault Duchanes aren't part of your organization, then whose?"

"You tell me. You must have ideas."

"I'd rather hear yours."

Of *course* Dorian had ideas—Alexei Rogozin, primarily —but he wanted to see how Chernikov would play this. The demon might claim ignorance, but if not—if he was actually willing to name names—Dorian knew the intel would be reliable.

False accusations? That's not how things worked in their world.

It wasn't *honor*, exactly, but people like Chernikov—like Dorian—didn't get where they were without adhering to some kind of code. Which was why Duchanes, for all his machinations, would never amount to anything in this city. Even if he succeeded in slaughtering Dorian's family and usurping the crown, he'd likely be overthrown by his own sycophants the first chance they got.

Such was the fate of every vampire king. Only two things could grant him a reprieve—commanding respect, or inspiring fear.

Dorian preferred the former.

His father had made a centuries-long game of the latter.

Duchanes wasn't strong or capable enough for either.

"I am not only demon in town," Chernikov said now. "The others… They've become pain in my ass—bigger pain than you know. And vampires? I thought you had them under control, yet always, they come to me. Favors for this one, for that one. It wasn't like this with Augustus."

"*Which* vampires, specifically? Duchanes?" Dorian asked, ignoring the dig about his father's superior leadership skills. "Tell me, *comrade*. Just how many favors *have* you granted the house plotting to overthrow the king?"

"I did not come here at ungodly hour to discuss my business practices." Chernikov shoved a finger in Dorian's direction. "Vampire mess is *your* problem. Your father would've handled it."

In the span of a heartbeat, Dorian grabbed the empty vodka bottle and blurred into Chernikov's space, smashing the bottle against the table and pressing the jagged end to his throat. "In case you haven't noticed, demon, I'm *not* my father."

Hellfire exploded in Chernikov's palm, and the demon

grinned, a trickle of blood leaking from the eye of his snake tattoo. "I didn't think Russian roulette was your game, bloodsucker."

The bottle cut into his flesh. Dorian held firm even as Chernikov's flames licked at his skin, hot and hungry.

"Try me," Dorian said.

Locked in a battle of wills certain to destroy them both, the men continued to glare at each other—a ridiculous competition neither could possibly win.

Finally, Chernikov backed down. With a raucous laugh, he closed his palm and extinguished the flame, and Dorian returned to his chair, pitching the broken glass into a nearby trashcan.

It was all a show, and they both knew it. But like their code, the occasional bit of dick-measuring had its place.

"You know why vampire is king and not demon?" Chernikov asked, flicking a few shards of glass from his suit jacket.

Dorian had several responses, all of which he kept to himself. "Enlighten me, Nikolai."

"Magic."

A dark chuckle escaped Dorian's lips, and he reached for his coffee, shaking his head. "It's that simple, is it?"

"Most things are that simple. We complicate them because we have human brains, and human brains like challenge. Makes us feel smart and superior, yes?" He opened a fresh bottle of vodka and poured another splash into his mug. This time, he didn't offer any to Dorian. "Your witches... They give you more power. Change your nature. Make you smart and superior."

Dorian sipped his coffee, waiting for Chernikov to circle back round to the bloody point.

"Demons? We have witches too," he continued. "Not as many, of course. Most witches find demons... unpalatable. But there are some who crave darkness. Crave chaos."

"Yes, the dark witches. A charming lot, to be sure."

"Charming, no. But powerful?" Chernikov shrugged. "Between this realm and hell, demons are always coming and going. It is dark witches who decide how many."

"They control the gateways."

"Yes. And they could open more, if price is right."

Dorian suppressed a shudder. Dark witches skirted the line, but they'd never been an outright threat. In Dorian's lifetime, they'd played their part in maintaining the balance, carefully controlling the flow of demonic entities to ensure none of the supernatural races overpowered another or became too great a threat against humans.

"Is that what you want?" Dorian asked, keeping his voice carefully neutral. "Demons, storming the gates and flooding the city streets?"

"*Nyet.* I like being big fish in small pond. Too many fish come into my pond, they get ideas about taking over—like your Mr. Duchanes. But Alexei Rogozin? He has other aspirations."

Rogozin. Just as Dorian had suspected.

Rogozin was currently number two among the greater demonic crime families, but if he could convince enough dark witches to fall in line, and they could turn up the tap on the flow of demons, and Rogozin united them all under the common cause of eradicating vampires and anyone else who got in his way…

"Many demons, many dark witches, all loyal to him," Chernikov said, confirming Dorian's fears. "This is Rogozin's perfect world order. And he's using traitor vampires to help build it."

"House Duchanes," Dorian grumbled.

"For now. But as soon as Rogozin is happy, he has no more use for Duchanes or *any* vampires."

"No, I'd imagine he doesn't."

It all made sense—everything from Duchanes attacking Chernikov's demons in Central Park the night of the Salvatore auction, to his bid for Armitage holdings, to his sirelings' attack on Charlotte at the fundraiser, to last night's brutality. Even the attempted alliance was fake—a move Dorian now realized was backed not only by the other vampires of his house, but by Rogozin's organization as well.

An organization whose leader—if Chernikov was right —wanted to wipe vampires off the map.

Rogozin was pulling all the strings.

Chernikov raised his coffee mug and gave a single nod. "So you see, this *is* mutual problem, like you say. We have common interests. Keep our city in check, keep humans from discovering us, run our separate territories in best way we see fit, keep Rogozin from making hostile takeover. Yes?"

"On all of that, we're in agreement."

"Perhaps we should make deal."

Dorian sighed. He couldn't imagine a worse idea.

Unfortunately, he couldn't imagine a better one, either. As he'd told his brothers in Charlotte's penthouse last night, his war was with Duchanes, not Chernikov. And while he didn't particularly trust the demons, he saw no reason to make an enemy of the most powerful one in the city, nor to allow him to be seduced by vampires eager to see Dorian's head on the proverbial pike.

Or Charlotte's.

The thought sobered him, despite his promises to eradicate thoughts of her from his mind.

As much as he hated to admit it, Aiden was right. Duchanes was completely unhinged. They couldn't simply leave the woman to fend for herself; even if she *did* have a connection to Rogozin, it hadn't prevented Duchanes from harming her. Dorian needed to ask Gabriel to bring her and Sasha back to Ravenswood, where they could be kept safe from further attacks.

As to her deceit... Dorian would settle on a fitting punishment later.

Right now, he needed to gather his allies—even the unsavory ones.

Especially the unsavory ones.

"And if we enter into this devil's bargain together," Dorian said, "what are you proposing?"

"I use my network to track Rogozin's activities, keep

watch on dark witches, and tell you about vampires asking for demon favors, shitting on crown."

"And in return? What is it you ask of House Redthorne this time, Nikolai?"

The demon's eyes glittered. "Two things."

"Name your price."

"I want access to Manhattan."

"Absolutely out of the question."

"My territory is—what is saying?" He puffed out his cheeks and patted his midsection. "Busting at seams."

"Manhattan is vampire territory. If I allow your demons access, we risk unsettling a very delicate balance—one that could have the rest of the factions revolting."

"You are clever and powerful, vampire king. I'm confident you can find way to make this happen. And if not?" Chernikov shrugged. "Then deal is off, and we watch Alexei Rogozin and his puppet Renault Duchanes take over our city, and delicate balance explodes like nuclear missile."

Dorian hated being outmaneuvered, but at the moment, he was dangerously low on bargaining chips, and Chernikov was right. Left unchecked, Rogozin could do a *lot* more damage than a few Chernikov demons setting up shop in Manhattan.

"I'll grant you limited access for a trial period of one month," Dorian finally said. "Weekends only. Your men will maintain the utmost discretion, avoid poaching anyone under the age of thirty, and make the terms of every agreement clear from the onset. No more fine print."

Chernikov nodded. "And after one month, we revisit longer option."

"Done. What's the second demand? You said there were two."

"I want only what was promised long ago, by your father."

"And we're back to the bloody statue." Dorian pinched the bridge of his nose, wondering if he could ever endure a demon meeting without getting a fucking headache. "Nikolai, how did you and my father come to meet?"

The demon considered him a long time, likely deciding how much to reveal. When he spoke again, his tone took on a note of reverence. "Children always want to think best of their parents, especially when they are young. But a father... He is not always hero his sons believe."

"I learned long ago the futility of believing in fairytales, Nikolai. I'm well aware my father lived and died as a monster."

"A *desperate* monster." Chernikov sipped his coffee, then let out a deep sigh. "As I've told you, your father and I knew each other many years. And in that time, we had many conversations, not unlike this one."

Many *deals*—not conversations. That was the implication.

A chill gripped Dorian's spine, rattling him from the inside out. Augustus Redthorne was the vampire king, brutal and powerful, unchallenged until his own experimentation with a cure aged him right into the grave. What desperate madness could've driven him to bargain with the demon lord—and more than once, if Chernikov's suggestion was true?

In exchange for the promised statue, what had the demon lord delivered?

And what else, over the course of their long and sordid friendship, had Augustus offered as payment?

"What interest does a demon have in the soul of a vampire?" Dorian asked. "Our souls are already bound for hell from the moment we make our first kill. And my father? He bought that one-way ticket sooner than most."

"Souls are not the only gift befitting a demon lord, vampire king."

...gift befitting a demon lord...

Something about the words prodded at Dorian's memories, but the harder he tried to grasp them, the faster they slipped away.

He drained the last of his coffee, then rose from his chair, more than ready to make his escape. "We're in agreement about Manhattan. As far as the Mother of Lost Souls, I have no further information."

"I am not only one looking," Chernikov said grudgingly.

The news that others may be seeking the sculpture—as well as Chernikov's obvious discomfort about that fact—set Dorian's nerves on edge.

Why was everyone so interested in a bloody Scandinavian fertility statue? One that was almost certainly buried on Dorian's property?

"If I find a reference to it among my father's belongings," Dorian said, "you'll be the first to know."

"See that I am, bloodsucker. You may not like me very much, but I promise you—I make better friend than enemy."

Dorian leaned across the table, so close he could see his reflection in the demon's beady eyes. "And I make a better king than assassin, Nikolai, but one never knows when he might have cause to learn a new trade."

With that, he helped himself to another bottle of Chernikov's vodka, turned on his heel, and marched out of the café, only marginally confident the demon wouldn't incinerate him before he reached the parking lot.

Safely back in the truck, he tossed the bottle to Cole, who caught it and let out a low whistle of appreciation.

"Consider it a down payment," Dorian said.

"On?"

"We've got some shoveling to do."

Cole set the bottle on the seat and pulled the truck out onto the road, flicking on the wipers as the first drops of rain splattered against the windshield. "I always say it's a true friend who helps bury the bodies, no questions asked."

"Yes, only this time, we're not burying the bodies." Dorian retrieved his phone from the center console and texted Gabriel, instructing him to bring Charlotte and her sister to Ravenswood. "We're digging them up."

CHAPTER FIVE

Sitting at the dining room table, Charley tried to sip her coffee, but her hands trembled so badly, she spilled half of it onto her bathrobe.

She and Sasha hardly ever ate in the dining room, always preferring the coziness of the breakfast bar. But today, Rudy had it all set up—the good dishes, the placemats, cloth napkins, taper candles flickering in brass holders. If Charley didn't know better, she'd say this was a celebration.

Instead, it felt like the last meal before an execution.

"Eat." He settled in across from her, waving the gun at her plate of runny eggs and charred bacon. "I didn't spend all morning cooking so you could turn your nose up like you just found a cockroach."

"Sorry," she whispered.

"What's that?"

"I'm sorry." She grabbed her fork and sliced off a piece

of egg, forcing it between her lips. The slimy texture made her gag, but she hid it well, chasing it with another gulp of coffee.

Seemingly satisfied, Rudy nodded and set the gun next to the juice carafe, so achingly close she could smell the sharp metal. All she'd have to do was reach for it... and hope like hell she was faster than her uncle.

That's what he wanted—for Charley to make a move. To give him a reason to take her out of the equation, once and for all.

She wouldn't take the bait.

Anger crept across her chest, heating her skin. *Screw* family ties. There was a time when she'd loved her uncle, but that time was dead, just like her father. Now, she hated everything about the man. His malicious eyes. The slurping sounds he made as he shoveled in his breakfast. The glint of candlelight on his tacky gold watch.

No matter how hard she'd tried to play the good little thief, Charley could never get the upper hand with him. Rudy always had another trick up his sleeve, another manipulation, another curveball to throw her completely off-balance.

"So help me understand something," Rudy said. "Last weekend, did you not waltz into my apartment and make a big speech about how badly you wanted to be involved in this? How badly Travis and I *needed* you to be involved?"

There wasn't a right answer, so she nodded and swallowed down another bite of egg, hoping Rudy would say his piece, finish the ego stroke, and get the fuck out of there.

"See? That's why I'm so confused, kiddo. You say one thing, but the moment I actually call on you, you can't be bothered to answer your phone."

"I forgot my phone at—"

"Let me tell you how this is going to work. I'll speak slowly, so you can follow along." He sipped his coffee, then blotted his mouth with the cloth napkin like he was some high-society prick trying to impress her. "No more games, no more delays, no more missed calls and ignored texts, no more going off the radar whenever you feel like it. Your only job right now is to convince your *boyfriend* to get rid of his brothers and whisk you away next weekend."

"Next *weekend*?" Charley blurted out, stunned. "You guys are making a move already?"

"We've got everything in place."

"But Uncle Rudy, I can't. It's way too soon. Getting them all out of the house on such short notice will be damn near impossible."

"Hardly impossible for a man of Dorian Redthorne's significant means and a woman of your significant talents."

Charley shook her head, adamant. "I need more time. You can't just—"

"I can, and I will."

"He's not—"

"*Enough!*" Rudy banged his fist on the table, sending his fork clattering to the floor. He leaned forward and gripped Charley's wrist, lowering his voice to an eerily soothing tone that belied the rage in his eyes. "Allow me to be *absolutely* clear, Charlotte. If you don't make this happen, my next visit will *not* be to cook you breakfast, and I'll be sure Sasha's home too."

Charley felt the blood drain from her face. The room spun, and she had to pinch her thigh to keep from passing out.

Rudy sat back, a gruesome smile sneaking across his lips. "Where *is* that little angel, by the way? Still with Darcy? I would've liked to see her today. Such a pretty thing. Reminds me of her mother, don't you think? So... *delicate.*"

"Stop," Charley said, alarmed that he knew about Sasha's whereabouts. How long had he been stalking her? "You know I'll do whatever you ask. This has nothing to do with Sasha."

"What I'm asking is for you to get us unlimited, uninterrupted access to the house next Saturday."

Charley shook her head. She needed to make him understand—to give her more time. "It won't work, Rudy. You have to trust me on this—as a *woman.* Dorian and I are just starting to spend time together. If I suggest a getaway— especially one that involves his brothers—he'll get suspicious right away."

The words sat between them like smoke, acrid and dangerous. A vein on Rudy's forehead pulsed blue against his skin, but Charley couldn't afford to stop. Stopping meant a lack of conviction—an easily exploitable weakness.

"I could plant the seed, though," she rushed to add. "I know he's busy with an acquisition at his company, but I'm sure when that's all wrapped up, he'll be itching for a vacation."

Charley didn't know much about the acquisition—Dorian had only mentioned it in passing—but it gave her claim some legitimacy.

"It's probably been in the papers," she hedged, hoping like hell it was true. Rudy had recognized Dorian that night outside the Salvatore; surely, he kept up with the business news. "He said something about ongoing meetings and investigations, and he really needs to be here for—"

"I'm fully aware of the pending acquisition. Travis' associates have been interviewing Redthorne and his staff, posing as corporate investigators."

"Seriously?" she asked. This, like most things in Rudy's game, was news to Charley. "What for?"

"Oh, Charlotte." Rudy snickered and shook his head. "Sometimes I forget how naive you really are. With a heist of this magnitude, we need to leverage every possible opportunity to gain information."

"But I'm getting intel direct from the source."

"And yet, it didn't occur to you that his employees might have valuable information pertinent to our interests?"

Charley's cheeks burned. No, it hadn't occurred to her. She'd been too busy melting under Dorian's exquisite, demanding mouth. And later, too busy fighting off demon attacks, saving his life, and nearly dying in the process.

God, I wish he was here…

"Then you probably understand better than me how

important FierceConnect is to him," she babbled on, desperate to convince Rudy that waiting was the right call. "He needs to be here to oversee everything. It sounds like a complicated deal, and—"

Rudy raised a hand to cut her off.

Charley hadn't meant to flinch, but it was instinctual; she knew what the man was capable of, and she was rapidly running out of second chances.

Stay calm. Stay strong. Don't let him see your fear...

She reached for the silver coffeepot and poured herself another cup, willing her hand not to tremble as her uncle glared at her, the air thickening with tension.

"I have a theory." Rudy tapped the table. Tiny ripples disturbed her coffee like a pebble dropped into a polluted lake. "Care to hear it?"

A bead of sweat trickled down the back of her neck, rolling between her shoulder blades. She swallowed hard, then nodded, knowing she didn't have a choice.

Rudy rose from his chair and came to stand behind her, towering over her.

Beneath the bathrobe, cold fingers latched onto Charley's collarbone, digging in hard. Her flesh screamed at the rough contact, but she forced herself not to jerk away.

"I think we have a conflict of interest here." Rudy's fingers crept dangerously up her neck. His enjoyment of the power game was obvious, every subtle move designed to elicit a reaction, but Charley didn't budge.

"I have no idea what you're talking about."

"Maybe," Rudy said, his breath stirring the hair at the top

of her head, "my little minx has *feelings* for the man. And in our line of work, kiddo, feelings are foolish." He ran his thumbs up and down her neck, deceptively gentle. "Deadly, even."

"I'm just doing what you asked. Keeping him close, getting him to trust—"

"Shut the *fuck* up!" Rudy fisted her hair and yanked her head back, forcing her to meet his eyes—the gaze of a maniac.

Blood rushed to her head, the headache returning with a vengeance.

If you're not an asset, you're a liability...

The old motto echoed. At this point in their fucked-up relationship, Charley had no doubt Rudy *could* and *would* kill her the moment he decided she was no longer an asset.

But still...

Something about his reaction was off.

Planning a big score like Ravenswood took forever—months, maybe even years—and timeframes often changed. You had to stay limber, had to have a backup plan, had to be ready to switch things up if the original plan fell apart—which it often did.

You had to adapt, and you couldn't throw it all together at the last minute, no matter how badly you wanted to get your hands on that score.

Rudy knew that.

So why the hell was he so insistent about hitting Ravenswood this weekend?

Still gazing up into his wild eyes, Charley opened her

mouth to try to talk him down, but Rudy shoved her head forward and gripped her collarbone again.

"I guess we can't help who we love," he said. "Poses a problem for me, though."

"But I don't—"

"Hush." Rudy's fingers dug deeper, grinding skin and muscle against bone. Charley pressed her lips together to keep from crying out.

"If you were to warn Mr. Redthorne, or let the authorities know about our plan…" Rudy chuckled, but beneath his twisted amusement, Charley again detected something off. He was losing control, acting desperate. Careless.

He'd always been cool and calculating. Not emotional. Not reckless.

What the fuck's got him so unhinged?

"You can imagine what kind of position that would leave me in," he said. "For the sake of the crew, I'd have to take immediate action. *Permanent* action."

Charley shuddered, frantically searching for some bit of logic to cling to in the face of his craziness.

No. He won't kill me here. Not like this. He still needs me to get Dorian out of the way. It's the middle of the morning. The doorman knows he's here. His fingerprints are all over the kitchen. Sasha could walk in at any minute…

The thought of Sasha witnessing the deplorable scene in the dining room sent a fresh wave of nausea through Charley's insides.

"And if anything should happen to me," Rudy went on,

"know that I've got layers upon *layers* of contingency plans in place."

"Contingency plans?"

"To ensure you and your sister are... taken care of. We are *family*, after all."

His grip was so strong, so unrelenting, Charley was sure her bones would snap if he didn't release her soon. Inside, she writhed in agony, but she didn't dare move. She had to keep talking, to keep asserting the lies.

She needed Rudy to believe she was on his side.

She needed him to calm the fuck down.

"Please," she whispered. "I understand completely. You can trust me. It's not about feelings, I swear. The acquisition timeline is legit. You said it yourself—Travis' guys interviewed him. They can vouch."

"I'm sure they can."

"Rudy, please!" Charley's voice was hoarse, her breath shaky and weak, but she had to convince him that he needed her. That she alone could handle Dorian and his brothers, could lure them away from the house long enough for the rest of the crew to get the job done. "I'll do what needs to be done—I swear. I just need a little more time. You have to understand that!"

"Don't tell me what I have to understand." His hands clamped around her throat, tightening. The edges of her vision faded, the dining room turning gray and spotty before her eyes.

This is it. He's really going to kill me.

Charley stretched forward in a futile attempt to reach the gun, bad ideas be damned, but Rudy held her back.

"You've always been a feisty one," he said. "I'm sure Redthorne appreciates that."

"Please," she croaked again. "Don't do this. Not here."

Rudy laughed, cold and cruel, finally releasing her. "Don't be so fucking dramatic."

Charley slumped forward in her chair, gulping in oxygen. Her neck and shoulders throbbed, fear pulsing through her limbs.

Without another a word, Rudy removed her plate from the table and brought it into the kitchen, leaving the gun. It taunted her, begging her to pick it up, take aim, and squeeze the trigger, just like she'd done when she'd tased the demon in Dorian's bedroom last night.

But no matter how badly she willed it—pictured it, even, his blood splattering on the kitchen wall, body dropping like a bag of rocks—she couldn't make her hands move.

And if anything should happen to me, know that I've got layers upon layers of contingency plans in place...

Charley didn't doubt it. Rudy had always been paranoid; back in the day, he'd even accused her father of cutting him out of a few deals. But now, it seemed his paranoia had exploded into full-on psychosis.

He'd said she and her sister would be "taken care of." Whether he'd have Travis do it, or some other lowlife associate she'd never even heard of, Charley had no idea.

Right now, she only knew one thing:

A dead Rudy meant a dead Charley and Sasha.

"Do you know the best part about watching you contemplate shooting me?" he asked from the kitchen, his voice dripping with mockery. "The gun isn't even loaded."

Tears slipped down Charley's cheeks, and her hatred for her uncle suddenly turned inward, zeroing in on a new target—herself.

She hated that she'd become the kind of woman who cowered in the cruel shadow of a man, who broke beneath the weight of his threats. She hated that as much as she'd tried to protect Sasha, one mistake could undo all of it, sending her beautiful sister to the grave. She hated that she'd become a pawn in a deadly game she'd never signed up to play.

And in this moment, she hated that all she really wanted was for Dorian Redthorne to blur into the room, tear out Rudy's heart, and sweep her into his powerful embrace, making her problems disappear with a deep, passionate kiss.

Maybe that made her weak—even weaker than the trembling mess of a woman Rudy probably saw when he looked at her—but Charley didn't care. Wasn't that what you did for someone you loved? Looked out for them? Saved them when they didn't have the strength to save themselves?

From the corner of her eye, she caught Rudy rummaging beneath the sink for the dish soap and a rag. She had a dishwasher, but Rudy turned on the faucet and soaped up the plate anyway, humming an old Italian lullaby her father used to sing.

The melody made Charley's heart ache.

A few minutes later, Rudy cleared his throat, and she finally looked up and met his gaze. He stood in the archway between the kitchen and dining room, watching her with unchecked disdain, clutching the dishrag as it dripped water onto the tile floor. A lone rose petal peeked out from beneath his shoe, red as blood.

She felt broken inside, unable to move.

When Rudy spoke, she flinched again, and the asshole smiled, eminently pleased with himself.

"Two weeks, Charlotte. Three at the absolute max. If we have to revisit this topic again, you and your mother's pretty little bastard will find out what it truly means to hurt. Understood?"

She nodded.

"I didn't quite hear that," he said.

"Yeah." Her voice cracked. She coughed and tried again. "Yes. I understand, Uncle Rudy. Two weeks, three tops. You got it."

"Good. Now clean up the rest of this mess before your sister gets home from Darcy's." He flung the dirty dishrag across the room, hitting her square in the face.

By the time it slid down and plopped into her lap, Rudy and the gun were gone.

CHAPTER SIX

Sasha's bathroom was closer, and Charley barely made it inside before her stomach convulsed, emptying its meager contents for the second time that morning. Even when she had nothing left, she still heaved, her tears unstoppable, her body trembling with fear and shame.

Unable to face herself in the mirror, she stripped out of her robe and pajamas and stepped into the shower, using an entire bottle of exfoliating bath gel to scrub Rudy's touch from her skin.

In the quiet fury of her work, she considered her options.

Even if she *wanted* to let the robbery play out, there was no way Rudy's scheme would work. She'd bought herself a few more weeks, but that was just a stalling tactic. Luring Dorian and his brothers out of the house for a weekend trip together? With her? Without arousing suspicion? Not happening. It wasn't just the FierceConnect acquisition either; Charley wasn't exactly versed in supernatural politics, but after last night, she was pretty sure a war was brewing, and the Redthornes were smack in the middle of it.

She could grab the passports, pack their bags, use the credit card to get out of the country with Sasha for good. The thought had crossed her mind before, but... No. Rudy controlled the credit card and would easily track her movements. She had a few hundred in cash hidden in a false-bottomed cookie jar, but how far would that get them? Buffalo? Toronto, if they were lucky?

She could turn herself in, cop a plea deal, try to take down Rudy and the whole crew in one fell swoop. But that wasn't a sure thing, either. Warrants took time, and time meant risking Sasha's safety. Rudy had been watching her, tracking her work schedule and social plans —he'd made that clear over breakfast. Charley had no doubt that if her uncle sensed the heat closing in, Sasha would be dead before the cops even kicked down his door.

Charley leaned her forehead against the tile and closed her eyes. Her mind spun in circles, searching for every possible loophole, but in the end, she only had one play left.

The truth.

She was in way too deep, and Rudy was quickly unraveling, growing more impatient every day.

Maybe she didn't need the fantasy version of a dark, deadly hero—a vampire in tarnished armor, charging in to slaughter her foes and save the day. But she *did* need help.

Without it, she couldn't protect Sasha *or* prevent the robbery.

Which meant Charley had to confess, once and for all. To look into the eyes of the man she was falling for—the *vampire* she was falling for—and admit she'd been plotting the heist of his entire estate.

He might call the cops, which would be bad.

He might tell his brothers, which would be worse.

He might even kill her. He was a vampire, after all—the king—and she'd betrayed his trust. Last night, she'd caught a glimpse of his primal fury—a fury unleashed by his enemies.

A fury unleashed by the threats against her life.

Seeing that fierce, brutal side of him... It had thrilled and terrified her in equal measure.

But how would it feel to be on the receiving end?

Charley opened her eyes and pressed a thumb to her wrist, the ghost of Dorian's mouth lingering.

A vampire.

Her mind still railed against it, even now.

But across the tumult of her violent, confusing, and even erotic memories of last night, one thread wove through them all, strong and certain: Dorian had protected her. He'd risked his life for her. So whatever anger her confession inspired, there was still a chance he'd be willing to help her figure this out—help her keep Sasha out of harm's way.

That was all Charley could think about now. She'd risk *everything* for her sister, no matter what the cost.

Even if it meant pissing off the vampire king.

Even if it meant walking away from the only man she'd ever truly fallen for.

That was the price of mixing her kind of business with his kind of pleasure. It was a price that kept on rising, no matter how many times she thought she'd already paid it.

Turns out she'd never even come *close*.

After the shower, Charley inspected her naked body in the mirror. The dark circles beneath her eyes had faded, but her shoulders and collarbone were raw, the pale flesh swollen and red. Dark, fingertip-shaped welts had risen to the surface, and no amount of scrubbing would erase them.

Fresh tears welled in her eyes, but a jarring knock on the bathroom door broke through her despair.

"Charley?" Sasha rattled the locked doorknob, her voice high and edgy. "Let me in."

"Um... Just a sec!" Frantic, Charley grabbed her bathrobe from the hook, yanking it around her body just as Sasha popped the lock and pushed open the door.

"What the hell is going on?" Sasha asked, gripping the butter knife she'd used to break in.

Charley forced a smile. "What are you doing home? I thought you were staying with Darcy until tomorrow."

"Rudy called me and said I needed to get home immediately."

Charley's blood ran cold. "What?"

"He said there was an emergency. I kept calling and

texting you, but you didn't answer." Tears of relief and frustration spilled down her cheeks. "God, Charley! I didn't know what happened and I just ran for the nearest cab and I was totally freaking out and—"

Charley cut her off with a tight hug.

"It's nothing. I… I wasn't feeling well. I think I ate some bad eggs." She pulled back, keeping her voice light. "Rudy was overreacting. I'm sorry—I didn't even know he had your number."

"Neither did I." Sasha folded her arms across her chest and leaned back against the doorframe, clearly not buying Charley's casual, everything's-just-fine act. "He also wanted to know how my psych presentation went on Friday. How the hell did he even know about that?"

"It must've come up in passing." Charley swallowed the knot of fear and anger in her throat. The last thing she wanted was for Sasha to worry, but Charley's nerves had just kicked into hyperdrive.

So not only does he know her work schedule and her social plans, but her class schedule too? Down to her presentations?

"When did you two start doing family breakfast, anyway?" Sasha asked, still suspicious. "And what happened to your flowers? Seriously, Charley. What the fuck is going on?"

Charley turned back toward the mirror, unable to bear the weight of her sister's astute questions. But Sasha stepped behind her, meeting her gaze in the reflection.

"Look at how miserable you are, Chuck." Sasha shook

her head. "No job in the world is worth that—not even for family."

"We have bills, Sasha."

"Let's just sell this place. We'll move. I'll take more shifts at work, go down to part-time at school. We'll figure something out."

Charley blew out a breath, wishing she could make her sister understand, but she couldn't—not without scaring the shit out of the girl. "I'll work it out with Rudy. He's not... he's not totally unreasonable."

"Are you kidding me? He's a classic psychopath! He meets all the criteria." Sasha held up a hand, counting down with her fingers. "Uses intimidation tactics for his own personal gain. Doesn't show remorse. Fakes emotion to get you to trust him. Manipulates you every chance he gets. Trust me—I've been studying this stuff all month, and Uncle Boss totally fits the profile."

Charley offered a sad smile in the mirror, but before she could give Sasha any more false reassurances, the doorbell startled them both.

Aside from Rudy, who technically owned the place now and had his own key—a fact Charley had never even considered until this morning's surprise drop-in—visitors had to be announced by the doorman.

Charley turned and grabbed Sasha's shoulders. "Stay in your room. Lock the door. Don't come out until I say so, okay?"

"*What*? Why? Should I call the police?"

"No, just stay out of sight. I'll handle it." Charley went

to the front door and looked through the peephole, heart in her throat.

But the man standing on the other side wasn't Travis or some unrecognizable thug sent to "take care" of them.

"Gabriel?" She opened the door, relief flooding her limbs at the sight of Dorian's youngest brother. He was cold and off-putting—very possibly dangerous—but Charley would take her chances with a Redthorne royal over her uncle's brand of cruelty any day.

"Ms. D'Amico." Gabriel gave a slight bow as he stepped inside. "My brother has ordered me to bring you and your sister to Ravenswood."

"*Ordered* you?"

He rolled his eyes. "The king says jump, the rest of us say how high."

Despite the obvious irritation, his mood was much more somber than the last time she'd seen him. Almost... compliant.

Charley didn't know whether to be relieved or afraid.

"What's Dorian doing back at Ravenswood?" she asked. "Did he tell you what happened last night?"

"I was here, Ms. D'Amico. All of us were."

"All of you?"

"With the exception of Aiden, who was sent to look for your sister. I'm told he wasn't able to locate her, though. Have you heard from her?"

"She's here, but... You guys were in my penthouse last night?" She closed her eyes, once again chasing memories that were still just out of reach. The men arguing in the living room. Colin, tending to her wounds with a mysterious woman. Dorian, frantic with worry, whispering that he'd fallen...

"Are you feeling better?" Gabriel asked. "Looks like your color has returned."

The sincerity in his voice shocked her, and she opened her eyes, her suspicion growing by a mile. "Gabriel. What the hell is going on? When did Dorian go back upstate?"

"As soon as we knew you were safe."

"But why? Has he heard any more from Duchanes?"

"Not yet."

She had so many more questions—why the fuck had Dorian left her last night? If he wanted to see her so badly, why had he sent Gabriel instead of coming himself? Was he still freaked out about drinking her blood? Was Duchanes still a threat?—but before she could find the words, Sasha bounced into the room.

"Hey!" Sasha said, beaming at their guest as if the last ten minutes had never happened. "I'm Sasha, Charley's sister. Who the hell are you? And are you staying for lunch? You totally should. Right, Charley?"

"Gabriel Redthorne." He bowed again, clearly uncomfortable at Sasha's attention.

"He's Dorian's brother," Charley explained. Then, realizing Sasha probably had no idea who Dorian was either, she added, "The guy I've been seeing."

"Oh my God! You're Mr. Already Forgotten's brother?" She turned to Charley with wide eyes and a huge smile, mouthing a single word: *hot!* "Why am I meeting your boyfriend's brother before I'm meeting your boyfriend?"

"Dorian isn't my boyfriend, Sasha. We're just..." She caught Gabriel's eye, hoping for an assist, but the vampire merely glared.

Charley glared right back. *My day's not exactly going according to plan either, buddy...*

"Don't stop digging the hole on my account," he said.

"Yeah, Chuck," Sasha teased. "Don't stop digging. I want the scoop on the *whole* family. Clearly, you've been holding out on me."

The light had returned to Sasha's eyes, and for that, Charley was grateful, even if the sight of Gabriel brooding in her penthouse—in Dorian's absence, no less—left her uneasy.

"Are you coming?" he asked Charley. "Or do I need to prepare for an argument with my brother?"

"Coming where?" Sasha asked.

"Nowhere." Charley shot him another warning glare, but the sudden concern in Gabriel's eyes made her adrenaline spike.

"It's not safe in the city," he whispered. "For either of you."

Charley sighed. He was right. In all the stress of dealing with Rudy this morning, she hadn't even fully processed last night's attack—what she could remember of it, anyway. But if Dorian hadn't heard from Duchanes, the vampire and his demons were likely still on the loose.

And she was probably still a target, which meant Sasha was also in danger.

Keeping her eyes on Gabriel, she said to Sasha, "Dorian invited us to visit his manor upstate. You in?"

"I finally get to meet Mr. Already Forgotten?" she asked, excitement bubbling from her voice. "And he has a *manor*? Seriously?"

"And an infinity pool and hot tub," Charley said, "so you might want to pack a swimsuit."

"On it!" Sasha disappeared into her bedroom, leaving a trail of exuberance in her wake, but Charley was still on edge.

Holding out her hand to the vampire in her entryway, she said, "Can I borrow your phone? I left mine in Tribeca."

"You can speak with him at Ravenswood, Ms. D'Amico. Please pack your things. We really need to get on the road."

Charley folded her arms across her chest and arched an eyebrow. It was barely ten in the morning, and she'd already puked multiple times, lost her roses, and survived a thorough manhandling by her psycho uncle. And even though Dorian wanted to keep her safe, his protective instincts—along with his feelings for her—would come to a spectacular, explosive end the moment she made her epic confession.

So if Gabriel wanted to stand there and have a fucking brood-off? Fine. She could do this *all* day.

"Do these childish antics work on my brother?" he asked with a look of supreme irritation.

But he also handed over his phone.

65

Charley tried not to gloat, but she knew this little win with Gabriel would probably be the highlight of her whole day—the very last thing she had to smile about.

Because the minute she heard Dorian's voice, she was pretty damn sure she'd fall apart.

CHAPTER SEVEN

By the time Dorian and Cole made it back to Ravenswood, the rain had soaked the grounds, making for slippery, messy work that left Dorian wet, cold, and thoroughly grouchy. It wasn't helping his injuries either—the wolf bites still burned, his healing slowed by the damp chill.

Fortunately, the weather didn't darken Cole's enthusiasm, and it wasn't long before he and Dorian were standing shoulders-deep in a soggy pit several hundred feet behind the manor, rotting planks creaking beneath their feet.

Coffins.

"Jackpot." Cole set aside the shovel and reached for his cigarettes, tapping one out of the pack. "Now, you mind telling me who's in there? I prefer knowing a little something about a man before getting up close and personal with his rotting corpse."

Dorian speared a coffin lid with the tip of his shovel.

The wood was soft with age and moisture, splintering easily. "Any corpses buried here are nothing but bones by now."

"Yeah, but *whose* bones?"

"Father never said." Dorian sidestepped a plume of smoke and glanced out across the vast acreage, the green grass so vivid it made his eyes hurt. In the distance, Ravenswood Manor stood sentry, a silent, immovable witness to more secrets than Dorian could imagine. "Two hundred-odd years ago, he dragged me and my brothers out here at three in the morning, right in the middle of a blasted storm, and ordered us to dig the hole. He'd already brought the horses round—two of them drawing the cart, jumping at every crack of thunder, the poor beasts."

"They brought the coffins?"

Dorian nodded, remembering the wet, earthy smell of the horses, the sucking sounds their hooves made in the mud. It was a wonder the cart hadn't overturned.

"Malcolm and I helped him lower the coffins into the hole, neither of us saying a word. When it came to Father's antics, we'd learned not to ask too many questions." Dorian stiffened, suppressing a shudder. "He waited until we'd buried them, and then he stood on top of the mound, lifted his hands skyward, and said, 'A gift befitting the lord of demons—may his eternal reign darken our doorstep only until we're ready to see the light.'"

Cole shook his head and laughed. "Your old man was a crazy sonofabitch. You know that, right?"

"Better than most."

At the time, Dorian hadn't the faintest idea what his father was on about. They'd all assumed he'd executed some poor, helpless humans in a ritual sacrifice—a gift for the demons, as he'd said.

It wouldn't have been the first time.

But this morning, as Dorian stalked across the Luna Del Mar parking lot after his meeting, Chernikov's words continued to chew through his mind, finally biting into the memory of that stormy night.

The coffins.

The befitting gifts.

And Dorian began to suspect it hadn't been a sacrifice at all… but an investment.

Tightening his grip, he jammed the shovel back into the wood, prying away the splintered pieces of one lid, then the other, finally revealing the contents.

"Those ain't bodies," Cole said.

"Those," Dorian said, crouching down to retrieve the child-sized bundles nestled inside the otherwise empty coffins, "are insurance policies."

The crypts beneath the manor were dank and dark, the stone sweating with condensation. Come winter, the passageways would be slick with ice, many of them inaccessible. But for now, Dorian paced the narrowest of them, giving Cole and Aiden a few moments to catch up.

After years of seclusion, the wolf's re-emergence in their

lives was a blessing in a season that had seen far too few, and watching the old friends embrace loosened the knot in Dorian's chest. Even Colin, normally reserved in his affections and expressions, couldn't help but smile when Cole reached out to shake his hand.

Considering last night's attack in Tribeca and the grays roaming the woods, all of them were glad to count the wolves among their allies. But for Dorian, it went even deeper; aside from Aiden, Cole was the last true friend he had.

Together, the four men headed into the tomb Augustus had used as his laboratory. Dorian set the bundles on the stone slab in the center, carefully removing their musty cloth wrappings to reveal the mysterious objects within.

One was a confirmation.

The other? Yet another mystery.

"So you're telling me Chernikov's had a hard-on for this thing for two centuries?" Aiden picked up the Mother of Lost Souls sculpture, carefully turning it in his hands. It was approximately eighteen inches tall, made of painted clay and polished stones. "I'm no art critic, but I find her a bit homely. I mean, honestly. The poor thing doesn't even have nipples."

"Yes, Aiden, I'm sure nipples would make a *world* of difference." Dorian scowled and relieved him of the statue, but he didn't disagree with the overall critique. She *was* homely. The stuff of nightmares, really.

The body was similar to many fertility goddess pieces

he'd encountered over the years, with exaggerated breasts and a belly swollen with child. The problem—missing nipples aside—was her face.

From the neck up, she looked more demon than human, with obsidian eyes, a forked tongue, and a nest of what Dorian suspected was human hair. Her teeth were jagged and yellowed, much too large for her mouth.

They reminded Dorian of the vampire fangs Cole had found in the woods.

"Why would Father go to all the trouble of burying this in a coffin?" Colin asked. "He didn't destroy it, so clearly it serves a purpose. Yet he kept it hidden from us. Why?"

"He probably didn't realize he was going to die so quickly," Aiden said. "If he had, perhaps he would've told—"

"No. He didn't trust us," Colin said, meeting Dorian's gaze. "He *knew* his days were numbered—that's obvious from the journals. He was surprised he'd lasted as long as he had. This was simply one more secret he intended to carry with him to hell."

"Actually, I don't believe that was his intention at all." Dorian set the statue on the table, gazing into her dark eyes. "Father didn't need our help that night, digging the grave. He could've managed on his own, but he *insisted* we join him. He called it a gift befitting the lord of demons—the same phrase Chernikov used. It can't be coincidence."

"That doesn't mean Father meant to tell us about it."

"The Mother of Lost Souls was no secret," Dorian said.

As much as he wanted to agree with Colin—to add one more checkmark to the terrible father column—on this, he couldn't. "We've all known about her from the moment Father stole her from House Kendrick. We knew he buried her at Ravenswood. Not in the crypts, as I'd always assumed, but still on our estate. He wanted us to find it, Colin. I'm certain."

"For what purpose?" Colin asked.

"I don't yet know." Dorian sighed, his father's long-ago words ghosting through his mind.

She is what makes us powerful. One day, you will see...

"Then she's useless to us," Colin said, "just like the man who buried her."

Hurt flickered in his eyes, but then he looked away, turning his attention to the second object they'd unearthed—some sort of ancient book. It was cold to the touch, but despite its long years in the coffin, undiluted magic hummed across the cover, preventing them from opening it as surely as it'd protected the pages from the elements.

"What do you make of it?" Dorian asked Colin.

"I'm not well-versed in demonic languages, but from the symbology on the cover, the closest translation I can come up with is the Book of Lost Souls."

"Brilliant," Aiden said. "A matched set. And Chernikov never mentioned it?"

Dorian shook his head. "As far as I know, he's only after the statue."

"Maybe it's an instruction manual." Cole ran his fingers

along the spine, tiny silver sparks following in his path. "Some assembly required."

"For fuck's sake," Dorian said. "This isn't a piece of furniture from Ikea. It's an ancient sculpture Chernikov believes belongs to his family—a piece he's allegedly been seeking for centuries. One Father obviously hid from him, despite his promises to the contrary."

"Cole might be onto something though," Colin said, his grim face suddenly brightening at the prospect of solving another puzzle. He was so much like their father in that way—a fact that intrigued and frightened Dorian in equal measure. "If we look at this objectively, setting aside our feelings about Father... All indications are that the book and sculpture are connected. Perhaps it's a grimoire, and it activates something within the sculpture itself."

"Wonderful," Dorian grumbled. "For all we know, it's a demonic beacon and it opens a portal to hell."

"Also a distinct possibility," Colin said.

"Demonic beacon?" Aiden took a step back from the table. "Perhaps we should put it back in the ground—forget we ever found it."

But Colin's eyes were already alight with possibilities. Dorian suspected he'd be spending all his time down here now, poring over their father's journals for clues about this new mystery... along with clues about the old ones.

Dorian rubbed his tired eyes and sighed. They hadn't even told the others about their father's alleged discovery of a cure for vampirism. So much had happened since Colin first shared the news with Dorian last night—the attack, dealing with Charlotte's injuries, the revelation of her treachery. There hadn't been time for a family meeting.

And now?

Bloody hell, Dorian hardly knew where to begin.

He *was* certain about one thing, though.

Now more than ever, the crypts and their expanding collection of secrets had to be protected at all costs.

Not just from Chernikov, who desperately sought the sculpture and likely didn't believe Dorian's feigned ignorance on the matter.

Not just from Duchanes, who was almost certainly plotting to claim the entire estate after murdering its present occupants.

Not just from Rogozin and the other demons pulling the strings, masterminding their own gruesome takeovers.

But from the woman—the *human* woman with whom Dorian had made the regrettable mistake of falling in love, whose loyalties remained a mystery, her motives as deep and muddy as the pit he'd just unearthed.

And now, Gabriel was in the process of bringing her here—straight to the scene of the yet-to-be-committed crime.

Telling himself he'd made the right call—that here, at least, he could keep a close eye on her and decipher her plans—Dorian turned back to the task at hand, hiding the objects among his father's things. He and Cole had just tucked away the statue when the phone buzzed inside his suit jacket, scattering his dreary thoughts.

Gabriel.

"Did you retrieve them?" Dorian asked.

"If by *them* you mean me and my sister," came the fiery, feminine, definitely-not-Gabriel reply, "then no. We're still in Manhattan, un-retrieved, waiting for an actual invitation. Or an explanation. Hell, I'd settle for a simple hello at this point."

The knot inside Dorian's chest tightened anew, the melodic sound of her voice filling him at once with repulsion and desire.

The battle between the two emotions made him ache.

Forcing a steely chill into his voice, he said, "Hello, Charlotte. I was hoping you and Sasha were already en route."

"En *route*? Do you hear yourself right now?" She paused, her footfalls echoing as she headed into another room and closed the door.

His thoughts immediately went to her bedroom, to the bed upon which he'd coaxed—through all their sinful, late-night phone calls—more orgasms from her body than he could recall.

The same bed where a handful of hours ago, he'd confessed his secrets over her nearly broken body.

"Dorian," she said, her voice soft and muffled, way more sensual than he cared to acknowledge. "What the hell is going on? Why did you leave last night?"

Pain laced her words, and Dorian was immediately sorry, knowing he'd been the one to cause it.

But then the truth rushed back at him with a vengeance, and he shored up his heart, determined not to waver.

Not again.

"As I'm sure Gabriel explained," he said coolly, "it's too dangerous in the city right now, and I don't have enough men to keep watch over you."

"I understand, but you can't just send your brother here to pick us up like we're the forgotten dry cleaning." She sighed into the phone, lowering her voice to a whisper. "Dorian, we almost died last night. When I woke up without you this morning, I thought... I thought something happened. I was worried about you."

Even at a whisper, the concern in her voice was clear.

Now, in addition to the desire and repulsion duking it out in his chest, molten guilt flooded in, burning away everything else.

He resented all of it.

He resented her.

He did *not* have time for this.

"Please don't fight me, Charlotte," he said, exasperation creeping into his voice. "Not on this."

"What aren't you telling me?"

Dorian nearly laughed. The answer could fill an entire library, and he could just as easily ask her the same question, filling a second.

Between the two of them, there were more unexplained mysteries than the ones lurking in the crypts—and most of them were almost certainly lies.

Not an ideal start to a relationship.

Which is why there will be *no relationship, you bloody fool.*

Nor any more carnal delights, no matter how readily the sound of her voice makes you hard as stone, even now...

"We'll discuss everything later," he said. "In person."

When I can read the lines of your deceptions in those beautiful, devious eyes...

By the silence that followed, Dorian knew he'd won her over. Charlotte was nothing if not pragmatic; she'd seen a glimpse of what a vampire like Duchanes could do, and there was no way she'd risk another altercation—especially not where her sister was concerned.

"Fine," she finally said, and Dorian tried not to sigh in relief. "We'll be there in a few hours."

"It shouldn't take you more than two, even with traffic."

"Sasha's in the process of convincing Gabriel to take us to lunch."

"*Lunch*? Did you not warn her he's the most ruthless Redthorne Royal of all? She's got a better chance of convincing the demon factions to attend afternoon tea at the Ritz-Carlton."

"You haven't met my sister. Her powers of persuasion are legendary."

"I imagine she learned them from you."

"Damn straight."

Dorian didn't know how the hell he'd deal with the two of them in his home together.

The thought brought an uninvited smile to his lips anyway.

But then it faded, the reminder of Charlotte's betrayal

blowing the warmth from his chest as swiftly as a late autumn breeze ushered in the winter.

He'd been waiting for it, he realized. Waiting for her to mention the notebook and floor plans he'd taken from her bedroom. To spin some elaborate tale he was all too eager to accept.

He wanted her to prove him wrong. To prove him a fool for ever doubting her. To spin back the clock to those moments when he'd cradled her hand in that bed and saw the entirety of their lives together, one breathless kiss at a time.

But she hadn't said a word.

Which meant she was either playing a *very* twisted game...

Or she had no idea she was about to walk into a minefield.

"Just get here, Charlotte." Dorian closed his eyes, admonishing himself even before the words slipped free from his mouth. "And please... be careful."

He ended the call and glanced up to find all three of the men watching him intently.

Colin, merely curious.

Aiden, his eyes narrowed with concern, as if he could sense the battle raging inside Dorian's heart.

And Cole, the only one who knew what Dorian had discovered about his woman last night, smirking at him like that bloody phone conversation had just proven every last one of the wolf's infuriating points.

I'll tell you what, Red. That look in your eyes? That's not the look of a man out for a few quick fucks...

Cole's smirk turned into a full-on laugh, and Dorian stormed over to the elevator, telling himself Cole was dead wrong. That a few quick fucks was all he truly wanted—all he'd *ever* wanted from that woman. His cock, still stiff from the sound of her voice, seemed happy to agree.

If only his fucking heart wasn't on fire, Dorian might've believed it too.

CHAPTER EIGHT

Despite a monumental amount of complaining from the so-called most ruthless Redthorne Royal, Sasha got her way in the end, and Gabriel took them for an early lunch at a gourmet soup-and-salad café near Charley's building—the first meal she'd been able to keep down all day.

The food perked her up, but the post-lunch ride to Ravenswood in Gabriel's BMW was long and awkward, with Sasha happily chatting away from the backseat while Gabriel attempted to drown her out with the news radio. It was the same story on every channel—something about a raid at a popular nightclub in the East Village, resulting in a major drug and sex trafficking bust. Charley couldn't imagine why he was so interested; she'd assumed vampires like Gabriel would be above the city's human dramas.

Still, Charley would rather listen to the depressing news than try to make conversation with Dorian's youngest brother. He'd never been particularly warm toward her—toward anyone, as far as she could tell—and the fact that he was suddenly following Dorian's orders without pushback meant the situation was even more dangerous than she'd feared.

She almost preferred the Redthornes to be at each other's throats. That, at least, would've felt normal.

Normal. Right. Like being attacked by crazy vampires and demons was normal. Like being threatened by her uncle was normal. Like confessing to Dorian that she'd been plotting to steal from him was normal.

Nervous energy zipped through her limbs, and she fidgeted in the front seat, alternately pulling threads at the hem of her sweater and wiping her damp palms on her jeans. She didn't even have a phone to distract her now—another situation totally stressing her out. She'd have to see if Dorian had been back to his penthouse—maybe he'd picked up her purse. If not, she'd have to send Rudy a text from Sasha's phone tomorrow. She didn't want to risk going off the radar for more than a day—not after his antics this morning. Plus, she wanted him to know Dorian had invited her and Sasha for a visit; she planned to spin it as an opportunity to gather more intel and charm Dorian into the idea of a future family getaway. Maybe it would keep Rudy off her back a few extra days.

By the time they pulled into the manor's circular drive, Charley's nervous system was damn near shot. The only thing that kept her from completely falling apart was Sasha

—the girl was over the moon at the sight of the manner, her slack-jawed appreciation of its grandeur making her look like a kid at Disney World.

"Holy *balls*," she whispered, taking it all in as they got out of the car. Charley kept stealing glances at the front doors, hoping Dorian would emerge, but the only vampire who'd shown up to greet them was Aiden.

"Good afternoon, Ms. D'Amico," he said with a cautious smile. "And this must be Sasha. Welcome to Ravenswood—we're so glad you could join us."

"This place is freaking amazing," Sasha said, her megawatt smile brightening the gray day.

"Wait until you see the grounds," Aiden said.

"Charley told me there's a pool?"

Aiden laughed. "Would you like the tour? I'm Aiden, by the way—friend of the family. I'd be happy to show you around, if it's okay with you, Ms. D'Amico?"

Charley nodded, grateful for his kindness. Pressing a kiss to her sister's cheek, she said, "I need to find Dorian. We'll catch up with you in a few minutes, okay?"

"I'll be fine," Sasha said. Then, leaning in to whisper in Charley's ear, "I'm officially mad at you for not warning me about the hotness level here. Had I known, I would've put a little more effort into my hair."

Charley laughed and pulled her in for a hug, squeezing extra tight. "*Behave* yourself, young lady."

"I may be young, but I'm legal," Sasha whispered, and with that, she twirled out of Charley's embrace and headed for Aiden, looping her arm through his and following him along the path into the gardens.

"How old is he, anyway?" Charley asked.

"An antique, like the rest of us," Gabriel said. "Why do you ask?"

"My sister's already smitten, and she doesn't even know he's a vampire. *That* would send her into crush territory in a heartbeat."

Gabriel grunted. Or maybe it was a laugh—hard to tell. "You've nothing to be concerned about. Aiden is a perfect gentleman—which is more than I can say for the rest of us. Especially our king."

His eyes glinted, but beneath all his cold, sharp edges, Charley had no idea if he was teasing her... or warning her.

A chill rattled through her bones, and she tugged her sweater sleeves down over her hands. "Where is he, Gabriel?"

"He's asked me to escort you to the dining room." Gabriel took her elbow, steering her toward the grand stairs that led up to the main entrance. "He's wrapping up a business call and will join you momentarily."

"What business call?" she asked. How could he think of business at a time like this? Didn't he have dangerous enemies to chase down?

"That's not your concern. Nor mine, frankly."

"Wait—what about our bags?"

"Someone will bring them in later."

"But I—"

"Ms. D'Amico, I realize you're used to a certain degree of latitude with my brother, but I have many things to do today, and answering questions in Dorian's absence is not one of them. My orders were to bring you to Ravenswood and deliver you to the dining room. If there is anything you'd like to discuss beyond that, discuss it with him."

Charley gaped at him, shocked by his blatant rudeness. She would've loved to tell him right where to stick it, but she didn't want to delay her reunion with Dorian another minute. So, zipping her lip, she nodded and followed him up the stairs and into the manor, where he led her through a set of carved pocket doors and into the massive dining room.

She'd gotten a brief glimpse of it the night of the fundraiser, but absent the guests and caterers, it looked even larger than she remembered, with stately, opulent furnishings, exquisite landscape paintings, and a large stone fireplace. Glass doors lined the far wall, opening onto a secluded rose garden whose blooms were still full and bright, despite the lateness of the season and the chilly nights. She wondered how they'd stayed alive so long.

Magic, perhaps. Another trick of the witches.

Rubbing a new chill from her arms, Charley paced the room, stopping before a rich mahogany sideboard along the wall opposite the rose garden. A large antique mirror hung overhead, reflecting the dark reds and pale pinks of the blooms outside.

Charley gave her own reflection a once-over, tugging down the collar on her cable-knit sweater to check her bruises. They were even more glaringly obnoxious now—a wide necklace of angry, purple blotches, courtesy of her uncle.

Somewhere in the distance, Sasha's laughter floated like a bright yellow bird on the air, but here in the dining room, Charley felt trapped and suffocated.

Tears stung her eyes. The dread of the morning weighed heavily, further solidifying her resolve to confess to Dorian. He wouldn't take it lightly, but he wouldn't turn his back on her either—not without hearing her out.

Of that, she was certain.

But the longer he kept her waiting, the less certain she became. She continued to pace, running her fingers along the gleaming oak table and chairs, admiring the artwork on the walls, counting the roses still clinging to the thorny bushes.

Ten minutes turned to thirty. When another fifteen minutes passed without word from anyone, she headed for the pocket doors, ready to go out in search of her man.

But instead, he'd finally come in search of her.

He opened the doors and stood before her, his gaze sweeping her head to toe, his golden eyes filling with relief.

At the sight of him—tired but nevertheless polished, dressed in a tailored charcoal gray suit and cream-colored dress shirt, hair sticking up as if he'd been running his hands through it—Charley nearly wept. She went to him, unable to hold back her smile *or* her tears.

But as soon as she reached for him, Dorian turned his back and closed the doors, locking them inside.

When he faced her again, the relief in his eyes had turned to ice, his mouth set in a grim line.

He folded his arms across his chest and glared at her, and Charley knew—before he uttered a single word—that something was very, very wrong.

CHAPTER NINE

"Dorian?" she whispered, her heart skipping, arms hovering in the space between them, still waiting for his touch.

But Dorian was unmoved.

It didn't make sense. Even when they were total strangers, he could barely keep his hands to himself. Now, after everything they'd shared—after last night's brushes with death—he was cold-shouldering her?

"Take a seat, Charlotte." He stalked past her and headed for the glass doors on the other side of the room. "We need to talk, and I prefer not to complicate matters with emotional outbursts."

Emotional outbursts?

She folded her arms across her chest, doing her best to hide the sting of his comments. "But I—"

"Sit *down*," he said again.

The seriousness in his tone left no room for argument, so Charley did as he asked, taking a seat at the head of the table in a stiff, high-backed chair, waiting for him to continue.

It felt like hours before he finally spoke again, and when he did, he kept his back to her, gaze fixed on the rose garden outside.

"That day in the mountains," he said, "you asked how I came to be a vampire."

Charley's breath caught, her heart thudding ominously. As badly as she'd wanted to know this part of Dorian's long, dark history, something about his tone and the tight set of his shoulders told her this wasn't the right time—not for either of them.

"Dorian, we don't have to talk about this."

"Oh, but we do." He finally turned to face her. The ice had melted from his gaze, but now it held fire instead, a sharp anger simmering in its golden depths. "You need to understand how we got here, Charlotte. How *I* got here. And how everything that happens after this moment, for good or ill, can be traced back to a single point in time, long before the parents of your parents were even born."

The ferocity in his eyes silenced her protests, and she sat back in the chair and held her breath, waiting for him to unleash the terrible truth.

"I was betrothed," he began. "Before."

Charley's eyes widened, a flicker of jealousy flashing through her heart. "Before?"

"When I was human. Her name was Evelyn—Evie."

"Wow. I... I had no idea." A million new questions exploded in Charley's mind. Betrothed... Did that mean they'd never actually married? Did she pass away? Did he love her?

Did he touch her the way he touched Charley?

Silently, she cursed herself, ashamed that her mind had even gone there. But she couldn't help it. She missed that touch, now more than ever.

"Evie was passionate and exuberant," he said, "but also evasive and prone to bouts of deep, dark melancholy. Being with her... Sometimes it felt as if I were standing on the shoreline just out of reach, watching her drown, knowing there wasn't a damn thing I could do to save her."

He lowered his eyes and shook his head, and Charley let out a broken sigh, wishing she could save *him*. But she knew all too well that no one could save you from your own darkness.

All she could do was keep the lights on and wait for him to return—to be here for him when he did.

If he did.

"She'd always told me she was estranged from her family," Dorian said. "In those days, it was unusual for a woman of noble birth to be on her own, but I took her at her word, never pushing for the details. But if I *had*..." He let out a bitter laugh. "Seems I've yet to learn that particular lesson."

Charley swallowed the tightness in her throat, her mind

connecting the dots. "Your fiancée... Evie... She's the one who turned you?"

She couldn't even imagine the pain of something like that. No wonder he didn't like to talk about it.

But Dorian shook his head.

"Evie didn't turn me. She merely lied to me." He glanced out again at the roses, sighing against the glass. "She was a vampire, Charlotte, as I'm sure you've deduced. But not just any vampire—the sole daughter of the king. I was ignorant, of course—too smitten to poke round the *many* holes in her story. Father wasn't fooled, though. As I learned later, he was quick to uncover her secrets."

"What did he do?" she whispered.

"What any doctor long obsessed with outrunning his own mortality would do. He tracked down her estranged family and brokered a deal with the vampire king: Grant the Redthornes the gift of immortality, and in exchange, the Redthornes would serve the king's house—House Kendrick —for ten years."

"Oh my God." Charley rose from her chair. "And you and your brothers had no say? No idea he'd made the deal?"

"My father was never one for consultation, particularly among his children. My mother was also kept in the dark."

"What happened when he finally told you?"

Dorian's chin dropped to his chest, and again, Charley wanted to go to him, to take him into her arms, to save him from the darkness before he drowned in it.

But she didn't dare.

Instead, she returned to her chair and took a deep breath, trying to keep calm, knowing the story was only going to get worse from here. It didn't help that the confession locked inside her was banging on the walls of her heart, desperate to break free. But how could she bring that up now? Her bullshit schemes, her struggles with Rudy, her father's death... In the shadow of Dorian's terrible past, her own bleak personal history felt like a fairytale.

"I suppose you never got the official tour," he continued, "but Ravenswood is a precise replica of our estate in West Sussex. My father worked for years coordinating the transport of our furnishings. The table, the sideboard, the chairs, the art, all of it. Back then, there were only ships and trains. Can you imagine?"

"Really?" It was all she could manage, the apparent shift in topics giving her whiplash.

"This room is a mirror image of the dining room we shared in England. It's where we held our engagement dinner—an intimate gathering, just the family and Aiden. My mother sat where you're sitting now, as proud and happy as I'd ever seen her, the fire crackling behind her. Colin, Gabriel, Malcolm—all of us toasted with fine wine and a decadent meal, revisiting family stories from our childhood, sharing our hopes for the future. The twins were there too—William and Fiona, the youngest Redthorne siblings, sixteen years of age. They'd always been enamored of Evie. And though she was in one of her low moods that night, I was still so happy, Charlotte. I truly thought it would be a turning point for us. For all of us." He glanced up at her, pain swimming in his eyes. "And it was."

"I'm sorry," she whispered, unsure what else to say. The torment in his eyes made her ache, her own eyes burning with fresh tears.

"Toward the end of the evening, when the staff had served the cake and we'd just opened the brandy I'd been saving for the occasion, there came a knock at the door. Father answered, promising us we were in for a rare surprise. The moment he ushered in the new guests, Evie bolted from the table in terror."

"Her father?" Charley guessed.

"Along with his three sons, yes. They'd come to honor the agreement—four royal vampires promising to sire the noble Redthornes, swiftly and thoroughly. They attacked us. They bit. They forced us to drink. They..." His voice broke, and he shook his head, as if that alone could erase the terrifying memories. "It was a slaughter, Charlotte. A brutal, horrifying slaughter that forever altered the course of our lives. Yet for House Kendrick and its king, it was no more than a business transaction, over and done in a matter of minutes."

Tears spilled unbidden down Charley's cheeks, splashing onto her jeans. "What about Evie? She didn't try to... to stop it, or change her father's mind, or... anything?"

A dark look crossed Dorian's face, and again his head dipped low. "In her father's eyes, Evie's desire for a normal life was an insult to her family and a dereliction of her royal duties. For the crime of falling in love with a mortal man, he ordered his eldest son to behead her. She turned to ash before her head even hit the floor."

Charley gasped in horror.

"My mother and the twins did not survive. William succumbed to his wounds almost immediately. Fiona held on a bit longer. Long enough for me to go to her. Her last words, as she lay dying in my arms, her blood spilling through my fingers like bathwater... Those words haunt me still. *Why didn't you help us, Dori?*"

Charley couldn't sit there another minute. She rose and crossed the room, joining Dorian at the glass doors and reaching for his hand.

He stiffened at her touch, but she laced their fingers together anyway, holding tight. Eventually, he relaxed and leaned in close, his cheek brushing the top of her head, his body trembling with sorrow and rage and a bitterness that had been festering for two-and-a-half centuries.

God, how she broke for him. Her heart and mind were shattered, the story hollowing her out inside. How had he lived for so long with so much pain? So much anguish? How had he not succumbed?

"I *despise* this room," he said softly, his breath warm in her hair. "Before today, I can't even recall the last time I set foot in here. Many times, I thought to burn it down, but I knew my father would only rebuild it. He always said it was a monument. To me, it's nothing but a tomb."

He pulled away from her touch and met her eyes.

"You absolutely *enchant* me, Charlotte," he whispered,

cupping her cheek. "You have from the very start. Even now, it's all I can do not to strip you bare, bend you over the table, and fuck you until it breaks beneath us."

"Dorian..." She swallowed hard and closed her eyes, tears still streaking her face. Despite the darkness hanging in the wake of his confession, her body warmed at his sudden closeness, his seductive words slipping beneath her skin.

"Evie's deception destroyed me," he said. "Destroyed my family. And though she died in the slaughter alongside my mother and siblings, hers is a betrayal I will *never* forgive."

Charley opened her eyes and searched his gaze for a lifeline, a faint glimmer of hope, but all she found was pain. Oceans and oceans of it, slowly pulling him under.

"Do you know why I've brought you here?" He slid his hand around the back of her neck, his voice taking on an eerie tone. "Why I've brought you to the one room in my *entire* manor that turns my heart to stone?"

Charley's stomach bottomed out, her own secrets and lies clawing their way up her throat. She had to tell him. No matter how foolish and childish, no matter how ridiculous her bullshit seemed by comparison, she could *not* keep lying to him—not with words, not with omissions, not even with the stolen, breathless kisses that had started it all.

"Dorian, I—"

"I've brought you here, Charlotte, because in the face of the *intoxicating* power you hold over me, I need to remember the past. The mistakes. The utterly *dire* consequences that come from entrusting one's heart to a beautiful woman." He tightened his grip and lowered his mouth to hers, his hot whisper a warning against her lips. "And you, my little prowler, need to learn that betraying the vampire king carries its *own* consequences. Deadly ones."

CHAPTER TEN

Before Charley could take her next breath, Dorian blurred out of her space, the sudden absence of his touch leaving her as cold and unbalanced as his warnings.

He stood behind her now, leaning back against the side of the stone hearth, arms crossed over his chest, eyes blazing.

She had no idea what Dorian knew, but it was clear he'd uncovered *something* about her. Her mind raced with possibilities, but in the end, it didn't matter.

By the time she left this room, he'd know everything. Every terrible truth.

"I fucked up, Dorian," Charley said. "Seriously, it's the worst mistake of my life—and it's not even just one mistake. It's a truckload of them, and every day I keep piling on more, and I just…God. There's so much I need to tell you."

"Oh, but there isn't. You see, Charlotte, I have a great

many connections, as you might imagine. Connections in the world of finance and government. In records and archives and law enforcement. In all manner of public and private sector agencies filled with people—human and supernatural alike—damn near tripping over themselves to do favors for the vampire king. In the time it took you to enjoy lunch and a leisurely Sunday drive with my brother, I've been on the phone." He tapped his lips, his words measured and even. "And do you know what I've learned?"

Charley shook her head, a tremble rolling from her shoulders to her feet.

"There is absolutely no record of Charlotte D'Amico at any art consultancy in the tri-state area," he began, "of which there are surprisingly few."

"I know. I can explain. I—"

"There is no record," he continued, taking a step toward her, "of Charlotte D'Amico ever having been employed in any capacity at any of the city's hundreds of museums. Not in Manhattan or the boroughs. Not in New Jersey or Connecticut or Pennsylvania."

"I'm—"

"In fact, no one has heard of you at any museum, gallery, art school, library, auction house, or antiques dealership on the entire eastern seaboard. As far as the legitimate art world is concerned, Charlotte D'Amico doesn't exist."

He was right, and he'd rendered her speechless. All she could do was stand there, waiting for the guillotine to drop.

"You live on Park Avenue," he said, taking another step

toward her. "You seem to be supporting yourself and your sister quite comfortably, yet you've got no verifiable source of income. You've never paid taxes on anything more than an inheritance from your father which, while sizable at the time, was hardly enough to sustain your current lifestyle."

The mention of her father unmoored her, immediately putting her on the defensive.

"You were in my home *one* time, in the middle of the night, in a moment of extreme duress," she said, as if she had a damn leg to stand on. It was stupid and desperate, but then, so was she. "You think that makes you an expert on my financial situation?"

Dorian was towering over her now, glaring down at her with barely contained fury. "Everything about you is a bloody *lie*. Look at me and tell me it isn't."

She met his gaze, but she couldn't tell him anything. Everything about her *was* a lie, and they both knew it.

"And you're a fucking *vampire*," she hissed anyway, desperate to feel something other than the guilt burning through her lungs. "Are we really making judgment calls?"

She felt the instant pressure of his impossibly strong grip on her arms, and then the room spun, the floor disappearing beneath her feet. When she finally found her footing again, she was clear across the dining room, hands braced against the sideboard, Dorian standing ominously behind her.

He leaned close and grabbed the edge of the mahogany, caging her between his arms from behind and meeting her gaze in the antique mirror.

She glared at him, her own anger rising to meet his. "Whatever you think you know about me? I promise you, you're not even scratching the surface."

"I *very* much doubt that."

"Then you can *very* much fuck off."

"Tell me, Charlotte," he said, voice low and menacing in her ear, so fucking sexy it made her thighs clench. "What's a suitable punishment for a liar and a con? For a woman who entered my life under false pretenses, and continues to stand here and lie to me in my own home, even now?"

He fisted the back of her waistband, his knuckles brushing her bare skin, sending a hot rush up her spine.

Charley swallowed hard, her mouth suddenly dry. For all his anger—and hers too—it was obvious they both still wanted each other. They were like two planets orbiting the same star, set on a collision course that could only end in a fiery, monumental explosion, yet neither seemed willing—or even able—to change direction.

"I could tear these clothes from your body and claim you right here," he said. "But you'd like that, wouldn't you?" He slid his hand around to the front of her jeans, deftly unfastening the button. Then, dipping his fingers into her underwear and sliding over her clit, "You're already wet for me. Already imagining my cock slamming into you from behind, *owning* you."

"Please…" Charley was hot and breathless, her skin flush beneath the heavy sweater, her core trembling for his touch.

"Please?" he repeated, dipping his finger lower, teasing

her entrance. "Are you begging me for something, Charlotte?"

"Yes. I..." She blinked rapidly, the last of her anger melting away as his fingers worked their devious magic. It was so easy to submit to him, to give him back the control he so desperately wanted. "Please, Mr. Redthorne."

With a swift tug, he pulled out his hand and yanked the jeans and underwear down to her knees, exposing her completely. In the mirror, she watched him lift a hand, and she bit her lip and held her breath, anticipation smoldering inside.

The punishment came hard and fast—two swift cracks against her flesh that echoed across the vacant dining room, unleashing her cry of pleasure.

He palmed her ass, rubbing away the sting as he nipped at her ear. "I always knew you were a bad girl."

"I... I am," she whispered, her head spinning. She needed to put an end to this before things went any further —to tell him the rest of the horrible story he'd yet to discover. But his presence was so overwhelming and intense, she couldn't think straight.

And *God*, how she wanted this.

But it wasn't right. Not like this. Not when she knew what had to be done.

"Dorian, there's more. I need to tell you the—"

"Shh." He reached for the button on his pants, quickly unfastening it and freeing his cock. A swift jerk of his hips, and the smooth tip slid between her thighs from behind, teasing her.

Close, but not quite close enough.

A soft moan escaped her lips. She couldn't help it.

"Is this what you want?" he whispered into her hair, his hand locking around her hip. The front of his suit jacket brushed against her backside, a cool contrast to the heat building between her thighs. "Me, fucking you hard and fast, one last time?"

"Y-yes."

"Say it. Tell me what you want. *Demand* it, Charlotte, and we shall see if the monster bends to your will."

"Please, Mr. Redthorne," she whispered. "I want you to fuck me one last time."

A slow grin slid across his lips, his eyes glinting with malice and desire and anger and loss, all of it burning bright.

"Then I *will* fuck you, enchantress. I will mark you. I will utterly *ruin* you for anyone else—mortal and immortal alike, from here to Manhattan to the very gates of hell. But I will *not* fall under your spell again, nor turn my back to offer a softer place for your treacherous blade." He fisted her hair, his whispered warnings falling across the back of her neck and making her shiver. "Open the drawer—top left."

With a trembling hand, she followed his order, sliding open the sideboard drawer where she imagined they'd once kept the silver.

But now, it held only papers. A notebook. Floor plans.

She recognized it at once.

Her intel.

He must've discovered it under her bed. Until this very second, she'd completely forgotten she'd stashed it there.

Fuck. Dorian knew about the heist. He already fucking knew.

That must've been why he'd left last night—he'd found the evidence.

The betrayal.

Fear and shame twined around her heart like serpents, squeezing tight. But before she could speak again, he slammed into her wet, aching pussy from behind, then pulled back out, slow and agonizing and perfect.

"I see we understand each other now, Ms. D'Amico."

Fuck... What game was he playing? He was furious— she could feel it coiled inside him, bunching his muscles, heating his skin, sending dark tremors through his voice. But his touch was as wild and electric as ever, his uncharacteristically slow thrusts forcing her to feel every hot, delicious inch.

"I... I was going to tell you," she stammered, knees weakening from the intense pleasure his cock delivered. "I wanted to..."

She trailed off, losing the ability to speak as he continued his slow, gentle tease, one hand still gripping her hip, the other tangled in her hair.

"Do you like that, Ms. D'Amico?" he whispered, rolling his hips against her backside.

"So much," she breathed. "You have no idea."

"And here I thought you liked it hard and fast." He slid

almost all the way out, then back in, so slowly she wanted to cry. "Perhaps even that was a lie."

Heat raced up her spine, her pussy throbbing as he held back just enough, clearly enjoying this divine torture.

So was Charley. No matter what he thought, that *wasn't* a lie.

She let out a soft sigh as her eyelids fluttered closed, but Dorian tightened his grip on her hair, forcing her to meet his gaze in the mirror once again.

"No, Charlotte. You're going to *watch* me fuck you. Watch me take my time, inch by inch, breath by breath." He pulled out, then slid back in, deeper this time. "And no matter how badly you want to come, no matter how close I push you to that blissful edge, you won't *dare*. You're not in a position to argue. You're only in a position to *obey*."

She bit her lip to keep from crying out. *God*, he felt so fucking good. She arched her backside to meet his next thrust, but again he pulled back.

"Is that clear?" he asked.

"Yes, Mr. Redthorne," she panted, dizzy for more of his brutal commands, his tortuous games.

He slid inside her again, angling to get even deeper. His gaze was as fierce and unrelenting as his cock, and right now, she was a slave to both. She wouldn't dare look away, wouldn't talk back, wouldn't come.

She and her vampire had blurred the lines between pleasure and punishment long ago, and now, trapped against the sideboard, completely at his mercy, all she wanted was to obey.

To submit.

To let go.

"Bloody *hell*, I hate that you feel so fucking incredible," he growled, his breath turning ragged. "Everything about you drives me insane."

"I'm sorry, Mr. Redthorne."

"I'll bet." He dug his fingers into her hip and shifted his angle, hitting her in an entirely new spot, making her shiver.

She watched him intently in the mirror, not daring to look away, no matter how badly she wanted to close her eyes and fall into this moment completely.

Dorian glared at her, his fury simmering, the tension building between them. But despite his raw anger, he still couldn't hide the desire raging in his eyes.

Or the pain.

Charley's heart cracked in half. He'd trusted her—took care of her—and she'd betrayed him. In that way, she wasn't much different from Evie, or even from his own terrible father.

A tear slipped down her cheek, her chest tight with sorrow and regret, even as her body hummed with intense pleasure, still so desperate for more.

Dropping the game for a brief instant, she reached behind her head and grazed his cheek. "I'm so sorry, Dorian. I never meant to hurt you."

A cocky grin twisted his lips, crazed and devilish as he continued to punish her with deep, masterful strokes. Without warning, he jerked his face away from her touch, and his eyes darkened, lips curling back as his fangs descended.

Charley's broken heart leaped into her throat. She'd never seen the transformation up close—after the attack last night, everything had happened so quickly; her only concern had been saving his life.

It wasn't just the fangs. The new brutality in his eyes changed his whole face—a chilling, ominous mask she hardly even recognized.

"You think you could hurt me?" he whispered against her neck. "You think I would allow *you*—a mere human *blip* on the timeline of a vampire's immortal eternity—to hurt me?"

"I... I don't know."

He dragged his mouth up the side of her neck, fangs grazing the skin just behind her ear, unleashing a flood of memories from last night.

The skin at her wrist warmed, the euphoria of that deep, penetrating bite rushing through her again, making her shudder.

Dorian pushed deeper inside, harder this time, his control starting to slip.

Her thighs trembled, her pussy clenching around him, her heart thundering, her body warring with her mind. She wanted so badly to give in, to let the explosion of pleasure burst forth, but she *couldn't* disobey him. Not now.

It was their final time, just like he'd said. And she needed to make it last.

She clenched her teeth and beat back her desire, muscles trembling with the effort.

"Are you frightened, little prowler?" he groaned, those sharp fangs dangerously close to her artery.

"Not of you, Mr. Redthorne." It was the barest whisper, but an honest one, and Charley forced herself to hold his punishing gaze, even though the words left her even more exposed than his hands. "I know you won't hurt me."

"You know nothing," he growled, his skin gleaming with a fine sheen of sweat as his own pleasure built. "I've slaughtered foes for lesser offenses."

Charley swallowed the tightness in her throat. She didn't need him to elaborate; she'd witnessed it firsthand the night of the fundraiser, when he'd ripped out the heart of a vampire who'd threatened her.

He could *do* that, she reminded herself now. Rip out hearts, tear off heads, kill without hesitation or remorse. He was, as he'd warned her so many times before, an apex predator. And in his powerful hands, at the mercy of his bite, Charley could easily become his prey.

Especially after what she'd done.

Still, she wasn't afraid.

Charley had spent her entire life around vicious, terrible men. Men who'd hurt women for pleasure, or because they were bored, or because they had some sick need to assert their power. She didn't have to look any further than her own fucked-up family tree for an example.

But when it came to the vampire whose fangs grazed

her flesh now, she trusted him. Completely and without question.

"You won't hurt me," she repeated, her confidence growing, her blood still singing for the rapturous bite those sharp fangs promised. "You *wouldn't*."

"Tell yourself all the pretty stories you wish." He stilled behind her and buried his face in her hair, inhaling deeply, his cock heavy and thick inside her. "But pretty stories can only keep the nightmares at bay for so long."

Still fisting her hair, he slid his other hand across the front of her hip and dipped down between her thighs. When he brushed her clit, she cried out, leaning back against the solid wall of his chest.

"How long, I wonder, can you hold out for me?" He nuzzled deeper into her hair and licked the back of her neck, his tongue a hot tease that sent tiny sparks skittering across her scalp. "I can feel it, Charlotte. You're so tight, so close, you can barely breathe. All you want is for me to say the word. To order you to come. Isn't that right?"

Despite the truth in his words, she did *not* want to give in now. To let him win.

But in so many ways—beautiful, impossible, dangerous ways—he already had.

She arched her hips, pulling him in deeper, another soft moan escaping.

Dorian growled behind her, and for a moment she feared he'd pull out completely—that he'd punish her for disobeying his commands by leaving her in this crazed, manic state of unfulfilled passion. Instead, he increased the pressure on her clit and rocked forward again, fucking her harder, the friction building, the heat making her gasp.

"*Watch*," he demanded, pulling her hair. "Watch me make you come. And don't make a *fucking* sound."

She pressed her lips together, and he fucked her harder, his fingers slipping faster over her clit, his jaw tight as the pleasure rolled through him, rising unchecked on his face in the mirror.

Charley saw the precise moment his control finally unraveled. The look in his eyes turned feral, his lips curling back over his fangs as he slammed into her one last time and let out a primal growl, his body shuddering as he came inside her and finally pushed her over that bright, tingling edge...

She fell, hard and fast.

The orgasm exploded inside her like fireworks, starburst after epic starburst, leaving her wet and trembling, chasing the very last breath from her lungs.

Through it all, she remained silent.

And in the end, when the last tremor rolled through her body, Dorian broke their gaze and rested his forehead on her shoulder, and Charley closed her eyes and tried, in vain, to count the stars swimming before them.

The moment was sweet, but fleeting, and after a few more blissful heartbeats, he finally pulled out from between her thighs and tucked himself back into his pants.

Charley wasn't ready to lose him, though. Not yet.

"I'm *not* afraid of you, Dorian Redthorne." She turned around to face him and lifted her hand, fingertips tracing a path from his brow bone down to his mouth. He opened at her touch, and she slid her thumb inside, grazing the edge of a razor-sharp fang.

At the barest pressure, it sliced through her skin, blood beading on the surface and dripping onto his tongue.

Another low growl vibrated from his chest, and his eyes turned from their rich honey-gold to a deep, dark red. It felt like watching the sun rise over the ocean, and it filled her with wonder.

My vampire king...

It was mysterious and impossible.

It was the sexiest, most incredible thing she'd ever seen.

Charley slid in deeper, and Dorian closed his lips around her thumb and sucked, moaning reverently. She brought her other hand to his cheek, and he fell to his knees, suddenly lost to the taste, the pleasure, the feed.

His soft, warm tongue stroked her skin, the delicious pressure of the suction winding her tight with new desire.

With power.

She let him take it—just for another minute—then dragged her thumb out of his mouth, lingering on his lower lip.

Dorian glanced up at her, his red eyes gleaming with so much hunger, she was certain he'd grab her exposed thigh and sink his fangs into her femoral artery.

But instead, he fisted the hem of her sweater and brought his mouth to her belly, kissing a hot path up to her breasts as he slowly rose from the floor. In a flash, he tugged the sweater over her head and tossed it behind him, then cupped her face, his mouth descending in a searing kiss.

She tasted her blood in his mouth, tasted his desire for her, tasted his pain. It was all wrapped up together, pulsating through his vicious kiss until there wasn't a single lie left between them—not one their bodies could tell, anyway.

Charley finally pulled back, staring deep into his eyes, once again bright and golden. His fangs had receded.

"Tell me you meant it," she whispered, knowing she was skating on the knife's edge, begging him for something she had no business wanting, but unable to stop the words. More than the story of the planned robbery, more than the desperate apology she'd rehearsed in her mind for hours, more than the pleasure he'd coaxed from her body, *this* felt like the true confession. The ultimate baring of her soul. "Last night... Tell me it wasn't a dream, Dorian."

His eyes clouded, and she knew at once he understood her meaning.

She was asking about his own true confession, a ghost that still whispered in her ear.

I've bloody well fallen in love with you, Charlotte D'Amico...

"Not a dream," he said, closing his eyes. "Only a momentary lapse in judgment. I assure you—it won't happen again."

"Liar," she whispered, taking his face between her hands, forcing him to look at her again. She could see it in his eyes—the embers still burning for her, the tenderness.

The love.

It was as new as the dawn on New Year's Day, as fragile as a soap bubble, but it was real.

Not a dream. Not a lapse in judgment. Not something that wouldn't happen again.

Despite everything, it was happening right now.

Fresh anger blazed in his eyes, as if he resented her for recognizing the truth, and he kissed her again, desperately working his way down her neck. Her hair hung low in front of her breasts, and he pushed it behind her shoulders, clearing the way for his hot mouth.

But then, without warning, he stopped. Pulled back. Gasped.

His fingers hovered over her collarbone, as if he was afraid to touch her.

His eyes widened, then filled with hot, new rage.

This time, it wasn't directed at her.

It was directed at the man who'd marked her.

CHAPTER ELEVEN

"Who… did… this?" Dorian could barely get the words out, fangs burning through his gums again, mouth filling with a taste for blood and vengeance.

Charlotte's skin was swollen and red, a row of fresh bruises decorating her collarbone like rotten grapes.

Dorian's vision swam, blood pounding in his ears. He thought he'd been angry last night, finding the robbery plans in Charlotte's bedroom. He thought he'd been angry when he'd cornered her in the dining room, confronting her with his dark past and her own bloody lies. He thought he'd been angry as he'd fucked her today, his traitorous heart still beating just for her, nearly breaking to think it might truly be their last time.

But seeing the perfect, silky-smooth flesh he'd eagerly kissed and caressed so many times before, suddenly bruised and battered…

I will find the man who did this, and he will beg *for death…*

"*Who?*" he demanded, fighting to keep his voice even, even as tremors of rage rocked his body.

Charlotte bent down to pull up her pants and retrieve her sweater, ducking his insistent gaze. She dressed quickly and covered herself up again, but now that he'd seen the marks, no amount of clothing would erase them from his mind.

"Charlotte, answer me." Dorian wanted to break something. Some*one*. Had this happened before? Was it the snake who'd shown up here the night of the fundraiser, claiming to be her driver? Was it the man who'd ordered her into the SUV outside the Salvatore? Some other soon-to-be-dead man for whom Dorian should promptly order a coffin and headstone?

His mind reeled, his fury desperate to lock in on a target. In that moment, if Charlotte pointed out a stranger on the street and named him as the one, Dorian would've ripped the man's throat out without a second thought.

"Charlotte?" he tried again, gently cupping her face. She looked up at him with wide, frightened eyes, her lashes wet with tears. "Tell me his name."

Charlotte bit her lower lip. She seemed at once determined and vulnerable, those eyes frantic, her mouth red from his kiss, her hair a mess. Even falling apart, she looked beautiful. Dorian didn't know how she always managed to get under his skin, but she did—every fucking time. And despite his intention of keeping a safe distance, all of his cool rationality—along with a good bit of his sanity and the last shreds of his self-preservation—had

SARAH PIPER

flown out the window the moment he'd seen those bruises.

Oh, who was he kidding? It wasn't just the bruises. His good intentions died the moment he'd laid eyes on her today, so clearly happy to see him, so confused by his cold response. He could no more keep his guard up than he could keep his mouth from devouring her lush, soft lips or his body from craving the exquisite taste of her blood.

Dorian ran a hand through his hair, closing his eyes in an effort to regain his composure. When he opened them again, she was still watching him, her own gaze desperate and frightened.

But not of him.

He didn't know whether to feel relieved or annoyed about that.

"Tell me this much," he said. "Are your injuries related to the information I found in your bedroom?"

At this, she finally nodded, letting loose a deep sigh. A strand of auburn hair stuck to her lips, fluttering in the shallow breeze of her breath. Dorian couldn't take his eyes off it. Off *her*, the woman who'd gotten him so turned round he could barely think straight.

"It was my boss," she admitted. "Rudy."

Rudy. Even the name enraged him, the sound of it setting fire to his ears.

"Was this the boss I met outside the Salvatore? The one who all but shoved you into the SUV and sped you away from me?"

"Yeah, and before you ask why I work for such a trash

114

fire of a person… Rudy's not just my boss, Dorian. He's my uncle."

"Your *uncle*?" Dorian didn't know why it surprised him. It wasn't as if his family was a stellar example of love and loyalty.

But still, it did.

He'd wanted better for Charlotte, he realized. Despite everything he'd learned about her, everything he'd speculated in the hours since discovering those floor plans, he'd still wanted her to be innocent. Not of the crime, perhaps, but in the sense that maybe she'd been spared some of life's harsher brutalities.

That had been a fool's hope, of course. She was as damaged as he was. In different ways, but nevertheless scarred.

He'd seen the darkness inside her the moment they'd first locked eyes in the Salvatore lobby. It had drawn him in deep, calling to his own shadows.

Even now, looking into her beautiful copper eyes, Dorian saw the gathering storm. And rather than run from it, rather than take shelter, he wanted to utterly *bathe* in it.

"He runs our crew now," she said. "He took over when my father died."

"And which crew would that be?"

"We're art thieves, Dorian." Charlotte pressed her fingers to her temples and sighed, clearly exasperated, but Dorian needed to hear her say it aloud. "It's the family business. I've been doing it professionally since I was Sasha's age. That's part of what I wanted to tell you today."

"Your father—the art lover. He was in the business too?"

"My father *was* the business. He built the entire empire from the ground up."

"Sasha?"

"I've kept her out of it." New fire burned in Charlotte's eyes at the mention of her sister. "She's got a chance at normal. I'm doing my best to give it to her."

Dorian's heart softened a bit more. But then the bruises flashed through his mind again, and he reached for her collarbone, tracing his fingers across the sweater.

"And this man... your uncle." He grit his teeth, keeping a tight rein on his anger. "He's the one who put his hands on you?"

Charlotte took a step back and wrapped her arms around herself, barely holding back a shudder. "It's the first time he's gotten so violent with me. Usually he just threatens."

"Excellent. So you won't mind if I drain him of his blood and bury his body out back?"

Her eyes widened. "Dorian, no! You can't kill him. You can't even threaten him. He's got too many fail-safes in place. If anything happens to Rudy..." She shook her head and lowered her gaze, but it was too late. Dorian had seen the sheer terror in her eyes.

Despite his earlier anger at her, despite his suspicion, despite every horrible thing he'd felt since last night, Dorian's heart bloody ached. It was all he could do not to take her into his arms and repeat the promise he'd made that day in the mountains—that he'd keep her safe forever.

He still bloody loved her. Even the worst kind of betrayal couldn't stamp out those feelings. And now, watching her tremble in the dining room that reminded him of his own hour of monumental helplessness, Dorian could *not* turn his back on her.

He took a step closer, the space between them shrinking again. Their bodies had always been highly attuned to each other, reacting instantly to a touch, a breath, a caress, even a look. Standing before him in her bulky sweater, Charlotte tried to cover her chest with her arms, but Dorian had already noticed her nipples, firm and erect beneath the fabric.

His cock stiffened as he tried desperately to rid his mind of the memories, the taste of her soft skin as he'd sucked those rose-colored peaks into his mouth time and again, teasing and biting, moaning her name as he drove himself into her hot, willing flesh...

"I hate asking this, but I need your help," she whispered, yanking him back to the moment. "It's truly a matter of life and death."

Against every warning in his heart, Dorian nodded. "I'm listening."

"Sasha and I are in danger. I know I deserve it—I made this bed, and now I have to lie in it. But she doesn't. I can't let him hurt her. I'll tell you anything you want to know about the heist, about the art, my family, all of it. But I'm begging you, Dorian. Please don't send me away."

Tears gathered in her eyes again, the coppery color bright against the bloodshot whites, and Dorian's breath caught. Since his discovery of her plans, he'd imagined all sorts of ways to punish her... but that didn't mean he wanted her to suffer. And Sasha had nothing to do with this. Even now, Dorian could hear her laughing with Aiden in the pool outside, her tone light and carefree.

He remembered the picture he'd seen of her in Charlotte's bedroom last night.

Who would want to hurt that sweet, charming girl?

Charlotte was losing her carefully controlled facade, breaking down before him in a way that couldn't—despite all evidence to the contrary—be an act. She was clearly withholding information—as usual—but she wasn't lying about Sasha being in danger. That much was obvious.

Dorian couldn't help himself. He needed to touch her again, to feel her skin, if only for the briefest moment. He reached for her face, and she leaned into his touch, her warm breath caressing his wrist.

There was more to her story. A lot more.

But right now, the question plaguing him most—the one that posed the most danger for all of them—was one she'd been dodging since before last night's attack.

And as much as he didn't want to push her into that corner again, Dorian needed an answer.

"Alexei Rogozin," he said, and Charlotte winced. "Are you and your... *uncle*... working for demons?"

Dorian held his breath, waiting for the denial. Desperate for it.

The Redthornes could take care of a human stain like

Rudy, one way or another. But if the demons were involved, their world just got a *lot* more complicated.

Seemed to be the running theme with Charlotte D'Amico.

"If you'd asked me that two days ago," she said softly, "I would've said no. But after last night?"

Bloody hell. Dorian lowered his hand from her face, his chest tightening. "Something tells me we're going to need alcohol for this conversation."

"Better make mine a double."

CHAPTER TWELVE

Charley scooted her chair closer to the fireplace in Dorian's study, pulling the blanket tight across her shoulders as he bent down to light the fire.

After cleaning up in the bathroom and taking a brief detour to check on Sasha—who was presently having the time of her life in the pool with Aiden—Charley had followed Dorian into the study, preparing to bare her soul. Not just about the planned robbery, but about her entire life —the heists, the high-end auctions, the hundreds of little mistakes that had led her to this moment, sitting in the manor of the vampire she loved, a million miles away from him.

Miles he might never let her cross again.

"I'll go fix the drinks," Dorian said, the fire roaring comfortably. "Try not to steal anything while I'm gone."

She took the hit, sucking it up without a response as he headed for the kitchen. He'd certainly earned the right to a few below-the-belt comments, but she hoped it wouldn't continue all day. She'd already hit pretty close to rock-bottom on her own; she didn't need the extra help.

Charley closed her eyes and let the fire warm her skin, the crisp, outdoorsy scent reminding her of the first time she'd been here, the night she'd discovered the Redthornes were vampires. That vampires existed at all.

It hadn't even been that long ago, yet so much had already changed. Was *still* changing, moment by agonizing moment.

Despite the insane passion that had overtaken them in the dining room, she knew it was over between them. It had to be. And she already missed him—his exquisite touch, his kiss, his smile, all of it.

What have I done?

Charley ached with regret, her heart mourning for all the things she'd destroyed. Things she'd never deserved in the first place.

"So you're a professional art thief. Cheers, then." Dorian was back, his voice startling her.

She opened her eyes, and he handed her a Sapphire and tonic, clinking their glasses. Icy liquid splashed onto Charley's hand. Absently, she wiped it on her jeans and took a deep drink. The alcohol was cold and strong—exactly what she needed.

Dorian settled into the chair across from her, not meeting her eyes. Everything in her ached to be close to him. She wanted to set down her glass and climb into his lap, to slide her fingers into his thick, silky hair. She wanted to whisper every reassurance, to kiss away the lines of doubt and worry she'd put on his face, to wrap her legs around his hips and show him how sorry she really was.

To pick up where they'd left off in the dining room.

But whatever tenderness and heat had filled his eyes then, now there was only ice.

She took another sip.

So did Dorian.

Both of them sighed.

Neither spoke.

The fire crackled.

And Charley was about to explode.

"So," she finally blurted out, "it's not like you wake up one day going, 'I think I'd like to steal priceless works of art for a living. Let's get to it!' I didn't choose this path, Dorian. It was chosen for me."

She took a deep breath and started talking. Slowly at first, then all at once, the words rushing out from a deep, dark place inside she'd never before opened. The longer she spoke, the more secrets she revealed, each one more painful than the last.

She told him about her childhood, growing up with her father and the crew after her mother split. How they'd taught her the con game, and how her first big score as a teenager had made everyone proud—had made her a bona fide member of the crew.

A phantom.

Ever since that moment, Charley's "career" had been a series of cons and heists, lies and manipulations, all of them virtually interchangeable. The only thing that had made it bearable was her passion for the art itself, the bright and colorful place she traveled to in her mind when all of life's other doorways had been shut.

"Everything I've told you about my love of art is true," Charley said now. "It's the one thing about my work I don't regret."

Dorian grunted into his glass. "Is that supposed to justify it, then?"

"Of course not. I just meant—"

"Because I love the art too, Charlotte. It's why I pay millions of dollars to acquire it legally. It's why people all over the world buy and make and trade it—because we love it, because it tells a story, because it makes us feel less alone. *Not* because we want people like you to steal it from us, and then sit back and talk about it like it's a bloody thing of reverence."

"I've kept things from you," she said. "A lot of things— really important stuff. But what I shared with you... That was real. You're the first man I've ever... No one else knows those things about me. Before you, no one else had even asked."

The admission left her naked, but Dorian seemed unaffected.

"Is this the part where you tell me I'm *different*?" he asked, making air quotes around the word. "That what we had was *special*?"

His mockery burned to the core.

"It *was* special," she said. "Say whatever you want—I

deserve it. But my mistakes don't change what we shared. It was real, Dorian, no matter how quickly it happened, no matter what circumstances brought us together. You can't go back and undo it."

Especially after the way you looked at me in the dining room...

"You undid it for me," he snapped.

"But I—"

"I know. You didn't have a choice. Right?"

"I grew up thinking this was normal. And by the time I figured out it wasn't, it was too late."

"Newsflash, love. It's *still* a choice. One you make again every time you wake up and decide to stay in the business another day."

Charley huffed, her defenses rising. "Like *you* wake up every day and decide to remain a vampire?"

"I *don't* have a choice about what I am."

"Rudy *owns* me," she said. "Not only is he my sole source of income, but he's also made it very clear that this is my job for life. If I try to leave him, if I make any more mistakes, if I don't follow through on my end of the deal, he'll kill me. He'll kill Sasha. So fine, maybe I *do* have a choice about whether or not to commit a crime. But when it comes to staying alive? To protecting my sister? Sorry— that's not a choice."

Dorian's eyes blazed again, but then softened, and he looked away, taking a long sip of scotch. Charley suspected he was thinking about his own brothers—what he might be driven to do if their lives were at stake.

No matter how much he'd bickered with them—even with Gabriel—Charley knew he cared for them. She could see it in his eyes.

After a long pause, Dorian said, "So the money... How exactly does it work?"

Charley told him about the hierarchy, the payouts, how Rudy took over after her father's death.

"He became the new boss, and he put himself in charge of everything—the books, the assets, the whole operation. We liquidated most of my father's personal collection, but because I was so naive, a lot of that money went straight back into the operation. I live in my father's penthouse, but I'm not paying for maintenance and upkeep—that's all Rudy. I don't manage my own credit cards. As pathetic and impossible as it may seem, I don't even have a checking account."

Charley's face burned.

Thirty-two years old, and I'm as dependent as a child.

Dorian stared into the fireplace, his jaw clenching. "What transpired this morning? Why did your uncle attack you?"

Charley looked at him through glazed eyes, her breath catching. They were getting closer to the specifics—to her role in the planned heist of Dorian's estate. Even after everything she'd shared, the idea of voicing those particular details left her burning with new shame.

"I screwed up my end of the deal," she said. "Rudy... He wanted me to convince you to take me and your brothers out of town next weekend, leaving Ravenswood clear." Dorian's eyes widened, but Charley pressed on. "I wasn't going to, Dorian. I told him it was too soon—that you'd get suspicious."

"Obviously, he didn't like that response."

"No. He accused me of… of having feelings for you."

Dorian raised an eyebrow, but Charley would neither confirm nor deny. What was the point? They were done. Hadn't he made that clear enough already?

"That," Dorian said suddenly, jabbing a finger toward her collarbone, where Rudy's handiwork still throbbed. "That's the kind of man you work for. The kind of man your father left you with. The kind of man who thought nothing of harming his own niece just because he didn't get his way."

She nodded. He wasn't telling her anything she didn't already know.

"So he's making his move this weekend, then?" Dorian asked.

Charley shook her head. "I bought another two weeks. Three at the most. I said you needed time to see the acquisition through before we could get away."

"He knows about the *acquisition*?"

"He knows nearly everything."

Shuddering under his accusatory, wounded glare, Charley gave him the play-by-play—details about Travis' surveillance of the estate, the fake interviews at FierceConnect, her own assumptions on how the actual heist would likely go down. Every detail felt like an arrow shot straight into Dorian's heart, but she forced herself to continue, all the way to the bitter end.

"Unbelievable. Truly." Dorian scowled and shook his head, unable to hide his disgust.

"Look, Dorian. I told you I'd come clean about the robbery. Judge me all you'd like—God knows I deserve it. But if you're going to keep asking me questions, don't act surprised when you hear the answers. I'm not a good person. I'm a fraud, a thief, a criminal. By all rights, I should be in prison."

"Yes, you should be. And your uncle should be eviscerated and hung by his worthless worm of a cock from the top of the Empire State Building."

A tiny smile broke across Charley's face as she pictured such a perfect act of revenge.

But it didn't last.

"Rudy's already made arrangements to have me and my sister taken out if anything happens to him," she said. "Besides, it's entirely possible we're dealing with more than just my sleazy uncle and a crew of human criminals. Right?"

"Rogozin," Dorian whispered, the muscle on his jaw ticking. "Tell me about your connection to him, Charlotte. Please. I need to know what we're facing here."

Charley took a long, deep pull from her drink, steeling her nerves. She hated going back to that terrible day in her father's car, that shady parking lot behind the pizza place and crappy apartment. But Dorian was right—she needed to put it all on the table.

She felt Dorian's eyes on her, but she couldn't meet them, focusing instead on the fireplace as she carved open her heart and gave voice to the story written in her scars, inside and out.

Where you off to, little girl?

Not so tough when Daddy's not around, are ya?

Don't struggle, D'Amico bitch...

She confessed it all, one painful word at a time, from the broken birthday promises to the stabbing to her stay at the hospital.

To the mystery that surrounded that day, even now.

"I don't know who my attackers were," she said, her throat as raw as her nerves. "At this point, I don't even know if they were men, or demons, or something else altogether. All I know is the client's name—Alexei Rogozin. That's who my father and uncle went upstairs to meet. They never mentioned him again, and I never asked. I don't know if Rogozin ever found out what'd happened to his guys, or if he was the one to send them after me in the first place. I have no idea if Rudy still deals with him or if that was their last meeting." She took another deep drink, then shook her head. "For all I know, they're old pals."

Charley may have been an idiot, but she wasn't stupid enough to believe her uncle was capable of any loyalty or compassion. Not when it came to her.

For a long time, Dorian sat in silence, staring into the flames. He didn't move. Didn't look at her. Didn't even blink.

Charley closed her eyes. She couldn't even imagine what was going through his mind.

Maybe he was thinking—just like *she* had thought in her own darkest moments—that she deserved everything that'd happened to her.

"*Fuck!*" Dorian's outburst tore Charley from her thoughts. Her eyes flew open just as he crushed the glass in his hand. Blood and scotch dripped from his fist.

"I… need a few moments alone," he finally said, cool and collected once again. "Please leave me, Charlotte."

Charley was at a loss, the emotional roller coaster taking its toll. Rising to her feet, she glanced around the study, but couldn't seem to make herself take a step. "I don't… Where should I…"

"There are thousands upon thousands of square feet in this manor, Charlotte. Inside and out. Take your pick."

By the time Charley returned from her exile in the rose garden, the broken glass was gone and two fresh drinks sat on the end table, one for each of them.

Dorian was back in his chair, gazing once again into the flames.

"I apologize for the outburst," he said without looking at her. "I shouldn't have done that."

"Understandable." Charley sighed and took her seat, pulling the blanket back over her shoulders. It was warm from the fire, the next best thing to a hug. "I dropped a few bombs on you. *Nuclear* bombs."

"It had nothing to do with you, and even if it had, that's not an excuse." At this, he finally looked at her, his gaze trailing down to her collarbone, where Rudy's fingerprints still stained her skin. "I know I've said things. I know I get... intense. I'm..." He closed his eyes and shook his head. "I don't want you to feel threatened by me. Ever, for any reason."

Charley sighed, resisting the urge to slip into Dorian's arms, to curl up against his strong, muscular chest. It was her favorite spot in the world, the place where she'd felt the most safe.

Threatened? How could he even *think* that?

"I don't," she said. "I never have."

Dorian opened his eyes and met her gaze, but his thoughts were completely veiled.

Waiting for him to speak again, she studied his face, drinking in the honey color of his eyes, his strong jaw, the perfect angle where his neck met his shoulder. She loved that spot—loved kissing it, biting it, nuzzling it, inhaling his clean, masculine scent.

She wondered now—selfishly, but there it was—if he still longed for her kiss as much as she still longed for his.

In that moment, Charley wanted to tell him all the things she'd left out of her confession, the feelings still roiling inside her. *Dorian, I'm in love with you too. I can't imagine my life—however screwed-up—without you. I'm so, so sorry, and I'll spend forever making it up to you if you'll just give me another chance...*

"I'm out," she said instead, surprising herself. "No matter what happens, I'm never going back to that life. I swear it, Dorian. I'm done with the con game. Whatever happens between us, I just... I want you to know that."

His eyes flickered in the firelight, but if he had a response to her latest confession, he wasn't sharing it.

"There's something still bothering me about the Rogozin connection," he said instead. "Vincent Estas."

Charley nodded. Dorian had told her about Estas last night—the demonic art dealer connected to both the Hermes statue and the LaPorte painting. He worked for Rogozin. It couldn't have been a coincidence.

"The big heist you told me about," Dorian said. "When my Hermes and LaPorte were first stolen. I presume it was one of your crew's schemes?"

"The scheme of all schemes," Charley said.

She took a deep breath to continue, but the words kept getting stuck, caught in a tight ball at the back of her throat. Like everything else she'd shared with him today, the story of her father's death was one she'd never spoken aloud. And now, sitting in his butter-soft leather chair, the smoky scent of the fire filling her senses, she had no idea where to begin.

Dorian sighed. "Charlotte, I want to help you and your sister. I *will* help you. But I need you to be honest with me. No more half-truths and cover-ups, no more sneaking around, no more lies. Whatever it is, we'll deal with it. I'm right here, and I'm not going anywhere. I promise."

Charley nodded, her eyes filling with tears at the sudden compassion thickening his voice. She didn't deserve to take comfort in it, but she couldn't help it. She felt so safe with Dorian, so protected. No matter how badly she'd fucked things up, he was a vampire of his word, and he was going to help her.

Even if he no longer wanted her in his life.

"My father... He was murdered," she whispered, so softly she wasn't even sure Dorian had heard. But his eyes changed in an instant, their fierce determination replaced with a deep, dark sadness. It was as though he could literally feel her pain—like she'd blown it away on a breath, only to have it land on his heart.

She shivered at the way he looked at her. At the power of her desire for him, still so real and intense.

Dorian offered no words, just a silence for which Charley was grateful. She didn't need apologies or sympathy, and Dorian seemed to sense as much.

Charley closed her eyes, trying to put the pieces of the story in order.

It's the perfect heist, baby girl. You go your whole life looking for a setup like this one, and we got it right here. We fuckin' got it.

Her father's words echoed, the memory of his sly smile lancing her heart. He'd been so certain it would go off without a hitch. Bones had officially christened it the One Night Stand—in and out, no strings attached—and the whole crew had pulled together to make it happen. They'd left nothing to chance.

It *had* been perfect too. Right up until the end.

Now, the more Charley thought about the whys and hows of that final imperfection, the more it confused her. Her father, betraying his own crew? Betraying his daughter without a word of warning? It had never made sense, but Rudy was always so sure. The other guys had been shocked at first, but eventually, they bought into Rudy's theory too.

Charley had always attributed her own lingering doubts to the haze of grief that had enveloped her after her father's death, and the fact that she'd been much too close to him in life to see the truth. By the time her head had cleared, Sasha had come into her life, and the past no longer mattered. Only the future.

Sasha's future.

But now, after five years, it was starting to matter again.

Solving the mystery of the botched heist suddenly felt like the most important thing in the world.

Charley's mind spun as she reviewed the facts.

Seventy million dollars in stolen art, boosted without a hitch, ferried away in a van that made it all the way through the Holland Tunnel, only to be stolen again somewhere on the Jersey side.

A "new guy" no one else but her father had ever met—a man he trusted enough to drive the van.

An uncle who'd taken over operations immediately, insisting his own brother had betrayed them.

The art itself vanishing without a trace, then resurfacing

years later in the home of Dorian Redthorne—Rudy's latest mark.

And never another word about the new guy—the one Rudy had walked away from with no talk of retribution, despite the fact that he'd allegedly whacked Rudy's brother and made off with the score.

In retrospect, it all looked too easy, too neat.

And Vincent Estas—the art dealer who'd sold at least two of the pieces from the missing cache—was a demon working for the same demon connected to a former client whose men had nearly raped and killed Charley.

"Charlotte," Dorian said softly, bringing her back to the moment. "Tell me what happened to your father, love."

She opened her eyes, took a steadying gulp of her drink, and started at the beginning.

"It was supposed to be the perfect heist..."

CHAPTER THIRTEEN

Fury tore through Dorian's chest like a blade, threatening to obliterate the last of his composure. He forced himself to remain outwardly calm, but inside was a war zone.

On one side of the battle sat Charlotte's betrayal—an enemy that had been festering in his heart since last night and had only gotten worse with her confessions.

She'd utterly played him. She'd spun her silky web, and he'd walked right into it. One kiss, one taste of her exquisite flesh, and he was eating out of her hand, ready to believe anything that had passed between her delicate lips. In trusting her, he'd put his entire estate, his closely guarded secrets, and his brothers' lives on the line.

It wouldn't happen again. He wouldn't allow it.

But on the other side of the trenches, an even darker enemy lurked, one whose very name left Dorian shaking with rage: Rudy, the piece-of-shit uncle who'd so brutally marked her. Who'd threatened the lives of Charlotte and her sister. Who'd been doing it—and probably much worse —for years.

Charlotte seemed unable to see it yet, but Dorian had a strong suspicion the man was behind her father's murder as well.

Dorian didn't just want him dead. He wanted him to suffer. Horribly. Along with Rogozin, and Estas, and Duchanes, and every man, demon, and vampire who'd *ever* brought her harm.

But it wasn't an option. Not yet. Charlotte had said as much—one wrong move against her uncle, and she and her sister would pay the ultimate price.

Never before had Dorian felt so bloody impotent.

It was a feeling to which he had no interest in getting accustomed.

He blinked hard, trying to clear the images of Charlotte's bruises from his mind, focusing instead on the pot of chili bubbling on the stove.

While Sasha and Aiden—who in the span of a single afternoon had become the best of mates—played a cutthroat game of Monopoly in the study, Dorian and Charlotte had relocated to the kitchen, where they'd volunteered to cook dinner so they might continue their conversation in private.

Now, he stirred the chili with a concentration bordering on obsession.

"We need to review our options," he said, keeping his voice low. "The primary goal is protecting you and Sasha at all costs. Everything else is secondary."

Charlotte leaned in beside him with a cutting board full of diced onions, scraping them into the pot. She gazed up at him, her eyes full of gratitude, but Dorian quickly looked away. He didn't want to see that look in her eyes. It was hard enough to be in the same room with her knowing he'd never hold her in his arms again, never feel those lips brushing against his chest, never hear the soft, delectable sigh she made right before he drove her to the edge...

He cleared his throat, retreating to the counter to open a bottle of wine before he got himself hard again. He needed to figure out this Rudy situation—lay down the options, pick the best one, and set the plan in motion—*not* fantasize about their mutually insatiable carnal appetites. Those steamy nights had been pure bliss, but they were over. As far as Dorian was concerned, this was a business arrange-ment now—a deal not much different from the hundreds he'd conducted over the years in the FierceConnect boardroom.

Yes, but you've never been in love with your business associates, you sodding idiot...

"We need to determine whether your uncle is still involved with Rogozin," he said, pouring two glasses of Cabernet. "And whether he knows Rogozin is a demon. If he does, it's likely he also knows I'm a vampire. And if that's the case, I guarantee they're after more than just my artwork, which complicates matters infinitely."

"I'm sorry." Charlotte sighed. "I wish I could remember more about Rogozin's men."

"It's a blessing that you don't." Dorian's chest ignited

again, imagining her as a girl younger than Sasha, fighting off those monsters. "For now, let's consider scenario one: your uncle is nothing more than a lowlife human, working with a crew of other lowlife humans to turn a fast buck, no supernaturals involved."

Charlotte nodded and stirred the pot, then brought the wooden spoon to her lips, sampling the chili. Dorian tried not to recall the feel of her velvet-soft tongue licking up and down his shaft in the guest house the night of the fundraiser, but it was no use. Everything about her turned him on, inside and out.

Forcing himself back to the urgent matter at hand, he said, "Under the lowlife human scenario... I'm assuming you don't have enough evidence of their former crimes to bring to the authorities? See if we might take your uncle out of the equation legally?"

"Not without implicating myself. I can't go to jail, Dorian. That would mean leaving Sasha. Rudy knows I'd never risk it—it's probably why he hasn't already killed me."

"So he knows your weakness."

"If by *weakness* you mean the one person in my life I'd willingly sell my *soul* to protect, then yes. She's my weakness."

"Loving someone isn't a character flaw, Charlotte," he said softly. "I simply meant... Look. Rudy knows exactly how to get to you. By threatening the one you love—explicitly or otherwise—he can keep you in a constant state of fear and obedience. As a royal vampire, I know the dynamic all too well."

"Yeah, but the difference is—I'm not a powerful immortal being. I'm a weak human." Charlotte covered the pot and turned it down to simmer, then grabbed her glass of wine. "And even if I had the physical strength to stand up to him, I don't have the courage."

Dorian frowned and reached up to tuck a lock of hair behind her ear. The contact made her heart skip—a soft beat that sang to him, drawing him closer. He couldn't help it. As long as they were in the same room together, he couldn't *not* touch her—no matter how badly he needed to keep his distance.

"You're the most courageous woman I've ever met, Charlotte. I won't have you doubting it. Not in my presence."

Her cheeks darkened, a shy smile touching her lips. "Is that an order, highness?"

"Indeed." He returned her smile, sliding his thumb across her lips, recalling how she'd done it to him in the dining room. The sweetness of her blood made his mouth water, and he leaned in closer, desperate for another taste...

"Cheese!" she said suddenly, pulling out of his grasp. "We need cheese!"

She darted for the refrigerator, and Dorian grabbed his wine, tipping back a healthy swig.

Bloody hell, the whole situation was growing more impossible by the second.

"So," she said, dodging his gaze as she grated a block of white cheddar into a large ceramic bowl, "any other ideas?"

Several, including but not limited to blurring you up to my bedroom and tying you to the bed, devouring you with kisses, and fucking you until you forget everything about your life but the feel of my punishing cock...

"Dorian?" she said, and he blinked, taking another sip of wine.

Right.

"What if we temporarily relocate you and Sasha to one of my properties in London," he said, "then let the robbery play out, at which time I'll have the thieves arrested onsite?"

"And then what? My sister and I live out the rest of our lives as fugitives? Rudy has connections, Dorian. Even if you had him arrested—hell, even if you took him out—the moment we set foot back in the States, we'd be dead. And that's assuming his guys didn't track us down overseas first."

"Fair point. All right, I could relocate my most valuable pieces to Tribeca. If they break in here, they'll only find a fraction of the estate, and perhaps they'll give up, moving on to something more lucrative."

"No good." Charlotte set the bowl of grated cheese on the table in the nook, then rummaged the cupboards for dishes and utensils. "Other than the Hermes and LaPorte painting, which I didn't mention because of the connection to my father's murder, they already know what's here. If it's gone when they make their move, they'll know I warned you."

Dorian bit back a curse. Of *course* they knew what was here. Dorian had been sleeping with a spy.

He reached for the bottle of wine, dumping the rest into his glass, the whole situation crashing down on him anew.

What a fucking mess.

"For fuck's sake, Charlotte. You really took me for a fool."

Wisely, she didn't deny it.

"I'll spend the rest of my life regretting that I betrayed you," she said, staring at the plate in her hands. "I've said and done a lot of fucked up things, hurt a lot of people… But you, Dorian Redthorne—you're my one."

"One what?"

Glancing up from the plate, she shrugged and said plainly, "I let you get away. Regrets don't get much bigger than that."

She held his gaze for so long, he was certain it was a dream. He bloody well wanted it to be—some garish nightmare from which they'd soon awaken, tangled together in his bed after another passionate night. He'd kiss the spot on her neck just beneath her ear, enfold her in his arms, and whisper to her about the craziest dream he'd ever had.

"Artwork aside," she said, returning her attention to setting the table, "what would you do with the cars? No way. It's too complicated."

Dorian's stomach bottomed out. "They're planning to go

after the cars as well? Bloody hell, Charlotte. How do you live with yourselves?"

"I don't. Being a thief? It's not a glamorous life. It's not a life at all. I don't have friends. I don't date. I don't work or explore new things or go on adventures. The dresses, the hair, the makeup... It's all funded by the operation. The only thing that gets me through the day—*every* day, no matter how terrible—is Sasha. When she showed up on my doorstep, everything clarified. My issues didn't matter anymore—not like that. She's my whole life, Dorian. My everything."

"I understand you love her, Charlotte, but she shouldn't be your sole reason for living."

"No, and I shouldn't be stealing. I shouldn't have dragged you into this mess. I shouldn't have let Rudy sell off my father's estate. I shouldn't have done a lot of things, but I did, and those are the cards I'm working with now. Obviously, it's not the greatest hand."

"Not the worst, either." Dorian offered a small smile. "You've got me, and I can be fairly resourceful when the need arises."

"Suffice it to say, the need has arisen." Charlotte returned the smile, but it didn't quite reach her eyes. "Any more brilliant ideas?"

"Just one. Final answer, love." Dorian downed the last of his wine. "I'm going to buy your freedom."

"What are you talking about?"

"Your dear Uncle Rudy isn't an art collector. He's a common thug. He's only in it for the cash. So here's how it plays out—I offer him a large sum, free and clear, no messy logistics like fencing and money laundering. He takes the bribe, and you get to live out the rest of your days on the right side of the law. You'll have to find a legitimate job, of course, and maybe move out of the penthouse, but—"

"No. He'd never go for it."

"We're not talking about a few hundred dollars." Dorian crossed the kitchen, joining her at the table. "Believe me, I'd make it worth his while."

"Dorian, I… You're not…" Charlotte finally abandoned the dishes, turning to slide her hands over his shoulders instead. Despite the pain of his still-healing wolf bite, her touch was electric, radiating pleasure up and down his back.

Fuck, he still wanted her. More than anything.

"I appreciate your offer," she said softly. "But this isn't the kind of job you just walk away from. I've seen too much. I know all their secrets, even if I can't prove them in court. The only way people like me walk away is if we've got enough hard, irrefutable evidence to keep the other guy in constant fear of its release, or if… if we die."

Immediately Dorian's mind flashed to her story about Rogozin's men—the type of danger her own father had placed her in. Over what—money? Power? Wasn't that what it always came down to?

Even as a human, Dorian had always been wealthy, a privilege he'd clearly taken for granted. He tried to imagine Charlotte as a child, doing her best to follow in her father's tainted footsteps, never realizing those footsteps would lead her straight to the grave.

The thought pierced Dorian's heart. Her father was as much a monster as her uncle. Daddy Dearest may not have put his hands on her, but he'd driven her to a life of brutality and violence just the same.

Exactly as Dorian's father had done to him.

Relocating Charlotte and Sasha, relocating the artwork, offering Rudy a buyout... None of his suggestions had really mattered, anyway. Deep in Dorian's gut, he *knew* they weren't operating under the human lowlife scenario.

Just as Charlotte had said about her own line of work, demonic entanglements weren't the sort of thing you walked away from. If her uncle had been involved with Rogozin in the past, he was almost certainly still involved with him now.

Which meant Charlotte and Sasha's lives weren't the only ones at stake.

It also meant something else.

Leverage.

"We're not out of cards yet, love." Dorian reached up and grabbed one of her hands, giving her a gentle squeeze. "Somewhere along the line, your uncle fucked up. Aside from me, I'm betting there are *many* others who'd like to see him dangling from his cock. Men, demons, vampires... the possibilities are endless."

"Okay. But what does that mean for us?"

"It means, my *incorrigible* little prowler..." Dorian

cupped her face and grinned. "It's time to put your special talents to better use."

She quirked an eyebrow. "Which talents, specifically?"

"You and I are going to do a bit of snooping," he continued, brushing a fingertip over the arched brow. "Your uncle has skeletons. We're going to dig them up. Every last bone, from every last grave, from every last cemetery. And then, when we find something incriminating, we're going to make that bastard an offer he *really* can't refuse."

Charlotte's eyes sparkled with hope, beautiful and pure, and Dorian lowered his mouth to hers, heart hammering in his throat, desperate for one more taste.

"Dorian, I... This isn't... We..." She was already melting into his touch, her protests dying in the air. Her eyelids fluttered closed on a soft sigh, and Dorian's lips brushed hers, sweet and silky and—

"Oh my *God!*" Sasha bounded into the kitchen, shattering the moment. "You guys are supposed to be cooking, not making out! I'm pretty sure that's a health code violation!"

Aiden stood behind her, desperately holding back a laugh. "Honestly, Dori. You're supposed to be setting an example here. Do better."

"Thank you, Aiden." Dorian pulled away from his woman. "Truly. You've just saved us from making a huge mistake."

"*Really* huge," Charlotte whispered, glancing down at his cock, which now stood at full attention between them.

He leaned in close again, nipping her ear and whispering a final warning. "This conversation is *far* from over."

With that, he excused himself and headed out to walk off his really huge... situation. By the time he returned to the kitchen, everything had changed.

The sight nearly brought tears to his eyes. It was one he'd never thought he'd see again, yet there it was—awkward and uncomfortable, slightly confusing, but bloody brilliant just the same.

There, crowded around the table at the breakfast nook, scarfing down bowls of hot chili and laughing at one of Sasha's endless stories, were his brothers.

Aiden, of course.

Colin, who'd finally wandered up from the crypts.

Malcolm, who'd just returned from the city.

And Gabriel, who—while not smiling, exactly—wasn't scowling, either. It was another rarity—one that soothed the ache in Dorian's heart.

Family. The word slid into his mind, fleeting but nevertheless real.

Blinking the sudden emotion from his eyes, Dorian took his place at the table next to Charlotte and grinned, pointing at his brothers with a spoon. "You bloody heathens better hope you saved enough for me."

CHAPTER FOURTEEN

"The penthouse was an utter disaster, as expected," Malcolm said. "The demons left no surface un-pissed-upon."

"Delightful," Dorian said, pouring himself a glass of scotch.

Hours had passed since they'd gathered in the kitchen—an enjoyable, all-too-brief reprieve from their usual bickering and plotting—and now the vampires of House Redthorne gathered in the study, gearing up for another round of political discourse before the crackling fire.

Dorian would've rather been elsewhere. Specifically, upstairs, making good on his threats to show Charlotte a proper punishment.

But he'd managed to think with his brain for once, ushering Charlotte and Sasha to their adjacent guest bedrooms at the end of the hall, refusing to extend the little thief an invitation to his own, no matter how desperately he'd wanted to.

Miraculously, he hadn't given in.

Not even when they'd passed his master suite, and her heart rate sped up, likely remembering all the deliciously naughty things he'd done to her there.

Not even when she'd mentioned wanting a shower, the invitation clear in her eyes.

Not even when Dorian had turned to leave her, catching the faint sound of her disappointed sigh.

He'd remained strong through all of it—a monumental effort that left him on edge and on fire, wishing he'd put his brain on a leash and listened to his cock instead.

Corralling his errant thoughts, he offered a nod of thanks to Malcolm.

Last night, after Dorian had ordered them to leave Charlotte's penthouse, Malcolm had spent the rest of the evening and most of today trying to track down news about Duchanes and his demons. Malcolm had been at Bloodbath during this morning's pre-dawn raid, but despite the very public closure of his precious club, Renault Duchanes himself never made an appearance.

Now, Dorian rifled through the file box containing the items he'd asked Malcolm to retrieve from the penthouse— Charlotte's purse and phone, along with most of the files and papers from his den. The files themselves weren't important; Dorian simply hadn't wanted to draw undo attention to the items he'd *really* wanted—the records of his darkest deeds.

Keeping the album tucked into the box, he cracked open the cover.

Crimson City Devil Strikes Again...

Dorian closed his eyes, a mix of shame and relief flooding his veins.

Closing the cover and replacing the lid on the box, he said, "Were you able to speak with security?"

"I met with the staff and viewed the exterior camera feeds," Malcolm said. "The video footage revealed two of the demons' marks—definitely Rogozin's guys."

"Thank the devil's cock." Dorian sighed as he settled into the chair closest to the fireplace. The blanket draped behind him held Charlotte's scent, and he leaned back, inhaling deeply.

"Forgive me, brother," Malcolm said, "but why do you seem consoled to learn that the demons who attacked you and vandalized your penthouse belong to Rogozin?"

"Because they *don't* belong to Chernikov. Chernikov and I made an agreement this morning, during which he assured me his organization was not involved. If I'd discovered he'd lied to me... Let's just say I'm relieved to keep my hands free of demon blood for another night."

Dorian updated his brothers on the meeting with the demon lord, including their mutual concerns about Duchanes working with Rogozin and Rogozin's potential plans with the dark witches and demon portals.

"That's *just* what we need," Aiden said from the adjacent chair, his tone uncharacteristically blue. "An endless supply of demonic enemies streaming in through the front door, fresh from hell and united against us."

"Let's not forget about the grays," Dorian said.

"*Grays*?" Gabriel, who'd been staring into the flames, finally glanced up. "As in, *vampire* grays? Are you fucking kidding me?"

"Cole Diamante and his associates are tracking a band of them in the area," Dorian said. "Now that he's come back into the fold, Cole has assured me he and the wolves will back us. But yes, the presence of the grays concerns me. After so many years without a sighting, the timing is quite suspect."

"Duchanes," Gabriel said.

Dorian nodded. "Chernikov has promised to keep me informed of anything he learns about House Duchanes and other vampires looking to ally with demons against the crown. He's also got an eye on Rogozin and the dark witches."

"And what will *that* juicy bit of intel cost us?" Malcolm asked.

"Weekend access in Manhattan for his underlings, with certain restrictions in place."

"Annoying," Malcolm said with a shrug, "but tolerable."

Dorian took a long pull from his scotch, bracing himself for the rest of the story. "He also wants the Mother of Lost Souls."

"Does he now?" Malcolm laughed. "Excellent! Just ask

him to kindly point us to its location, and he's welcome to it."

Dorian, Aiden, and Colin exchanged a loaded glance.

"We've... already located it," Dorian said. "And no, he's not welcome to it, nor to the demonic text that came along with it."

Gabriel and Malcolm remained silent as Dorian, Colin, and Aiden took turns filling them in on their various findings and theories—not just about the statue and the demonic book, but about what Colin had shared with Dorian last night before the attack.

Father's alleged cure for vampirism and other so-called supernatural ailments.

"So you're telling me there's a way to wipe supernaturals from the face of the earth?" Gabriel asked, his voice low and sinister. "And we're sitting on the bloody recipe card?"

"I've yet to locate the precise recipe, if that's what you wish to call it," Colin said. "But yes, I believe Father's journals contain such information—along with a great deal of other highly sensitive data that could become quite dangerous in the wrong hands."

"Then why are we standing around up here, jacking off?" Gabriel shot to his feet. "We need to get down to the crypts and burn it. All of it."

"I'm no sentimentalist," Aiden said, "but I would advise against it."

Gabriel wheeled on him, his deadly cold eyes shooting daggers of pure ice. "And *I* would advise against advising the royal family unless such advisement is specifically requested, which it wasn't. Furthermore—"

"Sit *down*, Gabriel," Colin said, his face stern and commanding, his eyes alight with an anger Dorian had never seen in the typically genteel vampire. "And for once in your immortal life, shut your sodding mouth. *Please*."

"*Thank* you," Aiden said. "Bloody hell, this family. Perhaps I should've taken my chances and stayed in England. Not that you lot could've survived as long without me."

"Agreed." Dorian raised his glass, offering a nod of thanks to his dear friend.

"Aiden is as much a part of the royal family as any of us," Colin continued. "And it's high time we start treating him accordingly. I, for one, appreciate his advice. And in this case, I happen to agree with him. But even if I didn't, I would welcome his thoughts. So, if you've got a problem with rational discourse, Gabriel, kindly excuse yourself from this meeting."

All of them were stunned into momentary silence by Colin's uncharacteristic outburst.

For a moment, Gabriel seethed, and Dorian worried he might escalate things—his favorite hobby.

But then he just nodded, sinking back into his chair with nothing more than an aggrieved grunt.

"Aiden," Dorian said, sharing a quick smile and a wink with his best mate, "please continue."

"Thank you, Colin. Dorian." Aiden cleared his throat. "As I was saying, I wouldn't be so quick to destroy the evidence, so to speak. For one thing, we don't know if there are other copies floating about, or if anyone else was working on the research with your father. It's possible he had assistance from vampires or mages in other countries. If this information were to find its way into the wrong hands through other means, the last thing we'd want is for House Redthorne to be in the dark."

"I understand your position," Gabriel said, albeit grudgingly. "But if Father truly died from this so-called cure, what's to stop our enemies from weaponizing it?"

"Nothing," Aiden said. "Which is why—in my humble, non-royal, unsolicited opinion, of course—I feel we've got the advantage here, and we need to hold onto it. If Colin can solve the puzzle from the source material, we'll be one step ahead of our enemies."

"How do you figure?" Gabriel asked.

"Like Augustus, Colin is a doctor. If he can decipher the cure for vampirism from your father's research, perhaps he can decipher a cure for that cure. Perhaps there are even applications beyond weaponry—applications that can help rather than harm vampires, or humans, or shifters, or anyone else with whom we share this beautiful, terrible world." He shook his head and let out a deep sigh. "Ignorance for the sake of enshrouding others in darkness is still ignorance. I understand the risks, Gabriel, but in this case, I prefer the light."

"I couldn't agree more," Colin said. "The material will be kept secured in the crypts. I shan't remove it, not even for a little bedtime reading. But it *will* be kept—not destroyed—for all the reasons Aiden articulated and more. Can we set aside our differences on that much, at least?"

All of them nodded in turn, even—however reluctantly —Gabriel.

But as much as Dorian agreed with Aiden and Colin, he couldn't help the new worry gnawing through his chest.

"There's… something else," he finally said, knowing he couldn't keep it from them for another moment. "In approximately three weeks, unless we can devise a way to stop it, a group of thieves will break into the manor and rob us bloody blind. I have reason to believe the ringleader is working for Rogozin, which means we have to assume the crypts are at risk as well."

"Thieves?" Malcolm rose from his chair. "How do you know about this, Dorian? Who is this ringleader?"

"A worthless cunt by the name of Rudolpho D'Amico." Dorian ran a hand over his face and sighed. "Otherwise known as Uncle Rudy. *Charlotte's* Uncle Rudy."

In the raucous volley of questions that followed, Dorian did his best to convey the severity of the situation without implicating Charlotte—a difficult task that left him even more wrung-out than his efforts to keep his hands and mouth from her luscious body.

Considering Dorian's terrible history with women—and the consequences such history had brought upon his house —his brothers took the news in stride, even showing concern for Charlotte and Sasha. It was as if the women's very presence in the manor today had loosened something inside all of them, shining a sliver of light into an otherwise dark, impenetrable fortress of blame and regret.

Dorian only hoped his willingness to help Charlotte wouldn't one day become another of those disastrous regrets, adding yet another layer of darkness to the brotherhood whose return he was only, just now, beginning to welcome.

"So," Malcolm said when Dorian finally finished, "we've got traitorous bloodsuckers siding with demons looking to make a major power play. We've got grays running unchecked in the woods—very likely released by those same traitors. We've got a tentative alliance with a demon kingpin who, by all rights, is our mortal enemy. And we've got a band of bloody thieves who not only pose a danger to the innocent women upstairs, but are also backed by the very traitors who cast the proverbial first stone."

"That about sums it up," Dorian said. Then, to Gabriel, "I'd like for you to look into this man. This… *Rudy*."

The name still left a bitter taste on his lips, no matter how many times he'd said it today.

Gabriel glanced up at him, and Dorian prepared for the inevitable argument. But then his brother nodded and said, "Anything in particular I should look for?"

"Firstly, we need to confirm the Rogozin connection. If they're still involved, someone will know about it."

"Did you check with Chernikov?"

Dorian shook his head. "Just because we have an agreement doesn't mean I trust the filthy demon. As far as I'm concerned, the fewer people who know about the planned heist the better. I don't want House Redthorne cast in an even weaker light."

"I'll see what I can dig up," Gabriel said. "Piece of shit like that is bound to leave a trail."

"Yes, and the sooner we can find it, the sooner we can follow it—and the sooner we can bring him down."

"Beyond the human stain," Malcolm said, "it's time to face the bigger facts here, brother."

Dorian bristled at the self-important tone. "To which bigger facts are you referring, *brother*?"

"We're outgunned in this fight," he said, crouching down to place another log on the fire. "House Duchanes may be the black sheep among the covens at the moment, but even if the other greater houses turn their backs on them, they've still got the numbers, the demons, and—lest we forget—a powerful witch who devised a poison strong enough to wholly incapacitate you."

"Don't forget the bloody grays," Gabriel added. "I'd bet my own balls Duchanes is responsible."

"The odds are certainly stacked against us." Malcolm rose from the hearth and dusted off his hands, making a show of furrowing his brow and tapping his lips as if he were channeling some utter brilliance from the great beyond.

To Dorian, it was all part of his endless scheming.

"For fuck's sake," Dorian said. "If I wanted to see a one-act play, I would've bought a ticket and put on a better suit. Out with it, Mac."

Malcolm met his gaze, his eyes sparkling with a determination Dorian already wanted to quash.

"Reunite the Council."

"The Council?" Dorian scoffed, dismissing the ridiculous suggestion at once. The Council was nothing more than a glorified vampire circle-jerk—a group of high-ranking, mostly ancient vampires who used to gather under the pretense of discussing the mind-numbingly endless politics of the various greater houses, when in fact they just needed an excuse to drink wine and congratulate themselves on their many uninspiring achievements.

They were so utterly useless that Dorian's father had disbanded the group decades ago, and the supernatural races had survived in their absence in relative, self-regulating peace.

Until now.

"I've no interest in resurrecting those dusty relics from the grave," Dorian said.

Malcolm folded his arms across his chest. "Need I remind you we're four vampires standing against—"

"Five," Dorian said firmly, glancing again at Aiden. "And we've got Cole and the wolves on our side as well, not to mention Lucien and Isabelle Armitage, whom I'm confident will align with us once we've eliminated Duchanes."

Malcolm shook his head, his face reddening with barely contained anger. "Even if that deal comes to fruition, that still leaves us gravely outnumbered. We need to take charge, Dorian. We—"

"You mean *you* need to take charge. That's what this is about, is it not? Your endless politicking, your scheming, your tiresome manipulations?"

"Who needs another drink?" Aiden asked, heading for the bar with a roll of his eyes. "Speaking of one-act plays."

"If I'm taking charge," Malcolm said, "it's because you refuse to. Dorian Redthorne, vampire king? Please. You wear the title as if it's nothing more than one of your bespoke suits—something to try on for a party and cast aside when—"

"I didn't ask for the crown. I wear the title because it's my duty."

"A duty you shirk at every turn."

"And you would do better? All this maneuvering, all these games, and you truly believe our situation wouldn't be just as dire—if not more so—with you at the helm?"

"I would at least *try*, which is more than I can say for a man who'd rather spend his days playing with his cock and kneeling at the altar of yet *another* hot piece of—"

Dorian had him on the floor in a heartbeat, his knee against Malcolm's chest, forearm pressed to his throat.

Malcolm's eyes ignited with rage, but he only laughed. "You're *pathetic*, highness. And when House Redthorne finally falls, I want all of us to remember this moment, and know we've only ourselves to blame."

"*Why*?" Dorian bellowed. "Why are you so insistent on undermining me and ruling our house? Our family? What do you *want* from me?"

"You have the audacity to talk to me about family?"

Malcolm's lip curled, rage vibrating through his muscles. "Do you remember when we were turned? When our *family* was decimated?"

The images, never far from Dorian's thoughts, rushed to the surface in stunning, brilliant detail.

The piercing screams of his mother and sister.

The sharp scent of blood mixing with the sweet scent of spilled brandy.

The twins, clinging to each other in fear.

Evie, her eyes wide and hopeless as her own brother swung the blade that ended her life.

Augustus, watching with little more than a sad acceptance as his newfound partners turned his sons into monsters, butchering his wife and youngest children in the process.

When it was time for Augustus himself to submit to the bite, he'd done so with pride, truly believing he'd just saved his family from eternal heartbreak. In that man's twisted mind, the losses were all part of the risk—a fair price for the eternal reward.

"Don't," Dorian whispered now, his heart banging in his chest as he tried in vain to beat back those awful memories. "Please."

He rose from the floor and backed away, finally allowing Malcolm to get to his feet, but the younger vampire would not relent. He'd seen a glimpse of Dorian's weakness, and he attacked it furiously.

Relentlessly.

Joyously.

"On that fateful day," Malcolm said, "as sweet little Fiona lay dying in your arms, do you know who lay dying in mine?"

Dorian didn't respond. Of course he knew—he'd replayed those brutal moments in his mind so many times, he saw them even in his sleep, like a movie he could never turn off, an ending he could never alter.

It was their mother who took her final breaths in Malcolm's arms.

"Mother's only concern was for her children," Malcolm continued. "What was left of them, anyway. She made me promise to take care of you—all of you. Do you know why?"

"She thought I was dying," Dorian said, and the others looked on in silence. In sadness. In shame.

"No. You were always strong of body and mind, Dorian. She knew if anyone were to survive, it would be you—her precious eldest son." He took a step closer, crowding into Dorian's space, his eyes full of the old hatred he'd never quite buried. "And do you know what her last words were, as she gasped and sputtered for air?"

Dorian shook his head. He'd been too focused on Fiona's last words to hear their mother's.

Why didn't you help us, Dori?

"You must look out for them," Malcolm said softly. "For I fear your brother's soft heart will be the death of you all."

A tear slipped unbidden down Dorian's cheek, burning his skin with shame.

"Compassion has no place in the royal court, brother,"

Malcolm said, reaching up to cup Dorian's cheek, swiping the tear with his thumb. His touch was gentle, but his eyes still burned with contempt. With disgust. "A lesson you've yet to learn."

Dorian turned away, unable to take another moment of Malcolm's judgment.

He was right, of course. Just as their mother had been right.

Dorian possessed a vile temper, an aloof disposition on the best of days, and a legendary lust for blood that was, at times, unquenchable.

Yet despite his violent past, despite the rage coiled inside him now, despite the monster endlessly rattling its chains, the heart that beat at his core was as soft as a rotten apple, and following it had brought House Redthorne nothing but pain and ruin.

Dorian closed his eyes, utterly defeated. One by one, he felt the silent departure of his brothers and Aiden, leaving him to duel alone with his many ghosts.

Hours earlier, he'd looked into Charlotte's eyes and told her that loving someone wasn't a character flaw. And maybe that was true for everyone else.

But not for Dorian Redthorne.

For the king of the vampires, love would always mean one thing, and one thing only: certain death.

CHAPTER FIFTEEN

Charley paced.

Thanks to Dorian, she was getting really good at it too. But even after dozens of laps from one side of the guest bedroom to the other, she still couldn't cast off the frantic energy buzzing through her veins.

Only one thing could scratch *that* particular itch, but despite their adventures in the dining room and the close call in the kitchen, Dorian had made it pretty damn clear it wouldn't happen again.

And if Charley had any doubts, her exile from the man's bedroom had sealed the deal.

To make matters *infinitely* worse, he was supposed to bring her some aspirin after her shower, but he'd been locked in the study with his brothers for at least two hours, talking about who knew what. Duchanes? Rudy and the demons? Her master plot to rob them of their most precious heirlooms?

If that was the case, Charley hoped they wouldn't all turn on her at once.

One vampire—*her* vampire—she could handle. But five?

He's not your vampire anymore, dumbass.

Letting out a deep sigh, Charley sat on the bed and pressed her fingers to her temples, gently massaging. The weight of the day had finally caught up with her. Her head ached, and her neck and shoulders throbbed in earnest, every tiny movement sending a bolt of pain down her spine.

Fucking Rudy.

At least they had a plan now. A sketchy, bare-bones, insanely dangerous one that could easily backfire, but it was a hell of a lot more than she'd had this morning when her dickbag uncle wrapped his hands around her neck.

A soft knock on the door startled her from her thoughts, and the vampire finally entered, carrying a bottled water, two ice packs, and an unopened box of aspirin.

"Dorian," she breathed, her eyes glazing with tears at the sight of him. Tears of relief, tears of joy, tears of frustration… It was all swirling together inside, making her heart pound.

His presence had always affected her, no matter how calm, cool, and collected she pretended to be on the outside. And now, denied his touch, all she wanted to do was give in to that seductive, magnetic pull, surrendering to the undertow, drowning herself in him.

Instead, she forced herself to remain still, a pleasant

smile plastered on her face as if the distance between them was perfectly acceptable.

It was the worst kind of torture.

Dorian's gaze swept down from her face to her baggy sleep shirt, stopping to rest on her exposed thighs.

A tiny smile touched his lips, his eyes glazing with desire, but before he took another step closer, he shook his head and blinked it all away.

When he met her eyes again, she saw only disappointment. Only pain.

"I apologize for the delay," he said. "Turns out we didn't have any pain reliever in the manor—I had to make a quick run into town."

"You went into town? For me?"

"I didn't want you to suffer, Charlotte." He passed her the water and opened the aspirin, shaking two into her palm.

After she downed the pills, he knelt on the floor by her side and instructed her to lie back in the bed.

Too exhausted to argue, she settled herself against the pillow and closed her eyes.

With a clinical but gentle touch, Dorian arranged the ice packs on her shoulders and neck, careful to ensure there wasn't too much pressure. The cold seeped into her skin, instantly soothing her aches.

"Better?" he asked, his voice soft and intimate.

"Much. Thank you."

With her eyes closed, it was easy for Charley to pretend this had all been a misunderstanding. That he was here because he loved her, because he wanted to take care of her, because he'd promised to look out for her.

"This should ease the swelling," he said. "Try not to move around too much."

For a few sweet moments, she lost herself in the liquid honey of his voice and the feel of his breath on her cheek, bargaining with God and the devil and anyone else who might've been listening to *please, please* let her have one more night…

But Dorian had fallen silent, the air between them so still, Charley feared he'd left.

"Dorian?" She opened her eyes, but he was still there. He hadn't moved. Hadn't left her side.

"I'm right here, love." He tried to smile, but it was guarded and dim.

The longer Charley stared into his eyes, the more they revealed: the pain and disappointment she'd caused. The confusion. The mistrust. And there, running like lava beneath it all, a hot, primal darkness she couldn't quite name.

Charley thought of him earlier in the study, crushing the glass in his fist.

The memory made her shiver.

"Too cold?" He brushed a lock of hair away from her face, trailing his fingers down her jaw.

"No, it's perfect." Charley sighed, a deep sadness settling into her chest.

That Dorian Redthorne still cared for her was obvious, no matter how many walls he'd erected to keep her out.

Yet for all the emotion he *couldn't* hide, his thoughts remained veiled.

"What are you thinking about, Dorian?" she whispered.

He lowered his eyes and shook his head.

Charley scolded herself for pushing. "Sorry. It's not my business."

Not anymore.

Dorian didn't respond, and Charley wondered if he'd finally had enough of her antics. She tried to think of something funny to say—something to get them back on neutral ground—but before she could speak, his deep, warm voice penetrated the silence once again.

"It *kills* me to see you like this, Charlotte. To imagine you there, totally alone, scared to death while that monster put his filthy hands on you. It killed me to see you last night, at the mercy of a crazed vampire using you to punish me. It killed me when I fed from you and watched the light drain from your eyes, and still, I couldn't stop. I nearly killed you. I was so, so close to—"

"But you *did* stop."

"It never should've gone that far."

She shook her head. "You could've died, Dorian. It *had* to go that far. I'm fine."

He sighed and caught her gaze again, his eyes full of shame and regret.

"And this?" he said softly, sliding his hand beneath the hem of her T-shirt, fingering the silver scar that peeked out from the top of her underwear, just above her hip bone. "You've lived your life at the mercy of monsters, and no one was there to protect you. Not even when you were a child."

In their short but explosive time together, he'd covered her body in kisses and caresses, exploring every inch. He'd lingered on the scar before, undoubtedly curious about its origins, but he never pushed for the story.

Now, he *knew* the story. It was all part of her life, part of who she was—who she'd grown up to become. Yes, she'd lived at the mercy of monsters. And nothing Dorian could say would make it any less terrible and brutal.

But she'd *lived*. Wasn't that the point? She'd survived. That was worth something, right?

His touch lingered, and Dorian closed his eyes, the muscles in his jaw tensing.

Charley didn't have the words to make it okay—not for either of them. So instead, she found his hand beneath her T-shirt and squeezed.

He brought her hand to his mouth and pressed a kiss to the center of her palm, the warm touch of his lips searing her cool skin.

Closing his eyes, he breathed her in, blazing a trail of soft, fluttery kisses from her wrist to the inside of her elbow, his stubble scratching the sensitive skin. With her free hand, she ran her fingers through his hair, urging him closer, the feel of his soft, thick mane as familiar to her as his touch, his kiss, his scent.

The ice packs slid from her shoulders, but Dorian's tender kisses were a better balm, brushing her injured flesh with no more than a whisper of lips and breath. Slowly, he worked his way up her neck to her chin, across the line of her jaw, up to her ear.

With a soft but possessive growl, he breathed the words she'd been aching to hear for an eternity. "It wasn't a dream, Charlotte. It wasn't a lapse in judgment. And try as I might, I can't promise you it won't happen again."

Charley's heart banged wildly, her chest heaving with desperate breaths as the current of Dorian's electric touch flowed through her body.

He pressed a kiss to her temple, tracing a delicate pattern across her forehead and down her nose, slipping his fingers through her hair, cradling her head in his strong, protective hands. All of her pain and regret melted away.

His lips hovered teasingly. Charley wanted so badly to take him, to press her mouth to his, to welcome the hot, wet slide of his tongue.

"I can't control myself around you," he whispered. "You unseat me at every turn."

"Then let go. Just for tonight."

Unblinking, Dorian considered her words, his gaze soulful and passionate and so vulnerable it made her heart hurt. Looking into his eyes was like getting a glimpse into a parallel world—the life she could've had if only she'd made a right turn instead of a left.

Dorian leaned forward, the barest brush of his lips flooding her core with heat and desire. Her thighs clenched, every nerve tingling with anticipation. She parted her lips, seeking the familiar warmth of his kiss, no longer caring what it meant—if it even meant anything at all.

Forever, for a night, for one single minute—she just wanted to taste him again.

But at the last possible second, Dorian pulled away, his face going blank as he reined in his emotions and shored up all the old walls.

The room turned as cold as the icepacks sliding down her chest.

Rising from the floor, he ran a hand through his hair and let out a soft sigh. "You should get some sleep. We'll talk again in the morning."

Charley pressed her fingers to her lips, still tingling from the near kiss. She ached for him, her body wound tight, every need unfulfilled, her heart tearing in two. "Dorian, please don't—"

"No," he said firmly. Edged in anger, the sudden resolve in his tone startled her. "It can't happen again. Ever. I mean that, Charlotte. We've got enemies in common, and because of that, I'm willing to help you—to keep you and your sister safe."

"So that's it?" Her head spun, the floor dropping out from under her. "You're only helping me because we've got enemies in common? Are you listening to yourself?"

His only response was a glare.

"That's bullshit, Dorian. I know you don't trust me, okay? I know I fucked up. But you can't look at me the way you do, and say the things you say, and touch me like that, and nearly kiss me, and set my whole body on fucking *fire*, and expect me to believe you don't care about me."

"What you *believe* is irrelevant." Dorian's eyes blazed

with fresh anger. "Regardless of my feelings for you, that's as far as our arrangement goes. If you've got other ideas, show yourself the exit."

"If *I've* got other ideas? You're the one who practically jumped me! And what was all that, 'it wasn't a dream, try as I might, I can't promise you it won't happen again' bullshit?"

"Apparently this is me, trying as I might."

"You're driving me insane! You can't just—"

"Good *night*, Charlotte. I'll see you in the morning." With that, Dorian clicked off the lights and stalked out of the room, closing the door behind him and leaving Charley alone with her guilt, her regret, and an ache between her thighs that would remain forever unquenched.

She readjusted the ice packs on her shoulders, trying to get comfortable, but it was no use. Her whole body was vibrating from Dorian's touch, her head throbbing, a single refrain echoing between her ears.

If only... If only... If only...

If only she and Dorian had met under different circumstances.

If only she'd been honest with him from the start.

If only she'd been born to a different family.

If only she'd made different choices.

That last one stung the most, because for the first time in the dumpster fire that was her life, Charley was finally starting to realize her own responsibility in lighting the fucking match.

For more than a decade, she'd been a willing criminal.

Ignorantly, yes, but Dorian was right—it'd still been a choice. One she'd make again to keep her sister safe.

But Sasha hadn't always been a factor, had she? Charley had worked with her father and his crew for years before Sasha arrived, and even though she'd never dreamed of standing up to her father back then, maybe she could have.

Maybe she *should* have.

Charley closed her eyes, dismissing the pointless thoughts. No good ever came from lingering in the past. All she could do now was move forward.

Tomorrow, and every day that came after, was a new day. A built-in second chance that *everyone* got, no matter how badly things had turned out the day before.

So tomorrow Charley would do better. She'd work hard with Dorian to dig up the kind of dirt that would silence Rudy for good.

And then, one day at a time, she'd build a new life. A better life.

Maybe even a decent one.

Charley opened her eyes, heart cracking beneath the weight of one last realization:

It just won't be with Dorian Redthorne.

CHAPTER SIXTEEN

Dorian always preferred to run at dawn, well before the sun rose high enough to make his eyes ache. In the city, he had to contend with garbage trucks and buses and all manner of pedestrian traffic, even in the early hours. But here in the mountains, his only obstacles were the trees, easily dodged as he threaded his way through the forest.

In the city or the woods, Dorian had been running regularly for decades, and the fresh air and physical exertion had never ceased to clear his head, calming him through even the most challenging business conflicts, stock market fluctuations, and irritable run-ins with his father.

But today, even after a punishing twenty-mile run, Charlotte's blood still pulsing through him like a fiery elixir, her beautiful face stayed lodged in his mind like a bad dream he couldn't shake.

Dreadful, conniving woman.

The words came easily, but deep down, despite all the

lies and schemes, Dorian knew Charlotte wasn't a bad person, or even a particularly devious one—just a desperate woman who'd been dealt a shite hand, made a few wrong turns, and gotten herself so deep into the game she no longer believed there was a safe way out.

Dorian was adamant about not letting her back into his bed—or his so-called soft heart, for that matter. But he couldn't turn his back on her, either.

He'd promised to help her and Sasha, and that was that.

His family, on the other hand…

No. *That* was a rattlesnake nest he wasn't quite ready to poke again.

Shaking off the memories of last night's argument, he revisited his conversation with Charlotte, combing through her story for details he might've missed. For something —*anything*—they might be able to use against Rudy.

Rudy.

Dorian could hardly think the name without seeing red, his entire body tensing for a fight.

But they'd find something. He knew they would. Rudy had spent the better part of his life committing heists and fencing stolen artwork, likely to demonic clients. There *had* to be a trail.

Dorian crested a rise, Cole's cabin now visible in the distance. He shifted course and headed toward it, forcing himself to go back to Rudy.

To Charlotte.

To her father.

To the One Night Stand heist.

173

The missing artwork.

The Hermes and LaPorte.

Vincent Estas...

Vincent *fucking* Estas.

Dorian sucked in a sharp breath. That was it—the linchpin connecting Charlotte's uncle to Rogozin's organization.

Charlotte's attack by Rogozin's men had happened decades ago, but the One Night Stand robbery was committed just five years ago, and Estas sold at least two pieces of the stolen artwork even more recently, which is how the LaPorte and Hermes pieces ended up in Dorian's collection.

If Dorian needed any more proof that Rudy was working with Rogozin, Estas was fucking *it*.

Suddenly, Dorian felt as if his shoes were winged like the Greek god's, speeding him down the other side of the rise toward Cole's place.

He had his man.

He just needed a plan.

And maybe... a volunteer.

"Found another one of them fuckers this morning," Cole said, handing Dorian a mug of coffee the consistency of motor oil. "He was in rough shape. Looked like the sun got him pretty good—probably been out there since yesterday."

Dorian took the chair at the small kitchen table and

forced down a swallow of the black sludge. "I assume you killed him?"

"Staked him on sight. Had some kinda pouch 'round his neck though. Nabbed it just before I ended it—thought you might wanna see." Cole shuffled through some of the clutter on the table and unearthed a small leather pouch tied with a red cord, knotted at intervals in a way that didn't look accidental.

"Did you open it?" Dorian asked.

Cole shook his head. "Figured I shouldn't mess with it before I showed you."

"Good thinking." Dorian brought it to his nose and took a quick whiff. It was pungent and herbal, tingling with magic.

Dark magic.

"We need a witch," Dorian said.

"Thought you Redthornes were fresh outta witches?"

"I keep a freelancer on hand."

"Right. The one who ignored you when you hooked up with Chernikov yesterday?"

"Something must've come up. She's normally quite reliable, if not outrageously expensive." Dorian removed his phone and snapped a photo, then sent it to Marlys.

Are you available this afternoon? he texted. *I've got a magical object of unknown origin that needs analysis and a tracing spell.*

Her response came at once. *Where did you come by this?*

I will answer your questions in person, he replied. *Can we meet?*

Sorry. I'm not available.

As always, I'll make it worth the trip.

I'm not available, she replied again.

I'll pay double.

I'm sorry, Dorian. I'm booked for the foreseeable future. I advise you to seek another witch. In the meantime, do NOT open that pouch.

"Problem?" Cole asked.

"Apparently, she's not as reliable as I believed."

That was putting it mildly. Marlys was clearly avoiding him, but why? Was she upset that he'd called her out of bed the other night to help with Charlotte? That he'd left Charlotte's penthouse in a rush before paying Marlys for her services? He'd transferred the funds to her account the very next morning, adding ten percent for the trouble.

Dorian glanced at the pouch, the soft leather stamped with symbols he couldn't decipher. It was no larger than a child's fist, and soft to the touch, yet looking at it now, Dorian felt a chill skitter down his spine.

Perhaps the object itself had scared her off.

In any case, something was obviously wrong. Marlys had never been so evasive or quick to brush him off before, especially when he offered double.

"You got another one of them witches on speed dial?" Cole asked.

"Unfortunately, I do not. I don't suppose you know anyone versed in the dark arts?"

Cole sucked down the last of his coffee, then nodded. "Your boy Nikolai. He's got witches, right?"

"That he does." Dorian sighed, the coffee turning to acid in his stomach, but the idea was a good one.

If he wanted answers about dark magic, he needed to go to the source.

He thumbed through his contacts and forwarded the photo to Chernikov, along with a text.

I have a job for a dark witch. Discretion is required.

Dorian had just enough time to swallow another mouthful of Cole's terrible coffee before his phone chimed with the demon's response.

Luna Del Mar, 12:00. Bring cash. Discretion is expensive.

CHAPTER SEVENTEEN

Eager to burn off the uncomfortable buzz of Cole's coffee—
not to mention the man's smug, barely contained laughter
as Dorian had confessed he'd not only agreed to *help* the
woman who'd betrayed him, but hadn't been able to stop
thinking about her for a single fucking instant—Dorian
half-ran, half-blurred his way back to the manor.

It was still early, and the main floor was blissfully silent,
neither vampire nor human in sight.

Certain he was alone, he stripped off his sweaty T-shirt
and raided the refrigerator for something cold to drink. He
hesitated at the ice dispenser, not wanting to wake Charlotte or his brothers, but then he remembered it was his
damn manor; he could do whatever he damn well pleased.
If they didn't like being startled awake by the grind and
clink of the machine, well... His brothers could fuck off
back to their homes out of state, and Charlotte could save
her *own* beautiful ass from the monsters at her door.

Feeling superior and bloody proud of it, he'd just pressed his glass to the lever when a heart-stopping clatter ripped through the silence.

It hadn't come from the ice maker. It'd come from the media room in the basement.

Charlotte.

She was in trouble.

"No!" she screamed. A crash followed, and she shouted again. "Get *off*! Die, asshole!"

Dorian dropped his glass and grabbed the closest weapon—a broom someone had left beside the refrigerator. He cracked it in half and blurred down the stairs and into the media room, adrenaline giving his tired, over-caffeinated muscles new life as he brandished his makeshift stakes, ready to impale the bastard who dared lay a hand on her...

But there she was.

Alone and unharmed.

Perched on a gaming platform in nothing but her long T-shirt, kneepads, and gaming gloves, her skin slick from exertion. She was panting hard, the shirt damp with sweat, the thin fabric clinging to her curves. On the screen behind her, a vampire avatar lay crumpled on the pavement, a female elf standing triumphantly behind him, one foot braced on his chest.

Midnight Marauder.

That's what she'd been screaming about.

"For fuck's sake," Dorian said.

"*You.*" Charlotte spun on her heel to face him, her eyes

flashing as she stabbed his chest with an accusatory finger. "You *deleted* me! I had to set up a whole new profile!"

He tossed the broken broom handles to the floor. "What the hell are you doing?"

"I can't *believe* you." She popped her hands on her hips. On the screen behind her, the larger-than-life she-elf mimicked her every move, shoulders squared for a fight.

Dorian felt like he was getting scolded by both of them.

"*Me?*" he said. "Who gave you permission to be here?"

"Aiden. And before you get all bent out of shape—yes, I signed the stupid NDA."

"You just couldn't wait, could you." Dorian shook his head. The adrenaline was fading from his blood, but the anger was fresh—anger that she'd made him so worried, anger that his ridiculous mind still allowed him to care.

But as his eyes drifted down from her face to her breasts, his resolve faded. It was hard to stay mad; those two perfect orbs stretched the fabric of the shirt teasingly, their dark centers raised beneath the thin cotton like a forbidden invitation to touch.

To tease.

To taste.

The kneepads urged his fantasies in another dangerous direction, flooding his mind with memories that made his balls ache.

"My stats," she said, counting down his apparent violations. "My high score. My outfits. My badges. Everything. You just…" She made a starburst motion with her fingers. "Poof! And I'm gone, just like that."

Dorian dipped his head, trying to hide his smile.

"This isn't funny, Dorian Redthorne! You *erased* me!"

"Yet here you are, love. In the flesh. And feeling much better than you were last night, I see. I take it the ice helped?"

When he met her eyes again, she was smiling too.

They faced off in silence for a moment, each trying not to laugh, the tension quickly evaporating.

"Good morning, Ms. D'Amico," he finally said.

"And good morning to you too, Mr. Redthorne." Her gaze slid down to his torso, leaving a trail of heat in its wake. "Why are you half-naked and sweaty?"

"I was on a trail run. I'd just returned home when I heard the—well, what I assumed was a struggle."

Charlotte grinned and pressed a hand to her chest, the T-shirt riding up her thighs to reveal the satin, rose-colored triangle of her panties.

Fuck, what he wouldn't give to press his mouth to that silky scrap of fabric...

"And you charged in to save me," she said. "Brandishing a broken broom. My knight in shining... half-nakedness."

Dorian raked his eyes over her scantily clad body. "I see we're well matched in that department."

"Twinning, as my sister would say."

She'd been teasing him, but now her eyes filled with raw desire, a deep and desperate look that nearly undid him. His cock bulged obviously behind the thin running shorts, picking a fight with his brain.

Just one more time.

Don't be daft.

What's the harm in giving each other a bit of dark pleasure?

She was plotting to rob your estate, you bloody idiot...

"Charlotte," Dorian said, finally forcing out the words, "I meant what I said last night. We can't—"

"Play Midnight Marauder?" She grinned again, deftly steering them away from a topic that clearly made them *both* supremely uncomfortable. "Yeah, I figured you'd say no. That's why I waited until you left, and asked Aiden to set me up down here. Had I known you'd *erased* me from existence—"

"*Virtual* existence. And what did you expect?" He raked a hand through his hair. "You damn near broke my bloody heart, woman."

Fuck.

He hadn't meant to say it out loud. Not like that. Quickly, smoothly, he hit the button on the wall to raise the second platform and booted up his Bone Crusher avatar, not sparing Charlotte a glance.

The media room at Ravenswood was significantly smaller than the game room in Tribeca, but still well-equipped, and soon they were both situated on their platforms, helmets and face shields in place, ready for a rematch.

"There's only one way to settle this," he said, scanning Charlotte's new stats. In the few hours he'd been gone, she'd done pretty well for herself, racking up a dozen KOs. Dorian was impressed. "Let's go, Miss Demeanor."

"Oh, Bone Crusher. Sweet, sweet Bone Crusher." Charlotte laughed. "Miss Demeanor's dead. You killed her, remember? The name is B.O.B. now. Guess what it stands for."

"I can only imagine."

"Breaker of *Balls*." She crouched into position, cracking her knuckles. The she-elf onscreen followed suit. "*Bring it, vampire king.*"

Ignoring the sight of her long, toned legs, the T-shirt hiding nothing as she crouched on the platform, Dorian nodded brusquely. "Oh, I *shall* bring it."

"Oh, I *shall* bring it," she mocked. Her English accent was bang on. "Shall you bring a spot of tea and some dainty little biscuits as well? Perhaps a bit of jam from your pantry?"

Dorian turned to say something witty, but the moment his eyes left the screen, she threw a sucker-punch. He tried to duck, but he was a beat too slow. Bone Crusher took a direct hit to the balls.

Dorian groaned. "Living up to the new name, I see."

"That's what you get when you sleep on B.O.B."

"Noted," he said. Onscreen, Bone Crusher regained his balance, faking her out and landing a solid right hook that sent Breaker of Balls skittering backward.

Charlotte huffed out a curse.

"Do you know what your problem is, Breaker?" he asked.

"Lack of decent competition?"

"No, love. You fight dirty."

"Gets the job done, doesn't it?"

"In Midnight Marauder, yes. But you lack technique. In a real fight—"

"I'd just grab your broom handle. And no, that's not a euphemism." She crouched low and kicked, trying to sweep Bone Crusher's legs out from under him, but he evaded the move with a quick hop, responding with a fierce kick to the chest that knocked Breaker flat on her back.

He could've ended it right there—pounced on her and gone in for the kill. But then he pictured Rudy—that greasy, despicable thug—jumping her in an alley, catching her totally unaware. He pictured Duchanes, biting into her neck. He pictured those other two vampire fucks from the fundraiser, batting her around the grass like a cat toy.

Rage boiled up inside.

"Listen to me, Charlotte," he said urgently. "In a real fight, you might not get a second chance—the other man won't look away. You've got to stay cool under pressure. Smart. You're not a large woman, so chances are you'll have to outthink rather than out-fight your opponent."

Charlotte removed her helmet and turned to face Dorian, her eyes somber and serious. The fact that she hadn't taken advantage of his momentary distraction told him she understood the gravity of his warning.

Suddenly, their little skirmish was no longer about a video game vendetta. It was about reality—Charlotte's reality. And the moment either of them forgot about that, her life—or Sasha's—could end.

Yes, Dorian could and would—with a fucking smile on

his face and a song in his heart—rip out throats and crush skulls and behead anyone who so much as *breathed* on Charlotte in his presence.

But she wouldn't always be in his presence. Especially once they dealt with her uncle and eliminated the threat of Duchanes.

After that, Dorian realized with a sick twist in his gut, he'd likely never see her again.

"You want to take the most effective shot you can," he said now, recalling the scrappy fights of his misspent human youth, knocking around in the stables with the other restless noble boys. "One that will take even the largest opponent down fast. The average man—and this goes for vampires and demons too—will expect a woman to kick him in the balls, scratch his face, or try to squirm out of his grip. But what's most effective?"

"Aside from fifty-thousand volts up the ass?" Charlotte shrugged. "Punch him in the gut?"

"You could try that, sure. But unless you've got proper technique and enough power behind the hit, it won't make a difference, and you might break your hand."

"Then I have no idea. I'd probably go for the eyes or the balls."

"Eyes are okay. But even better? A direct hit to the knee or a stomp to the foot. You can't always wriggle your way out of someone's grasp, especially with a man twice your size—even *more* especially with a supernatural man. But you *might* be able to knock a knee joint out of place or crush the small bones of his foot, right at the instep. No matter how big and powerful he is, that kind of impact can take him down. Even if it's just for an instant, it might be the instant that buys you an escape and saves your life." Dorian nodded toward the screen. "Let me show you."

He set her up in a few different positions, walking her through alternate scenarios—being grabbed from behind, rushed from the front, pinned on the ground. After a few tries, she started to get the hang of it, so Dorian booted up a new match—no more hand-holding, no holds barred.

Bone Crusher grabbed Breaker's arm and twisted, spinning her around backward and wrapping a meaty arm across her chest. Holding her in place on the screen, real-life Dorian resisted the urge to tell Charlotte what to do.

After struggling for a few seconds, Breaker of Balls finally raised her knee, then slammed her heel down hard, smashing Bone Crusher's foot. As his avatar hobbled backward, she spun around and jammed a heel squarely into his knee. He crumpled to the ground, clutching his leg in agony onscreen. Breaker pressed her advantage and finished him off with a kick to the face that laid him flat.

"Bone Crusher!" the game voice boomed. "You got *housed!*"

"That's how it's *done*, woman! *Yes!*" Dorian stripped off his gloves and hopped onto her platform, wrapping her up in his arms. "You did it! Look at that!"

"Did you see that?" she asked, looping her arms around his neck. She was beaming ear to ear, glowing with pride.

"I certainly did, love. The bad guys don't stand a chance."

"Does that really work?" she asked.

"You housed me, didn't you?"

"Don't I always?"

They both laughed, and for a moment it was as if they'd been transported to another realm, unaffected by everything else as their warm, slick bodies pressed together perfectly, hearts beating in sync. Charlotte slid her hands into Dorian's hair, her breath hot against his bare chest, the hard length of him pressing into her abdomen as he buried his face in her neck. He lowered his mouth to her skin, tasting her salty flesh, breathing in her scent.

Devil's balls, how he wanted to stay there with her, to hold her for the rest of eternity.

But letting his guard down was foolish. It was dangerous. And it only made the pain of their inevitable departure that much more unbearable.

Dorian pulled back, unable to meet her eyes. "I'm sorry, Charlotte. I got a bit carried away. We should probably just—"

"Eat," she said brightly, turning her back on him and hopping down off the platform. "I'm starving. Loser makes breakfast, right?"

Dorian shook off the weight of his regrets, telling himself for the hundredth time this was all for the best, ignoring the sting of her apparent rebound.

"Breakfast," he said. "All right, Breaker of Balls. I think I can manage that."

After their regrettably separate showers, Dorian whipped up a feast of mushroom-and-cheddar omelets, sourdough toast, and strawberry-banana smoothies. The sound of the blender brought his other house guests round, all of them crowding into the breakfast nook again, just as they'd done last night.

Everyone but Malcolm.

It was just as well. Dorian wasn't ready to face his brother yet. Not after the things they'd said to each other last night.

Forget knives and fangs. When it came to family, vicious truths had a way of cutting deeper than both.

Still, with Colin, Gabriel, and Aiden nodding appreciatively over the omelets, Sasha brightening the room with her impossibly sunny smile and endless tales of college life, and Charlotte singing the praises of those smoothies, Dorian thought again of that secret, hidden wish nestled inside him—the word that not so long ago had set his very teeth on edge, but had somehow snuck back into his heart, making itself at home.

Family.

It was a moment, a snapshot, perfect in all the ways but the one that mattered most:

It wasn't real.

CHAPTER EIGHTEEN

"Want to know what I love *most* about your boyfriend?" Sasha flopped on the end of Charley's bed—rather, her *guest* bed—and grinned. "I mean, there are a *lot* of things, right? But the whole pretending-to-sleep-in-separate-bedrooms thing? That's proper, next-level, old-world hotness right there, and I'm *here* for it."

"I told you, Sash. He's not my boyfriend." *And we aren't pretending.* Charley fluffed the pillows, trying to put the bed back in order after her night of tossing and turning alone.

After Dorian had left her, she'd tried to distract herself by compiling the notes he'd asked for—everything she could drum up about Rudy, about his known associates, his hangouts. She also made a list of the missing artwork from the One Night Stand heist.

After completing her homework, she'd only gotten a couple of hours of sleep, interrupted with alternating nightmares about Rudy strangling her to death...

And about losing Dorian.

When she woke up at dawn, she'd realized the latter had already come true.

"Then what is he?" Sasha asked now. "Just some rando who invited us to his manor and cooked us chili and omelets and looks at you like he wants to spend the rest of his life licking you like an ice cream cone? A thing that would be a lot easier if he skipped the whole separate-beds nonsense?"

Charley rolled her eyes and swatted Sasha with a pillow. "Shouldn't you be off pestering Aiden? I thought he was going to teach you how to play chess today."

"*Aiden...*" Sasha leaned back on the bed, letting out a dreamy sigh. "Speaking of licking someone like an ice cream cone."

"Sasha!" Charley gasped. "No! You're not allowed to get that crazy look in your eyes over Aiden Donovan."

"Why the hell not?"

"You're too young, for one thing. And he's too old. Like, *seriously* old. And he's a... No. Just no." Charley had enough trouble keeping Sasha out of the criminal life. Now she had to worry about keeping her out of the supernatural life too?

"Aiden's not a *no-just-no.* He's a *yes-hell-yes.* A hot, sexy yes I want to lick and—"

"I'm not listening!" Charley sing-songed, pretending to cover her ears, knowing damn well she could no more keep her sister from gushing over her new vampire crush than she could keep herself from obsessing over her own.

It didn't matter anyway. Once they figured out this Rudy business, she and Sasha would be out of Dorian's life for good. Out of Aiden's. Out of the lives of the entire Redthorne clan.

"*Anyway*," Sasha said, sitting up again. "Aiden's working today. But he told me there's a movie theater in town, and guess what? They're showing a double feature this afternoon—Romancing the Stone and Pretty Woman. I thought maybe we could go? And get a late lunch after?"

"Don't you have to get back to the city? I thought you had to open at Perk tomorrow. And what about class?"

"Darcy picked up my shift, and I already emailed my professors that I'd be out a couple days. I turned in my English paper early, so it's no big deal."

"Hmm. So you've got it all planned out, huh?"

"I like it here." She shrugged, her voice softening. "Don't get me wrong—I love the city. But here, I feel like I can actually breathe."

"It *is* beautiful," Charley said, her gaze drifting to the window. Her room faced some kind of orchard, the trees bursting with leaves the color of ripe apples. "Especially with the fall colors."

"Not just that, Chuck. I like *you* here too. You're way more relaxed. Not looking over your shoulder every five seconds, waiting for another stupid order from Uncle Boss." Sasha glanced up at Charley, her eyes glassy. In that moment, she looked as young as she had when she'd shown up on Charley's doorstep all those years ago. "Why can't you and Dorian just, like, get married or move in together or something? You deserve your happily ever after."

A deep despair welled up in Charley's heart, but she smiled through it, joining her sister on the bed and wrapping her in a hug.

Sasha was right. Charley *was* more relaxed here. Inside the walls of Ravenswood, it felt like her real life couldn't touch her. A momentary pause, sure—one that would shatter the moment she returned home to Park Avenue—but one she appreciated beyond words, despite her regrets over losing Dorian.

"It doesn't work that way, Sasha," she whispered, pressing a kiss to Sasha's head. "Besides, I already have a kickass roommate, and I wouldn't leave her for the world."

Sasha cracked up. "Who said anything about leaving me? We're a package deal, Chuck. Where you go, I go."

"I see." Charley nudged her in the ribs. "So this isn't really about me and Dorian finding our happily ever after. You just want a permanent invite to that pool."

"I mean, I wouldn't say *no*, but..." She pulled out of the embrace and blew a breath into her bangs, her eyes serious once again. "I really do want you to be happy. I want you to be okay."

"Me too, baby. Me too." Charley smiled and smoothed her hand over Sasha's ponytail. "Hey. Is that movie and lunch date still on the table?"

"Definitely." Sasha beamed. "Should I get us an Uber? We need transportation."

A slow grin stretched across Charley's face. "You leave that to me."

∼

After taking the scenic route to town, Charley pulled the Ferrari into the parking garage on the main drag, expertly guiding it into the spot.

"This car was made for you," Sasha said, still gaping. "You look so hot right now. Seriously."

"I know, right?" Charley fluffed her hair and laughed. She still couldn't believe Dorian had let her take it—she was sure he'd send Jameson to chauffeur them around. But then he'd surprised her by offering it up, with no more than a firm warning that she stick to the speed limit and not park too close to anyone else.

She had no idea why he was being so kind, given her treachery. But she wasn't about to look that particular gift horse in the mouth. For now, it was all part of her fantasy life—the one where she got to live in a beautiful manor and eat delicious food and spend a fabulous day tooling around town with her favorite person in the world—and Charley planned on making it last for as long as possible.

Linking arms, the girls headed down to the theater at the end of the block. They'd just reached the entrance when Charley noticed the creepster lurking outside, leaning against the brick facade and smoking a cigarette as if the tiny theater in the tiny town was his regular hangout.

Her stomach twisted, her heart giving her a swift kick.

She *knew* that fucking chain smoker.

And there was only one reason he'd be in Annendale-on-Hudson, mere hours after she'd gotten her phone back and texted Rudy that she and Sasha would be spending some time up here.

Her uncle had sent him to spy on her.

The man turned to glare at her, offering a fake smile.

"Why don't you head inside," Charley said to Sasha. "See what kind of candy they have. I'll be right behind you."

"You sure?"

"Yep. I just remembered I need to text Dorian about something real quick."

"Okay. Don't take too long—I want to get good seats." Sasha disappeared inside, and Charley stormed over to the spy, her skin hot with anger.

"How you doin', Charley-girl," Bones said, taking a drag of his Marlboro. "Been awhile."

"What the hell are you doing here, Bones?"

He shrugged and blew a plume of smoke into her face, not answering.

Jesus Christ. She'd practically grown up around the guy. And now, he didn't even have the grace to acknowledge how fucked up this situation was.

"If you don't mind," she said, waving away the smoke, "I'm here with my sister. Who's nineteen years old and has nothing to do with this. So please fuck off."

Bones shrugged. "No boyfriend today?"

Charley rolled her eyes. So Rudy had told him about Dorian, then.

Odd, considering she was pretty sure Rudy had cut the other crew guys out of the Ravenswood gig.

"What part of 'fuck off' was unclear?" she asked.

Bones didn't respond. Just stood there scratching his stubbled jaw, the cigarette burning to a nub between his fingers.

"I liked you better when you worked for my father," Charley said.

"Yeah, me too. Catch you later, Charley-girl." He exhaled another cloud of smoke, then flicked away the cigarette butt and walked off, disappearing around the corner.

That was it. No outward threats. No shake-down. No warnings.

Just an appearance. A reminder.

Charley leaned against the bricks and sighed. She wasn't afraid of Bones, but she hated being spied on. Hated what Rudy had done to her. Hated that he was doing it even now, intruding on the one place she'd wanted to believe he couldn't reach.

Rudy wasn't even trying to scare her—he could've sent goons to threaten her for that. No—he just wanted her to know he was watching. Always fucking watching.

"Who's the creep?" Sasha stuck her head out through the doorway, nodding toward the spot Bones had just vacated. "I saw you talking to him."

"Just some guy looking for beer money." Charley forced a bright smile. "Did you scope out the candy?"

"Yep. I've got it all planned out. Let's go."

As they waited in line for the ticket booth, Sasha hummed and bobbed her head, totally comfortable, totally content. For her, the future looked bright and happy, even if she had to navigate a few bumps along the way. Her seemingly endless joy was a firm reminder that Charley had done the right thing, asking Dorian for help.

Charley's own future didn't hold many bright spots, but Sasha's certainly did. And Charley would see that it stayed that way—no matter what.

"Two tickets for the double feature," Charley said to the kid behind the ticket window.

He pushed the credit card machine toward her. "Twenty-two even."

Charley swiped her card, but the machine wouldn't read it. She tried again—no luck. Just a series of angry beeps.

"Sorry about that," the kid said. "Thing's been wonky all day. I'll have to manually enter it."

She handed over the card, a trickle of unease rolling through her chest.

The machine beeped again.

"Sorry," the kid said again. "It says the card's declined."

"What? That's—forget it. I have another one." Charley fished out her secondary card and handed it over, but no matter how many times the kid tried the numbers, the machine kept up its incessant squawking.

"Did you put a fraud alert on your cards?" he asked. "It's declining this one too."

The trickle of unease turned into fear, sinking like a stone in Charley's stomach.

There was only one reason both her cards would suddenly be declined.

"I have no idea what's going on." She held out her hand for the card, cheeks burning. "I'll have to call the company."

"Sorry, I have to keep it. Do you have cash?"

Holy fuck.

The reality of her situation slapped her hard in the face.

Those cards were her only access to money.

Without warning, Rudy had just cut her off.

"Charley?" Sasha was at her elbow, tugging her arm. "What's wrong?"

She met Sasha's eyes, shame slithering down her spine.

I can't even buy my sister a movie ticket.

"Something's wrong with my cards," Charley said. "I have to call the bank, but for now, I can't get the tickets."

"That's *it*?" Sasha laughed, her brow crinkling with confusion, as if this were just some minor pothole on the road of life. "Damn, girl. I thought someone died. I'll get the tickets—it's no problem."

Charley tried to refuse, but Sasha was already handing over her debit card. The machine chimed happily, and the kid handed over two tickets.

"Enjoy the show," he said.

Sasha insisted on paying for the candy too, and as she

headed to the snack counter, Charley waited on the sidelines and took stock of her assets, wondering how far she could make them stretch: a few hundred bucks in the false-bottomed cookie jar, a monthly MetroCard that was good for another three weeks on the subway, a coupon for a free latte at Perk...

That was it.

Her mind spun with new worries. What if Rudy stopped payment on the maintenance fees of her penthouse? What could she do about it? Report him to the labor board for unfair practices?

Charley bit her lip, cursing herself for being so naive. She should've been taking cash advances out from the credit cards, a little at a time, squirreling it away for a rainy day.

Now, she was about to walk straight into a hurricane, and she didn't even have an umbrella.

Stupid, stupid girl.

Her whole life she'd been shuffled from one man to the next, never given the opportunity to grow, to change, to be anything other than Charlotte D'Amico, the phantom art thief. She was her father's, and then she became Rudy's, and in some ways, even Dorian's. He'd offered without hesitation to buy her out from Rudy's clutches—a deal Charley knew her uncle would never take. But even if that wasn't an issue, how could Charley accept those terms? Well-meaning or not, how could she allow herself to become indebted to another man?

She'd lived for decades in a constant shadow of fear, afraid to speak up, afraid to defy, afraid to truly live. But she wanted to. *God,* how she wanted to. It was more than just keeping her sister safe, dodging Rudy's threats, eking out some kind of living that didn't involve stealing. Deep down, she wanted to give her sister a *life,* and to build one for herself. She wanted to go to school, to study, to learn something, to *be* something, to find and follow her passions. She wanted to work hard. She wanted to be free to fall in love.

Love.

The last word stuck, echoing through the endless canyons of her heart.

She missed Dorian—missed the potential of what could have been. In all her years of loneliness and fear, she'd never once felt as scared and empty as she had yesterday in the dining room, when Dorian made her open that drawer. The moment she saw her notebook and floor plans, she knew she'd lost him forever, just as she knew—no matter what her future held—losing him would be the single biggest regret of her life.

I have to figure this thing out. No matter what.

Sasha returned with an armload of goodies—Reese's Pieces, M&Ms, a giant bag of buttery popcorn, and two jumbo sodas—grinning at Charley like the credit card issue was no big deal, like this sort of thing happened all the time. When they got inside the theater, there was only enough space in the back, but Sasha didn't mind. She was just happy to be with Charley, to be hanging out together, waiting for the lights to dim and their day of frothy, rom-com fun to begin in earnest.

Charley could barely pay attention to the movies, her mind racing with jagged thoughts and terrible memories, desperate to work out this puzzle and get Dorian the evidence he needed.

By the time they left the theater, Charley felt as used-up and wrung-out as a dishrag. Thankfully, Sasha wasn't hungry after gorging on all that candy and popcorn, so they decided to skip lunch and take a drive through the mountains instead.

Charley took the long way again, heading over toward Cole Diamante's property to show Sasha the view, knowing how much her sister would appreciate it.

Despite her anxiety, the hum of the road relaxed her, the sun warming her skin, the snap of the autumn breeze whipping through her hair. The fall colors ignited the surrounding forest in a fiery tapestry of reds and golds that nearly took her breath away.

It was enough to give Charley the faintest ember of hope —an ember she urged into a tiny flame.

"Okay, it's coming up," she said with a genuine smile— the first since they'd seen Bones outside the theater. She reached over and tugged on Sasha's ponytail. "Ready to see something amazing?"

"Hell yeah," Sasha said, trailing her hand out the window, surfing the breeze.

The hidden turnoff was coming up fast, and Charley downshifted, readying them for the turn.

In that moment, with her sister laughing at her side, the car humming beautifully beneath her, the sun shining relentlessly upon them, Charley felt—for just an instant—content.

Then something blurred in Charley's peripheral vision.

Sasha screamed.

Charley jammed on the brakes.

The car clipped something in the road and spun, careening to a stop on the shoulder, facing the opposite direction.

After checking to make sure Sasha hadn't been hurt, Charley unhooked her seatbelt and got out of the car to go see what had bolted out in front of them.

Huge. Fucking. Mistake.

CHAPTER NINETEEN

Dorian wanted to burn them all. Every last fucking gray, every last fucking enemy, until there was nothing left of them but a smudge of black ash.

He'd just wrapped up his meeting with Chernikov and the dark witch when he'd gotten Charlotte's frantic call.

Now, even as she stood before him in the gardens, very much alive and well, he still couldn't shake the feeling of dread from his heart.

She could have bloody *died* today. At the hands of a fucking gray.

"It jumped out at us near the turnoff to Cole's land," she said, pacing. "We clipped it. I thought it was a deer or something, but when I got out to check, I knew right away it was a man. But *not* a man."

She stopped long enough to glance up at him. The moonlight reflected in her wide eyes, making her look young and frightened and vulnerable.

"I've never seen anything like it, Dorian," she whispered, rubbing the chill from her arms. "I don't think I'll ever be able to scrub that image out of my mind."

Dorian hated seeing her in pain. He wanted to go to her. To wrap her up in his arms and promise he'd take her away from the cold, brutal world they lived in—from anything that would hurt or frighten her.

But he knew it would only confuse things for both of them. So instead, he stood in place on the garden path, gently urging her to continue. He needed to know exactly what had transpired today. What she'd seen.

"It... No, he. He was naked," she said. "His skin was blistered and cracked, like he'd been burned in a fire. Some of his ribs were poking out, and..." She closed her eyes and took a deep breath. "He had fangs—that's how I knew he wasn't human. His mouth and chin were covered in blood. He was just lying there and reaching up for me, his mouth opening and closing, but he couldn't get up. It was like the sun was just... just *cooking* him."

She shivered, tightening her arms around herself.

Dorian took a step closer. "Did you happen to notice if he had anything around his neck? Like a pouch?"

"Yeah, I guess he did. I didn't get a good look, but I'm pretty sure it had a red cord. The pouch itself was covered in blood."

"Did your sister see it?" he asked gently.

"No, thank God. I made her stay in the car. I told her it was a deer, then made a fake call to highway patrol to come remove it." Her eyes filled with tears, and she reached for his arm, her touch warm. "Dorian, I'm so sorry. The car seems fine, but the tires might be a little messed up. Or the brakes. I hit them pretty hard when—"

"I don't give a damn about the car, Charlotte." He cupped her face, unable to go another moment without comforting her. "You did the right thing. You kept yourself and Sasha safe."

The gathering tears finally spilled from her eyes. "Where did that thing come from? Are there more?"

Dorian brushed her cheeks with his thumbs, catching her tears. He wanted to lie, to tell her some story that would allow her to sleep at night, but lies are what got them into this mess in the first place.

"There are more," he said. "Though we don't know how many."

He told her about his reunion with Cole Diamante and the grays the wolves had been tracking.

He also told her about the pouch Cole had found this morning—likely the same kind she'd seen on the gray in the road.

"I've got a witch looking into its origins," he said, leaving out the part about Chernikov's involvement, "but I'm almost certain Duchanes and the Rogozin demons are behind this."

Charlotte nodded and pulled away from his touch, turning to look out at the rolling hills. The mist was creeping in again, blanketing the grounds in thin, white clouds that reminded Dorian of ghosts.

"You need to be prepared for other possibilities, Charlotte."

"You mean, something other than half-formed, mindless vampire monsters creeping through the woods and jumping out at cars? Burning alive in the sun? Eating people?"

"I mean…" Dorian sighed. "There's a very good chance if the grays are traced back to Duchanes and Rogozin, your uncle's got his hands in this mess as well."

"Wait. You're saying Rudy's involved with the *grays*? But he's just an art thief. What would he want with them? What would he stand to gain?"

"There's a historical connection between your uncle and Rogozin. That alone is enough to warrant further investigation—and extreme caution."

Charlotte dropped onto the stone bench, her eyes welling again.

Dorian could only imagine the memories haunting her now. The attack by Rogozin's men when she was a girl? Her uncle's threats? Her dead father's unsolved murder? The ghoulish creature who'd crossed her path this afternoon?

Charlotte may not have been ready to hear it, but Dorian was convinced all of those things were connected.

And one way or another, he was going to find out how.

"I need to ask you something about that heist," Dorian said, taking a seat beside her on the bench. "About your father's death."

Charlotte nodded.

"Why did your uncle immediately assume his brother

had betrayed everyone? In my mind, it seems equally likely your father himself was the victim of a double-cross. Even if Rudy thought your father's betrayal was obvious, why not at least look into it? Put the word out, as it were?"

"I wondered the same thing." Charlotte pulled her sleeves down over her hands, knotting them together in her lap.

Dorian stole a glance at her profile, her skin soft and luminous in the moonlight, her jaw set even in the midst of another day of setbacks.

He knew she was a fierce woman, that she possessed a deep inner strength that had kept her alive in even the most dangerous circumstances. For all her softness, Charlotte was a fighter, strong-willed and determined, fueled by a deep inner fire he'd felt smoldering inside her many times —when they flirted, when they argued, when they played Midnight Marauder, when they fucked. She was fearless— no doubt about it. But now, sitting on the bench with her hands tucked into her sleeves, her hair in a messy bun, makeup erased by her tears and the stress of the day, Charlotte seemed young and lost and utterly defenseless.

The sight filled him with rage. He wanted so badly to sort it all out for her, but even if he could keep her safe from the supernaturals lurking in the shadows, he couldn't change her past—including the part where she'd conspired to rob him.

"We *all* wondered about it," she continued. "But Rudy kept telling us he wouldn't waste resources on a traitor. To him, it was cut and dried—my father had vouched for the inside guy he'd used, and that guy had double-crossed them. Rudy grieved—in his own way, I guess—but after that, his top priority was planning the next score. He said he'd keep an ear to the ground, but unless he heard otherwise, we were all to assume the obvious—my father tried to screw us over, and it bit him in the ass."

"But you said the crew was tight. Granted, my knowledge of professional thieves comes entirely from heist movies, but I'd always assumed a tight crew was like a family."

"A really messed-up family, sure." Charlotte went quiet, lost for a moment in thought. After a few beats, she said, "No one wanted to believe it about my father. But one by one, they all fell in line—Bones, Trick, Welshman. I was the only one who maintained his innocence. I still do. I know it sounds crazy, but he wasn't a traitor, Dorian. He'd never do that to us. He really was an honest thief."

"And the other man?" Dorian asked. "The insider your father brought on?"

"Vanished with the artwork. That's the great mystery."

Dorian shook his head. It was all so obvious to him, but Charlotte didn't seem to get it. "Charlotte, Rudy was involved in this."

"Of course. He was my father's brother and second-in-command, right up until—"

"I'm talking about your father's death. If he didn't pull the trigger, he knows who did. He was calling the shots all along. It's the only explanation that makes sense."

Charlotte looked away, absently playing with her hair,

untwisting and re-twisting her bun. She'd heard his words, but she neither agreed nor disagreed, offering nothing further. Dorian sensed this wasn't the first time she'd considered the theory, but she'd obviously dismissed it back then, just as she was dismissing it now.

Denial and self-preservation were powerful forces.

"Think about it, love." He reached for her hands, and her hair tumbled down over her shoulders, wild and beautiful, filling the air with the citrus-and-vanilla scent he loved. Dorian had to resist threading his hands into those auburn locks, pulling her mouth close to his.

Instead, he traced his thumbs over her palms in slow, gentle circles, focusing on the feel of her skin, on the familiar softness and warmth he kept on craving no matter how badly he tried to stop.

"Think about what?" she asked.

"Even if he'd found *irrefutable* evidence of your father's betrayal, no thief on your uncle's level would let that kind of score vanish without a trace."

"What choice did he have? It was just... gone."

"I don't buy it. We both know what kind of man Rudy is. There's no way he'd turn his back on a seventy-million-dollar score he'd spent months planning. No way he'd chalk it off to a double-cross. He'd have men on the street immediately, shaking down every criminal and lowlife he'd ever worked with until he'd exhausted all possible avenues."

Charlotte considered this, but then shook her head. "We had other work, other clients, other scores. We had to move on. There was no time to chase after a ghost. As far as Rudy was concerned, that's all my father was."

"But it wasn't about your father—don't you see?" Dorian slid closer to her on the bench, their thighs brushing, a familiar heat simmering in the air between them. "It's ego. Trust me, love. The only way Rudy walks away from that kind of money—and the potential blow to his reputation—is if he knows the money never disappeared at all."

"What do you mean?"

"It sounds to me like Rudy set your father up."

The longer they talked, the more holes Dorian poked in Charlotte's old theories. He felt bad being so blunt about it, but she needed to be disabused of the notion that Rudy had any loyalty to her father's memory, to Charlotte, or to any of the other members of his crew. It was obvious to Dorian that Rudy had sold them out five years ago, just as he'd likely sell them out again after the Ravenswood heist.

Only this time, the demons were involved.

For all Dorian knew, they'd been involved last time too.

Regardless, Charlotte's and Sasha's lives were at stake. And Dorian—no matter what had transpired between them, no matter what he'd have to walk away from when all was said and done—would find a way to put that bastard down for good. To finally give Charlotte and Sasha their lives back.

"I made the list you asked for," Charlotte said. "All the artwork I could remember from the missing cache. Do you think it will help?"

"It will definitely help."

"What about that Estas guy? Do you think he knows anything?"

Estas. The name echoed through his mind. Dorian had already decided the art dealer was the logical next step; tonight's conversation with Charlotte only solidified his determination.

This morning, after he'd updated Cole on the situation with Charlotte and her sister—and Cole had given him the requisite amount of I-told-you-so shit about his obvious feelings for Charlotte—Cole had jumped at the opportunity to help nail Rudy to the wall. He'd been on standby ever since, awaiting word from Dorian on the plan.

Now that Dorian had the list of artwork from the missing cache, that plan was finally solidifying.

"How do you feel about Maui?" he asked suddenly.

Charlotte's brow furrowed.

"For our romantic getaway," he said. "I do hope it suits you, because I've already chartered a private jet and booked a very expensive, very lush package at a gorgeous seaside resort for the whole family. Sasha too."

Dorian pulled out his phone, then emailed Charlotte the reservation details. A moment later, her phone beeped with the notification.

Her smile lit up the misty night. "Maui? Really?"

"Forward that to your uncle—proof that you've secured the weekend at Ravenswood for him, as ordered. That should at least buy you a bit of breathing room."

Her smile dimmed. "Oh, right. That's... Thank you. It's brilliant." Charlotte turned away to redo her bun, then forced a laugh Dorian suspected was for his benefit. "I guess you've thought of everything, Dorian Redthorne."

"It's in my nature, love. Business strategy, tying up loose ends, et cetera."

"I've never been to Hawaii."

"No?" Dorian's thoughts drifted to the islands, conjuring up images of the two of them swimming at the resort's private beach at dawn, chartering boats and dining on extravagant seafood dinners, cruising the coastline beneath the stars...

He rose from the bench, dropping the pointless fantasy. The jet, the expensive package—it was all a sham. Reservations booked and paid for, but never to be used, all to make Rudy believe he'd gotten the upper hand.

With any luck, the bastard would be dead before the yacht even left the harbor.

"When this is over," Dorian said, "perhaps you can take your sister. I'm sure you'd have a lovely time."

A wounded look flickered in her eyes, a pain that threatened to knock down the last of Dorian's walls. He had the urge to bend down and scoop her into his arms, carry her up to his bedroom, and peel away every last layer of clothing, every last scrap of fear and doubt. He ached at the memory of her soft skin, her silky kiss, her tight, hot flesh...

But that kind of fantasizing could only end in heartache.

"I'd like you and Sasha to stay the duration," he said coolly, using the tone he normally reserved for his staff. "Until we've taken care of your uncle and Duchanes."

Charlotte looked up, surprised and a bit confused. "Here? At Ravenswood?"

"Your uncle suspects you've tricked me into falling in love with you. Lovers spend their nights together. As for Duchanes…" He curled his fists, resisting the urge to pummel the stone bench. "It's not safe for you in the city. Not until we've located him and eradicated the threat."

"After what I saw today," she said, folding her arms across her chest, "you can't tell me we're any safer here, Dorian."

"Here I can at least keep an eye on you."

"Every minute? Of every day? Because that's the only way I'd feel safe *anywhere* right now." She closed her eyes, a shiver rolling through her body. When she spoke again, her voice was soft and broken. "Besides, I need to get back home. I've got some things to take care of."

"What things?"

"Just… some personal things."

"*What* personal things?" he demanded.

"Seriously, Dorian?" She opened her eyes and got to her feet, that beautiful fire sparking to life once more. "I'm not your staff, or your younger brother, or your loyal subject, or even your fucking girlfriend. I don't owe you an explanation about my personal affairs. In fact, you don't even get to *ask* about my personal affairs. You surrendered that right the minute you decided we were over."

"I'd just discovered you were a thief, woman! What was I supposed to do? Roll out the bloody red carpet? Yes, do come in, make yourself at home, take anything you'd like.

Shall I fix you a sandwich and a drink while you're fleecing me?"

"I said I was sorry and I meant it. You don't get to keep throwing it in my face. Do you need to hear it again? Fine. I'm sorry, okay? I'm sorry!"

"Not as sorry as I, believe me."

"Oh yeah?"

"I'm sorry I ever laid eyes on you."

"Eyes. Right. *That's* what you laid on me."

Dorian shook his head, a bitter laugh rushing from his lungs. "You *seduced* me, woman. All part of your con, no doubt."

"*I* seduced *you*?"

"What else do you call it when a woman wantonly throws herself upon a man at a private auction, distracting him from the fact that she's—oh, right. Plotting yet *another* heist!"

"You are so full of yourself, highness. It's a wonder your brothers can fit in the manor with your ego taking up so much room!"

"And *you've* got an attitude problem the size of the Empire State Building. It's a wonder your sister hasn't run for the bloody hills!"

"Run for the... You know what? Just... just *bite* me, vampire."

He grabbed her and blurred her against the stone wall, pinning her wrists above her head, trapping her body with the hard press of his hips.

Her eyes flashed with a mix of anger and desire, her breath quickening right along with her heartbeat.

"That smart mouth is going to get you in trouble one day, Ms. D'Amico," he warned.

"Let. Me. *Go*." She struggled against his hold, glaring at him as if she could conjure demon fire of her own.

Dorian swept his gaze from her eyes down to her mouth, full and soft and kissable. He recalled that night in the basement at the fundraiser, the first time he'd lost control and stolen a taste of her exquisite blood.

A pulse of desire throbbed in his balls.

"Is that what you want, little prowler?" he whispered, tightening his grip on her wrists, grinding against her warm, soft body.

She gasped at the press of his stone-hard cock, arching her hips to meet him.

His muscles trembled with barely contained lust, his blood racing, pulse pounding like a drum between his ears, drowning out the sound of her frantic heartbeat. The scent of her desire flooded his senses, the energy between them crackling like a gathering storm.

Her earlier taunt echoed.

Bite me, vampire…

Dorian *wanted* to bite her. To absolutely *ravage* her.

"Fuck," she breathed, her eyelids falling closed. She cursed again, then shook her head, leaning back against the wall, her resistance evaporating. "Option two. I want option two."

He was on his knees in a heartbeat, yanking down her

thin leggings and lacy black thong, burying his face in the smooth, wet heat that had fueled his fantasies for weeks.

Tonight, there would be no teasing, no holding back, no exquisite restraint.

Only his raw, primal hunger, unleashed and untamed, reclaiming what was rightfully his with every delicious stroke.

Taking her.

Marking her.

Owning her.

Charlotte fisted his hair and gasped, and he gripped her thighs and plunged his tongue inside, fucking her with deep, wet strokes, the savory taste of her filling his mouth and driving all else from his mind. She pulled him closer and rocked against his face, her own desires as insatiable and demanding as his.

Another moan escaped her lips, her fingers tightening in his hair. "You're... still... a... monster..."

Yes, he was a monster. Dark and depraved. Wicked.

Savage.

He growled against her flesh, her warmth radiating across his lips. Why had he denied himself the pleasure of such divine seductions?

No more. She was *his*.

His to command. His to fuck. His to claim.

His fangs descended, the exquisite burn driving him harder, and he grazed them over her clit, flicking it with his tongue until her thighs quaked and her blood rushed to the surface, darkening her pale skin. And then, certain she was teetering on the edge, he plunged inside her once again.

"Oh, *fuck*. That's… Oh, God. Right there… I'm… Don't stop… Fuck! *Dorian*!" She shattered for him, as she always did, with a wild bucking of hips and hot, breathy moans, his name on her lips like a curse, like a prayer, like the last words of a woman who'd looked upon the face of death and no longer feared her imminent demise.

Dorian rose to his feet, drunk on the taste of her, dizzy with lust as he unzipped his pants, fisted his cock, and pushed it between her bare thighs. "Tell me what *else* you want from your monster, love."

"More," she whispered, fisting his shirt. "I need—"

He claimed her mouth in a deep kiss, his own still glistening with the evidence of her desire.

She bit back a whimper of pleasure and arched her hips, but before he could give her what she wanted—before he could fuck her against the wall, so hard and deep he left *no* lingering doubts about his claim—a whispered curse and a dramatic clearing of the throat shot across the darkness like a warning.

"Dorian," Gabriel called from the shadows, his tone laced with annoyance. "You're needed in the study."

Dorian stilled inside her. Never before had he so longed for his brother's swift demise. *"Now?"*

"It cannot wait."

"Fuck," he whispered, burying his face in the crook of her neck.

Charlotte sighed, a chill rattling her limbs.

Dorian was still hard, still aching with need, but the dark spell that had ensnared them both had finally dissipated, the sparks between them fizzling like fire in the rain.

He pulled away from her, and they reassembled their clothing in silence, Charlotte's cheeks dark, her eyes veiled.

"I'm... sorry," Dorian said. "For the unfortunate interruption."

She nodded, still not meeting his eyes. Then, in a weary, defeated voice, she said, "My sister and I are going back to the city tomorrow, Dorian. I won't budge on that."

He nodded, knowing there was nothing more he could do to convince her to stay, short of taking her prisoner. "I'll have Jameson take you home whenever you're ready."

"Thank you."

"But... Charlotte?" He waited for her to meet his eyes again, then said, "My brothers and I will be keeping watch over you and Sasha as needed. I don't trust your uncle or Rogozin, and just because we haven't heard from Duchanes since the attack doesn't mean he's not still a threat to you."

Dorian held his breath, expecting her to fight back, to hit him with one of her feisty Charlotte-isms.

Do it, he thought. *Break through my walls, shatter my chains. All I need is one solid hit. Just fucking do it...*

But Charlotte only sighed, resignation filling her eyes. "I guess that's probably a good idea."

A good idea. Yes, very practical. Perfectly reasonable.

Perfectly fucking awful.

Dorian didn't want good ideas. He wanted bad ones.

The ones that left them tearing at each other's clothes, pulling hair, sucking and biting and tasting...

"Goodnight, Dorian." Charlotte yawned.

"You're going to bed?"

"You're... needed elsewhere. And I'm wiped. Today was a long day, and I want to get up early tomorrow—try to beat rush hour."

With nothing left to say, Dorian walked her back inside and watched her disappear up the stairs, forcing himself to stop thinking about the taste of her, the feel of her, the uncomfortable bulge in his pants—a constant hazard in her presence.

For all his talk, Dorian knew the truth, right down to his soft fucking heart.

She was the one who owned *him*.

And once again, he'd let her slip away.

CHAPTER TWENTY

The meeting was brief but grim. Gabriel had been asked to deliver a message from Malcolm, who'd been staying in the city since their argument and still wasn't speaking directly to Dorian. Three dead humans had just been discovered in the service alley behind Bloodbath, beaten and exsanguinated, clearly the work of vampires.

They hadn't even attempted to hide the bodies.

Malcolm believed it was a message from Duchanes— retaliation for the police raid against his nightclub.

Dorian agreed, the news darkening his already oil-black mood.

Vampires attacking humans in Manhattan. Grays attacking upstate. Demons plotting against them all.

They were living in a powder keg, holding their collective breath to see which of the many matches would strike first.

It was time for Dorian to make his move.

After wishing his brother goodnight, he locked himself in his bedroom, ignoring the depressing sight of his empty bed, and called Cole.

Despite the late hour, the wolf answered on the first ring.

"What're we in for, Red?" he asked.

"I need someone who can bullshit his way through a conversation about art. Someone who can pose as an eccentric but wealthy collector."

"I'm listening."

"Aiden and I can set up the meeting, but I can't meet the dealer face-to-face. He'll recognize me at once and immediately suspect foul play."

"Who's the dealer?"

"A high-ranking Rogozin demon by the name of Vincent Estas."

Cole hissed into the phone. "Fucking demons."

"My sentiments exactly. I don't suppose you know anyone who might be willing to play the part?"

"Yeah, you know what?" he asked, and Dorian could already hear the grin in his voice. "I got the *perfect* guy in mind. Artsy, rugged, *devastatingly* handsome. A wolfish charm, some might say."

"Yes, I'm sure they might."

"When do we roll?"

"Soon—I'll let you know. But Cole, you can't wear flannel. You realize that, right?"

"Believe it or not, Red, I do own a suit." Cole laughed. "It's older 'n shit, but still fits like a glove. Powder blue too. *Real* nice."

Dorian sighed. "Send me your measurements, wolf. I'm calling my tailor at once."

CHAPTER TWENTY-ONE

Fuck. That. Guy.

By the time Charley and Sasha returned to the city the next morning, Charley was on *fire* with determination.

She had a new assignment. No, not one from her asshole boss. One she'd given herself. One she couldn't wait to accomplish.

The credit card disaster may have thrown her for a hell of a loop, but Jersey girls were nothing if not resourceful. If Uncle Rudy thought she was going down *that* easily, he was in for a rude fucking awakening.

Hopefully in a coffin. Nailed shut. Encased in cement. Dropped in the ocean.

She felt it in her gut—the sea change coming her way, the vestiges of her old life drying up and falling away like the autumn leaves. It was time to bring the bastard down. Time to find her way out of the game. Time to start over.

And with the help of one *very* dark, *impossibly* sexy vampire, Charley was going to do just that.

But first? She needed to figure out this money situation.

And that meant hitting the pause button—better yet, the *delete* button—on the fantasy playing on repeat in her mind.

Dorian's commanding tone, making her wet with every word.

That smart mouth is going to get you in trouble one day, Ms. D'Amico...

His hot kiss, descending on her flesh.

Is that what you want, little prowler?

His tongue, deep and relentless and divine.

Tell me what else you want from your monster, love...

Nope.

Delete, delete, delete.

Last night was a mistake. An epic, heat-of-the-moment, ought-to-be-illegal mistake that needed to make like her Miss Demeanor profile and go *poof*.

From that moment forward, Charley was officially on the VDD—Vampire Dick Detox. And by *dick*, she also meant mouth. And fingers. And...

Focus, girl. Focus.

Standing inside her penthouse, her head at least eighty percent back in the game, Charley took a deep breath, downed an espresso, and got to work.

All she needed was one idea. One game-changing idea that would save her suddenly broke ass and end her dependence on Rudy for good.

You've got this, girl. Come on.

It was true. Despite her monied existence, Charley knew how to tighten the purse strings. It was a hard lesson, but one she'd mastered quickly after her mother walked out, leaving Charley and her dad in the double-wide they'd rented, nothing to call their own but a few half-empty cupboards and a rusty 1990s Toyota Corolla with questionable brakes.

Somehow, with a bit of sacrifice and a whole lot of ingenuity, the D'Amico dad-and-daughter duo had made it work, finding creative ways to weather the storm until her father discovered his true calling as a criminal mastermind, finally launching them into wealth and status.

Illegitimate wealth and status, but a status that had kept her fed and comfortable for a long, long time.

Charley looked around the penthouse now, taking stock of her beautiful furniture, the pristine home accessories, the luxury items lining her multiple closets.

She'd come a long way from her trailer park days, but as the saying went...

You can take the girl out of the trailer park, but you can't take the trailer park out of the girl.

And just like that, the scrappy, resourceful Jersey girl re-emerged.

And that bitch knew just what to do.

Charley grinned, the idea solidifying in her mind.

No, she didn't have cash.

But she *did* have a whole lot of expensive shit—shit Rudy had paid for. Shit that could be sold, pawned, and quickly converted into those sweet, beautiful greenbacks she so desperately needed.

Starting with the closet full of designer dresses she'd never actually liked, shoes that made her feet hurt, and jewelry she'd rather flush down the toilet than wear again, Charley got busy.

One outfit at a time, she dressed and accessorized herself like Barbie, shooting enough selfies for a celebrity Instagram feed. Each outfit reminded her of its corresponding heist—the forest green wrap dress and emerald tennis bracelet from the Killian job, the black pantsuit from the Washburn-Higgins job, the sable sweater dress and Louboutin pumps from the Porterfield assignment. As she stripped them from her body and placed them in the sale pile, she felt like she was shedding more of those desiccated leaves, revealing the soft, new growth underneath, almost ready to emerge.

A few hours later, one quick posting on her building's community Facebook page—*Dozens of luxury brands! Gently used—some never even worn! Cash only, everything must go!*—and the penthouse "garage" sale was officially on.

By lunchtime, her neighbors had already shelled out over a thousand bucks, more than happy to take the beautiful dresses and jewels off her hands.

To them, it was a steal.

To Charley, who was done with stealing, it was a lifesaver.

No, a thousand bucks wasn't enough to live on in New York City—not for long. And maybe it was small potatoes for someone like her billionaire vampire social media tycoon.

But still. They were *Charley's* fucking potatoes.

And for the first time in her life, she started to see the faintest glimmer of light illuminating a new path. The one that would lead her and Sasha out of the *now* and into the *someday* she'd been dreaming about.

By the end of the day, Charley had a lot more space in her closets... and close to three grand in cash in her hot little hands. She stashed the day's earnings in a box of tampons in her bathroom and grinned at herself in the mirror, that tiny ember of hope inside flickering back to life, warming her heart.

Operation Fuck That Guy was in full effect.

CHAPTER TWENTY-TWO

"Half a million," Aiden said, leaning back in Dorian's FierceConnect office chair and propping his feet on the desk. "That's as low as the man is willing to go."

Cole let out a low whistle. "That's a lot of dough for a statue of a cat, Red."

"Technically, she's a lion," Aiden said. "Well, half lion, half woman. Sekhmet was an ancient Egyptian warrior goddess known for drinking the blood of her enemies."

Cole grunted. "You don't say?"

"It was actually her downfall. After a particularly brutal slaughter, she was so crazed with bloodlust, the only way the gods could stop her from destroying all of mankind was to trick her into getting hammered on beer they'd dyed to look like blood. Quite crafty, that lot."

"For fuck's sake." Dorian scrubbed a hand over his jaw. Cat, lion, blood of the enemy, what did it matter? Five hundred grand—in cash, no less—for a gilded statue the size of his arm in which Dorian had absolutely no interest... It was bloody extortion.

Still, his gamble had paid off, and for that, he was grateful.

Dorian knew he needed to get close to Estas. He was the link who could eventually reveal—intentionally or not—the demon connection to Charlotte's uncle, along with other damning evidence they could use against the rotten bastard. After reviewing Charlotte's list of the artwork from the One Night Stand heist, the idea had taken root.

Apparently, the collector they'd robbed was particularly fond of the Egyptian deity; the list contained several statues and busts. Hoping Estas still had access to at least one of them, Dorian had Aiden contact the demon, posing as the assistant of a wealthy collector interested in Egyptian art.

Emphasis on wealthy.

Now, they had the demon on the hook. As for their next move, that's where Cole came in, posing as the collector interested in the statue. If all went according to plan, he'd meet with Estas, make the buy, and establish a rapport.

Dorian wasn't sure what came next. Getting a foot in the door had to come first. He'd figure out the rest later.

"He wouldn't budge on price," Aiden said.

"I suppose I haven't got a choice, then," Dorian said.

Aiden shrugged. "Not if we want to get close to Estas. A real wheeler-dealer, this demon. Cole needs to earn his trust, mate. Cash is the only way to prove we're serious. Unless you'd rather your pretty little thief be involved."

Dorian glared at Aiden, but there was no real ire behind it, just as there was no ire behind Aiden's dig.

This morning, as they drove together from Ravenswood to the city, he'd finally come clean to Aiden about Charlotte's involvement in the planned heist. He'd already told Cole and didn't want to keep his best friend in the dark.

Aiden was understandably upset—he'd grown rather fond of Charlotte and her sister during their brief stay at Ravenswood—but in the end, he was on Dorian's side.

If Dorian was willing to set aside his anger and mistrust in order to help her, then so was Aiden.

Cole had expressed the same sentiments.

Dorian was more than grateful for the backup, but setting up a deal over the phone was very different from meeting the vile demon in person. And not just any demon, but a demon who worked for their enemies, dealt in black-market art, and was very likely connected to the murder of Charlotte's father.

Just like her bloody uncle.

"Estas works for Rogozin," Dorian said. "We aren't exactly walking into friendly territory. And Cole's going in as a spy. If anything were to tip Estas off about our true motives..."

Dorian sighed. He didn't need to spell it out; demonic hellfire could roast a wolf shifter as easily as it could a vampire.

But it was more than that. Much more.

Aiden narrowed his eyes, immediately picking up on Dorian's unease.

"Why are you so cagey?" Aiden asked.

As usual, the vampire could see right through him.

Dorian pulled the top folder from the stack on his desk and tossed it to Aiden.

"What's this?" He flipped through it, scanning the report.

"It's the dark witch's analysis and tracking details on the pouch Cole found on that gray."

"Bloody hell," Aiden whispered. "They're resurrecting them?"

"That was her assessment, yes."

"But how? When the grays die, they turn to ash as sure as any other bloodsucker."

"Not if they've got one of those pouches." Dorian clenched his jaw, reining in his frustration.

According to Chernikov's witch, the pouch contained the symbols and ingredients of two extremely ancient, extremely advanced, and highly illegal demonic spells. One prolonged the precise moment of death indefinitely, preventing a slaughtered vampire from turning to ash. The other resurrected him, infusing him with demonic energy that allowed him to essentially rise from death again and again to continue his mindless mission.

Fuck. Kill. Feed.

It meant that the grays wearing those amulets couldn't be killed—not unless the pouches were removed or destroyed first.

And since grays couldn't heal like other vampires, whatever wounds they sustained, whatever killing blows, they'd suffer through them without reprieve.

Dorian almost felt sorry for the gruesome creatures. Their existence wasn't comfortable by any means, nor was it their fault. The dark amulets only ensured their endless torment. And, if enough could be produced, made for one hell of an indestructible army—particularly against humans. Not because the amulets were difficult to remove, but because—according to the witch, anyway—they were just the first-pass prototypes.

In her opinion, it was highly likely the witch who'd created the spells would continue to refine them, eventually devising something that didn't require the grays to wear anything external—anything that could be destroyed.

Dorian summarized the rest of the witch's findings, sparing Aiden the trouble of further reading.

"Now, *that's* some six-ways-from-Sunday fucked-up shit," Cole said, scratching his beard. "I don't suppose Chernikov's witch has any idea who's makin' these things?"

"She knows exactly who's making them." Dorian sighed, recalling the kind, blue-eyed witch he'd met at his fundraiser. The same witch who'd—under Duchanes orders and probably a good bit of duress—devised the poison that had nearly decimated him. "Jacinda Colburn. The witch bound to House Duchanes."

"And the hits just keep on coming," Aiden said. Then, glancing at Cole, "Dorian's right to be concerned, mate. Maybe we should find another way to get to Estas. If he's working for Rogozin, and they're involved in this business with resurrecting grays, I don't think you should go anywhere near it."

"Look," Cole said. "I appreciate the concern, guys. But you said it yourself, Red. We want evidence against this Rudy sonofabitch? Estas is our man. We follow the stolen art—that's our best shot. Besides, if I ran off with my tail between my legs from every demon, dark witch, and bloodsucker to cross my path, they'd probably castrate me and revoke my membership card to the shifter race."

Dorian wanted to argue, but he'd learned long ago that once Cole set his mind on something, there was no talking him out of it.

Especially when he'd made a promise to a friend.

Besides, this truly was their best shot. If there was evidence to be found against Rudy D'Amico, it started with Vincent Estas. Dorian knew it in his gut.

Dorian leaned forward, knocking Aiden's feet off the desk and turning back to Cole. "You realize you're putting yourself at great personal risk, Cole."

Cole waved away the suggestion as if it were the most ludicrous thing in the world.

"I mean it," Dorian said. "Estas, Rogozin, D'Amico, Duchanes, the grays… Things could get ugly."

"Can't be much uglier 'n *you*." he said.

"He's got a point, mate." Aiden gestured at Dorian's face and winced. "I've been staring at that hideous mug for two hundred fifty-odd years, and I'm still alive. Nauseated, but alive."

"Be serious," Dorian said. "If anything were to—"

"I'm totally serious," Aiden said. "Have you *seen* your face?"

Dorian grabbed the FierceConnect standard-issue stress ball from his desk, crushing it until his fingers went numb. *Fucking Aiden. Fucking Cole.* Dorian wanted to talk them both out of it. To thank them for entertaining his crazy scheme and implore them to walk away before they got in any deeper.

But one more glance at his friends—at the steel in their eyes, the strong set of their shoulders—and he knew his efforts would be futile.

"Thank you," he managed, emotion tightening his throat. He trusted these men more than he trusted his own brothers.

He trusted them with his life.

With *Charlotte's* life.

The men nodded, and after a beat, Aiden frowned and said, "I'm sorry, mate. I knew Charlotte was a bit unpredictable, but a thief? I truly didn't see it coming."

"You couldn't have," Dorian said. After all, Dorian himself had been right next to it—in *bed* with it—and he'd been blindsided too. "But... thanks."

Aiden shrugged. "You're clearly still in love with her, and I still think you're a crazy obsessive bloody damn fool, and after this, if you so much as *smile* at a woman, I'm fingerprinting her, microchipping her, and putting her through every psychological screening test known to man. But I've always got your back, mate. You know that."

Dorian nodded. He *did* know that. And it meant more to him than Aiden could imagine.

"So what's our next move, Columbo?" Cole asked.

To Aiden, Dorian said, "Call Estas and tell him it's a go. Set up the meeting for Saturday night. Cole will meet him for the exchange, and you and I will follow—from a safe distance, of course—to make sure everything goes smoothly."

"Sounds like a plan," Cole said.

"Excellent." Aiden rose from the chair and stretched, cracking his neck as if he were limbering up for a fight. "I'll have someone from H.R. send up the paperwork for my raise."

Dorian chucked the stress ball at Aiden's head. "Sod off, you bloody racketeer."

"Forty percent ought to do it. A nice, round number."

"How about dinner and a few pints?"

"Eh…" Aiden considered the offer. "Throw in dessert and a movie, a little cuddling afterwards, and you've got a deal."

CHAPTER TWENTY-THREE

ECHOES OF CITY'S DARK PAST SEEN IN CHILLING EAST VILLAGE
DISCOVERIES; AUTHORITIES FEAR CRIMSON CITY DEVIL COPYCAT

NEIGHBORHOODS ON EDGE AS BODY COUNT GROWS

MIDNIGHT CURFEW IN EFFECT FOR MANHATTAN; POLICE URGE
EXTREME CAUTION IN WAKE OF GRISLY MURDERS

Dorian tossed the Friday edition of the Times into the bin. The gruesome headlines capped off the end of a long, hellish week, the days growing darker on all fronts.

This morning's discovery of three more human victims in the vicinity of Bloodbath put Duchanes' body count at two dozen since the raid on the club. The increased police presence and constant media speculation continued to drag Dorian into a past he'd never quite outrun.

Upstate, the grays were multiplying at an alarming rate,

growing bolder and stronger, with Cole and his wolves reporting more sightings and fewer kills. Worse, they were starting to spread into populated areas. Since Tuesday, four humans had been slaughtered in towns around Annendale-on-Hudson, all of them written off as animal attacks—a ridiculous assumption that would only result in more casualties. The pack seemed to be moving south along the river, likely heading for the most densely populated place in the entire country: New York City.

Dorian's fucking city, where—if left unchecked—they'd eventually merge with the so-called "civilized" Duchanes vampires in a vicious tsunami of death and mayhem no human would survive.

Brilliant bit of strategy, that. A city in chaos was a city ripe for demonic takeover—a threat that, while presently unconfirmed, still loomed large in Dorian's mind.

More than ever, Dorian needed his brothers united behind him. But Malcolm still wasn't speaking to him, Colin had become so obsessed with solving their father's great mysteries he was all but living in the crypts now, and Gabriel was spending the better part of his evenings trading favors among his network of unsavory supernatural associates in Las Vegas, all to dig up dirt on Charlotte's uncle.

Here at FierceConnect, while talks with Armitage Holdings had cooled significantly in the wake of the tensions with House Duchanes, Dorian continued to endure the parade of Rudy D'Amico's spies masquerading as investigators, their questions becoming more invasive, their demands more ridiculous. The various regulatory bodies involved in the acquisition process were already starting to balk, undoubtedly suspicious about the on-again, off-again status of the deal and the constant schedule changes.

It was, in so many ways, the perfect storm. Yet despite the gravity of his many responsibilities, Dorian's mind was locked almost entirely on another matter.

Charlotte.

Soft, beautiful, fiery Charlotte.

In the days since they'd parted ways at Ravenswood, he'd sent her five dozen roses each and every morning, telling himself it was all part of the romantic ruse they needed to carry on for her uncle, should the bastard pay her another visit.

He'd emailed her more details about their fake Hawaiian getaway, telling her how much he was looking forward to it.

He'd typed up lengthy texts—hot, filthy, depraved—only to delete them before hitting the send button.

He'd conjured her memory in the shower, in the bedroom, in the closets, recalling the feel of her soft, wet mouth as he stroked his cock to no avail.

Her presence was all around him—flooding his senses, filling his memories, haunting his dreams. Everything about her made him constantly hard, constantly frustrated, and constantly worried.

In that time, he'd seen her only from afar, alternating shifts with Aiden and occasionally Gabriel to keep watch over Charlotte and her sister from a distance, hoping to grant them a modicum of privacy. Only once had she spotted him on the street, and though he hadn't approached her, she'd waved at him, and the smile that broke upon her face had felt like the dawn.

He was still thinking about that smile now, just after close of business at FierceConnect, as the rest of his employees took off for the weekend. And though it was probably a terrible idea, the moment he was certain he was alone in the office, he grabbed his cell and made the call.

"Chateaux Noir," he said when Charlotte answered, "makes the most exquisite Coq au vin in America. Believe me, I've tried them all."

Charlotte laughed, the sound immediately warming him. "Sounds divine. Is that what you're having tonight, *monsieur*?"

"It's what *we're* having tonight, *madame*. Six o'clock?"

Her silence spoke volumes.

"It's just dinner, love," he said softly. "An early one, at that."

Still no response.

"Charlotte, I know we're not exactly..." Dorian sighed and raked a hand through his hair, searching for the words that'd clearly abandoned him. "It's just that... I was hoping..."

Bloody *hell*, why was this so damn difficult? Not four nights ago, he'd gone down on her in the garden as if it was his last fucking meal, and now he couldn't even invite her on a simple date?

"Dorian..."

"You're over-thinking it," he said. "Don't."

"I'm sorry. It's—"

"There's no reason we can't enjoy each other's company over a nice meal and a bottle of wine," he said, biting back his irritation. "I haven't been out in the city on a Friday night in an age."

Charlotte sighed, and he pictured the curve of her eyebrow, the wrinkle that appeared when she was deep in thought. His thumb ached to smooth it out.

"I would love to, Dorian. But I already have plans tonight. Rain check?"

Dorian's heart thudded.

Plans? As in, a date? Did she have a fucking date?

I will kill him without hesitation...

He tried to dismiss it, but the thought wormed its way into his mind, burrowing deep, taunting him.

Haunting him.

"Of course," he said. "Enjoy your evening, Charlotte. Be safe."

He ended the call and pitched the phone across his desk, anger and frustration pushing him to his feet.

He knew he should let it go. Just head back to Ravenswood, call Aiden and Cole to make sure they were all set for Saturday's meeting with Estas, review the additional Armitage files his corporate lawyers had sent over, work on his Midnight Marauder stats, test the new gaming gloves one of his programmers had delivered from R&D...

Anything but give in to the idea presently slithering through his mind.

But he couldn't.

If Charlotte was seeing someone new, it could jeopardize everything—the entire show they'd been putting on for Rudy, her safety, Sasha's, all of it. Whether she realized it or not, Dorian and his family were risking a *lot* to help her; one way or the other, he had a right to know what she was up to.

At least, that's what he told himself as he poured a glass of scotch from a bottle he kept in his desk. The alcohol burned, but it steadied his nerves for the task ahead.

One way or the other.

CHAPTER TWENTY-FOUR

After waiting in the limousine across the street from Charlotte's building for nearly an hour, Dorian finally spotted his woman exiting the lobby.

She wore a simple black dress and a sheer, wine-colored wrap, her hair and makeup expertly styled. With every step, she carried herself with purpose, poise, and stone-cold determination.

Blood rushed to Dorian's head, his heart thumping frantically in his chest.

Stunning.

In so many ways, the moment reminded him of the night they'd met, when he'd first caught sight of her in the Salvatore lobby, her smile lighting up the darkness.

"Do you see her?" Dorian leaned forward through the privacy window, pointing her out to Jameson as she marched down Park Avenue on foot. "Black dress, fucking gorgeous?"

"Of course, sir."

"Follow her. Don't get too close."

As Jameson pulled the car into Park Avenue traffic, a flicker of guilt burned in Dorian's chest. Although he and Aiden had kept tabs on Charlotte and Sasha all week, this was different.

Dorian told himself it was only to keep her safe, but that white-hot guilt eating through his guts called him a bloody liar.

He was spying on her.

Because deep down, all dangers and threats to her life aside, Dorian was a desperate, lovesick, jealous asshole who couldn't stand the thought of some filthy human lowlife putting his hands—or any other body parts—on his woman.

What was her type, anyway? Thieves and con artists? Stockbrokers? A lawyer, perhaps?

Dorian scoffed.

Pathetic.

But… wait.

A new fear jammed into Dorian's skull like an icepick.

What if her new man wasn't human at all? What if she'd fallen for another vampire?

"Don't lose her," Dorian snapped.

"She's just ahead, sir."

Already he was itching to bolt from the car, to chase her down, to make a fucking scene. But he took a deep breath and forced himself to calm down, keeping a close watch as

Jameson trailed her to Eighty-Fourth Street, where she cut west toward Fifth Avenue.

It was a one-way street; they couldn't follow.

"Sir?" Jameson asked.

"Cut down Eighty-Third. We'll beat her to the other end and…Never mind. I'm going after her."

"But Mr. Redthorne, are you certain that's—"

"Yes." Ignoring Jameson's voice of reason, Dorian exited the car and followed Charlotte's path, spotting her midway down the block. She was heading for the park, charging down the street like a woman on a mission, wobbling each time her spiked heels hit the sidewalk.

Dorian kept his distance, following her right through the park until the path spilled them out onto Central Park West.

Why was she walking? In heels and a dress, no less? Where was her date? What kind of classless twat made a woman walk across town for a date?

A dead twat, that's what kind.

Rage boiled inside him anew. He couldn't wait to wrap his hands around the bastard's neck. Perhaps he'd get a meal out of it too. Sink his fangs right into that fat, juicy artery and—

"Bloody hell."

The breath whooshed from his lungs as he finally figured out where she was heading.

In a sharp, terrible instant, Charlotte's so-called plans came into focus.

Not a date. A fucking job.

Just a few yards ahead of him on the sidewalk, she slipped away like a shadow beneath the blood-red awning, disappearing into the Salvatore.

Moments later, Dorian stormed inside, promptly compelled the doorman, and stalked into the elevator, more than ready to make that fucking scene.

The auction was set up in the same penthouse as before, but it looked nothing like the place in his memory. Gone were the bar and the high-end furnishings, the caterers and bartenders that had previously served the bidders. Tonight, the place was stripped to its barest bones, the walls stark, the hardwood floors scuffed from heavy foot traffic. There was no socializing—only the business of selling off the family's final few pieces of artwork.

Even the security guard that had chased them off the property was nowhere to be found.

Standing in the shadows at the back of the main room, Dorian scanned the attendees. No vampires this time, but two demons were seated just in front of him— Chernikov's, already taking advantage of their new weekend freedoms.

Still, what the hell were they doing at an auction? He hadn't pegged Chernikov's foot soldiers as art collectors.

With a sinking feeling, he wondered which of the humans they were after—which of the wealthy elites was ready to sell his soul.

No matter. Dorian had other business tonight, and he quickly turned his attention back to the other guests.

He'd expected Charlotte's absence, and was more than ready to hunt her down in the study, self-righteous and smug. He'd wanted it, he realized. She'd promised him she was out of the game for good, and he wanted to catch her in that lie.

It would've made things so much easier.

Give me a reason to end this for good...

But there she was, seated at the front of the room alone, beautiful and aloof, a touch of sadness weighing on her soft shoulders.

Dorian's heart sputtered. He wanted to go to her. To rewind the past few weeks, erase them, call a do-over on the entire mess. They could be strangers once again, crossing paths for a few brief moments of passion, nothing more.

And then he could turn on his heel, walk back into the elevator, and forget all about her.

Oh, for fuck's sake. Who was he trying to convince? He'd never take that deal, just as he'd never forget her. Not in an eternity.

The artwork set up on the platform was covered with sheets, and now the auctioneer approached, revealing the few remaining pieces—two sculptures, a handful of smaller paintings, an antique tea set, and...

Oh, Charlotte...

Dorian stifled a curse. She wasn't working a job after all.

Without preamble, the auctioneer began the event,

selling off three small paintings and a sculpture before getting to the painting that had captured all of Charlotte's attention.

One that had come to mean something to Dorian too.

"*Adrift*, by Heinrich Von Hausen," the auctioneer said. "We'll open the bidding at five thousand dollars."

On the night they'd first crossed paths, Charlotte had told Dorian the painting of the ship on a stormy sea reminded her of her father—that she'd seen it with him on a trip to the Smithsonian as a child.

Charlotte raised her bid card, but she was trumped by three others in quick succession. She tried to keep up, raising each bid by another thousand, but when the bidding reached five figures, she quietly tucked the card into her purse, her head low.

Dorian knew she didn't have money—not even the five grand she'd first bid.

She wasn't here to buy it. She was here to see it off. To say goodbye.

She remained seated, and Dorian watched as the auctioneer made quick work of closing the deal, the final bid coming in at $350,000.

Charlotte nodded once at the painting before her, then rose from her chair and headed for the exit.

Dorian remained in the shadows along the back wall, but his caution wasn't necessary. She walked right past him, so closely Dorian could smell her intoxicating scent, could see the tears glittering in her copper eyes.

She hadn't even known he was there.

He caught up with her in Central Park, lingering on a bench not far from where they'd shared their first dinner. The memory made him smile as much as it made him ache.

"Had I known hotdogs were the way to your heart," he teased, "I wouldn't have led with the coq au vin tonight."

Charlotte didn't smile. Didn't glance up to meet his eyes. She barely acknowledged his presence.

Standing over her, his shadow eclipsing her face, Dorian said only, "I'm sorry."

"So you saw—"

"Everything, yes."

"I don't know why I came here. I knew I wouldn't be able to buy it." She slipped off her shoes, leaning forward to rub her feet. "I don't even have money for a taxi."

"You *what*?"

She waved the words away. When she sat up again, she patted the bench beside her, finally inviting him to join her.

Dorian sat down and put his arm around her shoulders. She stiffened at his touch, but then leaned into him, resting her head on his chest and letting out a deep sigh.

"I miss him, Dorian," she said, her voice thick with emotion, and he knew at once she'd meant her father. "Sometimes I still wake up thinking he'll be in the kitchen —like, I swear I can *hear* him in there, flipping pancakes, humming some old Italian song his nona used to sing, waiting to tell me about his latest scheme." She pulled back to face Dorian, her eyes full of so much pain and vulnerability, it nearly gutted him. "How can I still love someone who was so... so *bad*?"

"Unfortunately for us, love doesn't discriminate." He shook his head, offering a gentle smile. "Or... I don't know. Perhaps it's a fortunate thing after all."

"It hurts," she whispered, pressing a fist to her heart, her tears spilling.

"I know, love. I know."

Charlotte rested her head on his chest again, and Dorian buried his face in her warm, silky hair. They sat like that for a long time, looking for all the world like a pair of lovers comforting each other, but the truth was so much more complicated than that.

With neither warning nor precedent, Charlotte D'Amico had broken upon the shores of Dorian's heart like a tidal wave, unleashing feelings he'd never experienced—never even thought possible—overshadowing all else.

Then, just as quickly as she'd arrived, she was gone—a traitor, a liar, a thief from whom he should've hid every last one of his valuables.

Especially his heart.

But there, sitting on a bench in Central Park, his arm wrapped tight around her, her body leaning into him with an aching need he was certain they shared, Dorian was done pretending.

He missed her.

He wanted her, more than he'd ever wanted anything in his life.

And despite everything—*everything*—he still loved her.

Love.

Devil's balls. All this time, he thought he'd understood the meaning of the word.

But he hadn't understood a damn thing.

With a deep sigh, Charlotte sat up again, slipping out from his protective embrace. "I didn't mean to cry on your shoulder. Um, literally." She smiled and wiped away her tears. "Thanks for... listening."

She held his gaze for an eternity, the darkness in her eyes rising to the surface, swirling together with pain and regret and fear and loss and things Dorian could only guess at. More than anything, he wanted to take it away from her. To bear it, so she wouldn't have to.

"Dorian," she whispered, "I need to say something."

"You can talk to me about anything, love." He took her face between his hands, brushing her satin-smooth cheeks with his thumbs. "I'm not going anywhere."

And he wasn't. Not again. Whatever confessions fell from her lips now, whatever treacheries new or old, whatever spells or curses, he would *not* turn his back on her. Not again.

"What I did was... It was unforgivable," she said softly. "And it wasn't just what I did to you, but to every family and person and museum I've ever... You're just... You're the one that kills me the most, because what we had?" She reached up and wrapped her hands around his wrists, her touch warm and electric. "Maybe it started as a ruse, but for me the ruse ended the minute you kissed me in that study. I can't go back and change the past, but I guess I just... I wanted you to know how sorry I am. Truly. I know I don't deserve your forgiveness, but... Maybe I'm asking for it anyway."

Forgiveness. Now *that* was a word whose meaning he'd never pretended to know.

When he'd found those floor plans under her bed, Dorian swore she was dead to him. Swore he never wanted to see her again. If vampires could've compelled one another, he would've grabbed the first one he'd stumbled across and ordered him to erase the damnable woman from his mind.

And every day since, he'd tried to remind himself of that. To convince himself that's how things had to be. That he could never trust a woman who'd lied to him, who'd misled him, who'd conspired against him.

But all of it had been in vain.

And now, staring into her infinite eyes, Dorian realized it was already done.

He'd forgiven her the moment she'd uttered that first tearful apology in the dining room, bent over the sideboard as he fucked her slow and deep, swearing it would be the very last time.

Dorian supposed that made him a liar too.

Without another thought, he lowered his mouth to hers, claiming her in a possessive kiss.

She sighed into the kiss, sliding her hands into his hair, parting her lips and drawing him in deeper. As the tears fell down her cheeks, she kissed him as if it were their last chance, as if she were dying, as if the world was set to end and this was their epic goodbye.

Fuck, she tasted so good. So fucking right. So bloody perfect his head was already spinning, his cock bulging uncomfortably in his pants.

He wanted her—*all* of her. Her mouth biting his shoulder. Her hands stroking him hard and fast. Her perfect ass reddening beneath his commanding touch. Her toned thighs wrapped around his face as he sucked and licked and teased, her hands fisting his hair as she screamed his name, over and over...

Dorian broke their kiss, his whole body trembling with the need to possess her. "Fucking *hell,* woman."

He couldn't take it anymore. The kissing, the soft sighs, her hands in his hair...

It wasn't enough. It would *never* be enough. He needed more, and he needed it right fucking now.

He grabbed her shoes and rose from the bench. Then, scooping her into his arms, he gathered his woman close, nuzzled her neck, and whispered his next command—one he wouldn't allow her to disobey.

Not tonight.

Not ever again.

"I'm taking you home, Charlotte D'Amico."

CHAPTER TWENTY-FIVE

"Strip," Dorian demanded, jamming the button to close the privacy window. "Now."

He'd just blurred Charlotte across the park and deposited her into the waiting limousine, and now she sat on the leather bench seat across from his own, still trying to catch her breath.

Her lush lips, red and swollen from their earlier kiss, parted in surprise. "In *here*? Are you crazy?"

She glared at him across the darkened space as though she'd already made the diagnosis, and hell, maybe he *was* crazy. Utterly certifiable.

In that moment, he didn't care.

"Perhaps I was unclear, Ms. D'Amico," he said, his tone as relentless as the rock-hard bulge in his pants. "That *wasn't* a request."

New heat flared in her eyes, bringing a dark splash of color to her cheeks.

Oh, how he'd missed making her blush...

As Jameson smoothly navigated them through Friday rush-hour traffic, Dorian continued to hold her gaze.

Moments passed.

City blocks passed.

An eternity passed.

Dorian was beginning to fear he'd pushed too hard, too soon. But then, miracle of bloody miracles, she lowered her eyes and slid the wrap from her shoulders, a seductive smile stealing across her lips.

His heart lurched sideways. It was *everything*, that smile. Radiant and beautiful. Sweet and sultry. Devastating.

And by its light, Dorian knew, at long last, Charlotte was his to command once again.

The realization sent a throb to his cock.

"Yes, Mr. Redthorne," she said, lowering the zipper at her side. Slowly, torturously, she peeled the dress from her body, revealing her soft skin, one provocative inch at a time.

Dorian's gaze traveled across her collarbone, skimmed over a delicate lace bra the color of ripe raspberries, straight down to the matching lace below, all of it making his mouth water.

Charlotte folded the dress in her lap, then carefully set it aside, raising an eyebrow as if she were daring him to issue another command.

Don't worry, love. We're just getting started.

"Forgive me," he said, stroking his jaw, "as I'm *quite* advanced in years and my memory is unreliable at best. But I could've sworn I ordered you to strip. Did I not?"

"You did, Mr. Redthorne. I'm sorry." With a mischievous grin, she unclasped her bra and tossed it aside, gifting him with the sight of her full, perfect breasts, dark pink nipples hardening at the barest brush of the car's air conditioning.

She removed the matching panties next, slowly dragging them down her long legs.

Before she could set them aside, Dorian's hand shot out, gesturing like a greedy child at the cookie jar. "*Mine.*"

She tossed the panties to him, and he caught them and brought them to his mouth, inhaling deeply.

Fuck... The heady scent of her desire almost made him come. He wanted to blur into her space and bury himself to the fucking hilt.

But... no. He'd just gotten her back. And thanks to rush-hour traffic, they had two long hours before they reached Ravenswood, trapped together behind the darkly tinted windows, nothing to do but reacquaint themselves with their favorite sinful delights.

Naked before him, Charlotte leaned back against the soft black leather, arms at her sides, her legs slightly parted.

Dorian took a moment to drink her in, his gaze raking over every inch of newly bared flesh, heart slamming against his ribs, cock straining behind his zipper.

"Anything else, Mr. Redthorne?" she asked, further parting her thighs to reveal the dark, wet heat at her center, already glistening with desire.

Dorian unfastened his pants and slid his hand down the front, finally unleashing his cock, hard and eager for her.

Across the darkened space, Charlotte let out a soft gasp

and bit her lower lip, shifting on the leather seat as if it was suddenly difficult for her to sit still.

Her eyes glazed, and he flashed a smirk, wondering if she was recalling the last time she'd taken him in her mouth.

Dorian certainly was.

"Come to me, Charlotte," he ordered.

Charlotte hesitated, a silent war waging in her eyes, a smile twitching at the corners of her mouth.

"Is there a problem, Ms. D'Amico?" Dorian teased. "Something you find... unsatisfactory?"

"Damn," she whispered, the smile finally breaking through in earnest. "You're a very bad influence, Mr. Redthorne. I'm supposed to be on the VDD."

"VDD?"

"Vampire dick detox," she said, as if it made perfect sense.

Dorian laughed. "I see. And how's that working out for you, love?"

"It *was* working out just fine, until you..." She gestured at his cock, still fisted tightly in his hand.

"The VDD," he mused. "Well, this *is* an unfortunate turn of events. But not entirely unworkable." He stroked himself once, twice, long and slow, her eyes following the movements of his fist. "I suppose we'll have to get creative."

Charlotte sighed, nibbling again on that plump lower lip.

Dorian wanted to bite her.

But *that* would have to wait.

She reached for him, already moving from her seat, ready to follow his commands.

"Easy, love," he teased. "You're on a restricted diet, and I respect that."

"Dorian, I—"

"*Dorian?*"

"Mr. Redthorne," she said, adorably exasperated. "Please let me touch you. *Please.*"

Ignoring her, he hit the intercom for Jameson.

"Yes sir?" came the reply.

"Jameson, I'd like you to take the long way home, if it's not too much trouble."

"No trouble at all, sir."

He turned off the intercom, then said to Charlotte, "There's a compartment beside you. Open it."

She did as he asked, finding a small ice chest, freshly refilled. He heard the change in her heartbeat, the quick skip as the realization set in. He knew at once she was thinking of their rendezvous in the game room in Tribeca, just as he was.

Without being asked, she retrieved an ice cube from the chest and brought it to her lips.

"Suck on it," he whispered, tightening his grip on his cock.

She wrapped her lips around the ice cube and slid it into her mouth, obeying his command. She closed her eyes and moaned softly, working the ice as if she were working *him*.

Bloody hell, I could die right here and call it a life well lived…

"Open your legs," he demanded, and she did, her sweet

blush spreading from her cheeks to her neck, cresting over the tops of her breasts. "Touch yourself for me, Charlotte. Show me what you do when you're all alone in that bed at night, thinking of me. Remembering all the dark, wicked ways I've made you come."

Charlotte moaned again, dragging the ice cube from her lips to the hollow of her throat and down to her breast, slowly running it over one nipple, then the other, rivulets of water dripping down her skin. A low growl vibrated in Dorian's chest, and he stroked himself again, following the trail of melted water with his eyes, recalling the sweet, addictive taste of every soft curve, every dark hollow.

"Charlotte," he breathed, his own heart rate matching hers, beat for rapid beat as she slid the ice cube down between her thighs.

She gasped at the shocking cold, but didn't stop, her head falling backward against the headrest, her hips tilting up as she swirled the ice over her clit, then dipped inside, fucking herself for his pleasure.

"That's it, love," he whispered, his breath ragged and hot. "*Show me.*"

"Oh, *fuck*," she breathed, a sound of pure ecstasy as the ice finally melted and she took over with her wet fingers, stroking herself faster, the blood singing through her veins, her heart pounding as she pushed herself closer. "I'm... God, Dorian. You're... impossible..."

"Don't stop, Charlotte," he warned, his voice strained.

The moment threatened to overwhelm him, Charlotte melting at her own touch before his eyes, the limo purring hypnotically along the highway, her scent invading his senses, his balls tightening, desperate to unleash everything he'd been holding back for a fucking *eternity* as they'd spent their nights apart…

"Please, Mr. Redthorne," she whispered, trembling and desperate. "I'm so close."

"I know, love."

"It's you I want," she breathed. "It's you I *always* want."

Dorian tightened his grip, forcing himself to resist the siren call of her begging. "Not yet, love. Not until you come for me."

She caught his gaze, her eyes dark and glassy, defiance sparking in their coppery depths. But Charlotte was, as ever, eager to obey. With another desperate moan, she closed her eyes and slid her fingers inside, then back out, frantically circling her clit, harder, faster, faster still…

"I'm… Dorian… Oh my *God*! I'm there… I'm… Fuck! Yes! *Yes!*"

She came for him hard and wild, the blush spreading across her skin like a sunset, chasing the waves of her orgasm until she was spent and panting, her body glistening with a thin sheen of sweat, her legs trembling, her heartbeat like a thunderstorm.

When she finally met his eyes again, Dorian growled, hungry and possessive. Fucking *feral*.

He'd never seen a sight so beautiful.

And she was his.

Right. Fucking. Now.

CHAPTER TWENTY-SIX

A deep, erotic growl rumbled through Dorian's chest—Charley's only warning before he blurred into her space, capturing her shoulders and pushing her onto her back.

He pinned her down on the backseat and kissed her mouth, her neck, her throat, her collarbone, his cock pressing hard against her thigh. Everything about the moment conspired to sweep her out to sea, lost to those dark, dangerous currents she so craved.

Charley was drowning in him again, and she didn't want it to end. The possessiveness in his gaze, the weight of his powerful, muscular body as he settled between her thighs, the teasing brush of his cock against her already aching pussy...

Hell yes. Yes to this. Yes to all of this...

"I can't get enough of you, Charlotte," he whispered, nipping her neck. "You've entranced me again, and I don't even care. If this is nothing but a dark spell, may it never break."

"It's not a spell. It never was." Charley reached for his shoulders and pushed off his suit jacket, desperate to feel his bare skin beneath her hands. She'd just started in on his shirt buttons when the limo hit a bump, jostling them both. Dorian fell forward, his chest briefly smothering her face before he righted himself again.

But it was too late.

That moment—however brief, however unintentional—changed everything.

The dam broke, and memories flooded her mind, making her sick and panicked.

She was no longer in the back of a limo with the vampire she'd fallen in love with. The one she knew, logically, would never hurt her.

She was in an old sedan outside an abandoned pizza joint on Long Island—a thin, scrappy child trapped by two impossibly strong men.

Don't struggle, D'Amico bitch...

Fear gripped her chest. Her throat closed on a scream, and Charley thrashed, shoving hard against Dorian's shoulders, desperate to escape.

To make it all go away.

"Charlotte?" Dorian stilled, his voice tight with concern. "What's—"

"No! Stop! *Stop!*"

He backed off in a heartbeat, and Charley sat up and

scooted to the far side of the seat, curling in on herself, squeezing her eyes shut to block it all out.

"Tell me what you need, love," Dorian whispered, gently draping her in his suit jacket, careful not to crowd her.

Charley sucked in a deep, shuddering breath and slid her arms into the sleeves, willing his warmth to penetrate the sudden chill. She opened her eyes, and slowly, the limo came back into focus.

Outside, the city had already faded away, the highway a dark and comforting escape.

You're safe, girl. Just a bad memory. Let it go.

"I'm okay," she said, her voice thin and watery. "I just... I need a minute."

Dorian backed off completely, giving her some much-needed space, though the air between them was heavy with his obvious concern.

Charley's hands and feet tingled with the leftover effects of the panic attack. She tried to slow her breathing. Her lungs ached, her throat burning with unshed tears.

God dammit. She was naked in the back of a limo, and instead of putting that nakedness to good use with her sexy, commanding, hot-as-fuck vampire, she was sitting there shivering, embarrassed, and pissed off—at herself, at those fucking animals who'd hurt her when she was a kid, at her father and uncle. She wanted her fucking life back. Yet every time she got a little closer, the past stomped right back into her heart and snatched it away.

Was this her eternal punishment? Would she always be

a scared little girl inside, chasing after those big-girl dreams that would forever remain just out of reach?

"I'm sorry." She finally turned to face him again. "For a split second I couldn't breathe, and you were on top of me on the seat, and I just... My mind flashed back to a *really* shitty place."

"Rogozin," Dorian whispered, and she nodded.

He knew. Of course he knew.

"Charlotte..." Dorian's eyes filled with compassion, but she rushed in with another apology, shame heating her cheeks.

"I'm sorry, Dorian. You didn't do anything wrong. It was stupid. It was all me."

"No, love. You didn't do anything wrong either." He took her hand and squeezed—a soft, supportive gesture that meant more to her in that moment than he could've possibly imagined. "Don't *ever* apologize for that. It wasn't your fault. Not what happened back then, and not what you're feeling about it now."

A tear slipped down her cheek, but his words calmed her, and she leaned back and rested her head in his lap. He traced soft patterns across her forehead, and they rode in silence for several minutes until the panic fully subsided and she finally felt like she could breathe again.

"Thank you." She gazed up into his honey-brown eyes, centering herself, slowly finding her way back.

His only response was a soft smile, but it was all the encouragement she needed.

"I know that was a bit of a mood-killer, but... I still want to... to be with you." Charley sat up, her shame melting away in the wake of his strong, silent support. "If you still want to?"

He laughed. "Charlotte, when it comes to you, I *always* still want to."

Feeling a little bit braver and a whole lot better, she slipped out of his jacket, crawled into his lap, and straddled him.

Dorian buried his face in the crook of her neck, inhaling deeply. "You're sure you're all right? We don't have to do—"

"I want to. I promise." Charley's smile returned, along with a little more bravery. "But maybe... just for tonight... I think I need to be in charge."

She'd never asked for it before—never even wanted it. She'd always loved submitting to him, loved their games, loved his sexy demands and his firm, punishing touch. But it felt important tonight—a chance to snatch something back from the old ghosts still trying to control her. She didn't want to be afraid of them anymore. Didn't want to constantly relive that ancient trauma. It would always be part of her history—part of who she'd become, for better or worse. But it didn't need to be part of her present.

Maybe, calling the shots in the limo with a man she trusted—a man she loved—would help her.

Dorian's eyes softened, and he nodded without question.

He spread his arms across the headrests and leaned

back, already hardening beneath her. "You set the pace, love. I won't touch you unless you ask me to."

A surge of power shot through her body, and she reached down between her thighs, sliding her fingers over his smooth, perfect cock.

Dorian let out a soft moan, growing even harder at her touch.

"You're… certain?" he breathed.

"Absolutely."

"Hmm. And what happened to the VDD?"

Charley laughed. "*Fuck* the VDD."

Who was she kidding? She didn't want to detox from him.

She wanted to fucking *overdose*.

Now, gently guiding him to her throbbing center, she sank down onto that hot, hard perfection, closing her eyes as he filled her completely, bringing her back to herself.

"That's… incredible," she moaned, gripping his shoulders and taking him in deeper, rolling her hips to get the perfect angle.

Dorian let out a satisfied sigh, his eyelids drifting closed as she continued to ride him, harder and faster, taking exactly what she wanted, exactly what she needed.

True to his word, he didn't touch her, though she could feel the twitch and strain in his muscles, desperate for it. Still, no matter how hard it must've been for him to hold back, Dorian gave her the reins, and Charley had never felt more alive, more turned on, more powerful.

She let out a soft cry, and Dorian met her gaze again, his eyes dark and hungry. "Doing okay?"

"Amazing." Charley threaded her fingers into his hair and tugged him close, arching her back to press her nipple to his mouth.

"Suck," she commanded, and he obeyed, teasing her nipple with maddening strokes of his tongue, then sucking it between his lips, his soft moans vibrating across the stiff peak.

"*Harder*, Mr. Redthorne."

Again, he obeyed, sucking her in deeper, teeth grazing her flesh, making her ache. Between her thighs, his cock was hot and slippery, every stroke bringing her closer to that magnificent fall.

But suddenly, it wasn't enough. She needed more than just the graze of his teeth against her nipple, more than the hot slide of him, more than his soft moans.

With a dark rush of desire, she knew exactly what she wanted next.

His bite. His *real* bite.

It was a dangerous pleasure, but one she knew they both enjoyed. Knew they both—after all the arguments and lies and near misses and hurts and fears—needed.

She waited until Dorian released her aching nipple, then pressed her wrist to his mouth.

"*Bite*," she demanded.

He kissed her soft skin, but then pulled back, glancing up at her with wide eyes, a dangerous current running just behind his desire. "Charlotte, that's not... a good idea."

"I'm sorry, Mr. Redthorne, but *I'm* in charge tonight. Was that unclear?"

Heat flared in his eyes, but still, he shook his head.

"Are you refusing my command?" she asked.

"I'm protecting you from making a terrible mistake."

"I want this," she said softly. Sincerely. She pressed a kiss to his neck, slowly working her way to his ear, rolling her hips to take him in deeper. Then, in a dark whisper, she said, "Let me give this to you, Dorian. Please."

"But last time—"

"—is not *this* time."

She pressed her wrist to his mouth once more, and his eyes filled with new lust, another moan escaping his lips. He licked her skin, then sucked, and she pressed harder, urging him, *begging* him for that delicious bite as she rode his cock and felt the first waves of her orgasm building.

And then—finally, brutally, deliciously—he bit.

It was nothing like she remembered.

Without the adrenaline that'd come from the penthouse attack, without the fear of losing him, the pain was infinitely sharper, shooting up her arm and across her chest, straight into her heart.

But then, Dorian began to suck.

He held her gaze, and as the first twinges of red leaked into his golden irises, the pain of the bite faded, chased by a pleasure so intense, it bordered on rapture. It filled her completely, heating her from head to toe, her blood buzzing through her veins, her skin tingling with warmth.

Holy. Fuck.

She was so close. It felt like her whole body was about to come undone, every nerve ending sizzling, building to the same inevitable end.

She wanted to feel it with him. Every beautiful, dangerous moment.

Charley leaned forward and nibbled his earlobe, then ran her tongue along the edge, whispering the words she could no longer hold back. "Come for me, vampire king. Make me *feel* it."

He groaned against her wrist, his dark red eyes devouring her, unwilling to look away. He sucked her harder and arched his hips, slamming into her, meeting her every wild thrust.

She felt his abs tighten, and then he tore his mouth from her wrist and let out a guttural cry that rattled through her chest.

"*Fuck*! Charlotte!" He came hot and hard, his body shuddering beneath her, pushing her to the edge of that dangerous cliff...

And right fucking over it.

"Dorian!" she cried out, and the orgasm exploded inside her, her pussy clenching as the erotic thrill of the bite combined with wave after wave of white-hot bliss. Blood ran warm down her arm, and her vampire licked a hot path from her elbow to her wrist, his lips as red as his eyes. Together they rode out the aftershocks, zooming along the highway like they were leaving the rest of the world behind.

When they finally came back to earth, she took his face

between her hands and pressed a soft kiss to his blood-stained mouth, warm and salty and familiar.

It was hers. It was home.

Dorian had given her everything she'd asked for, and when he looked up at her now, Charley felt amazing and beautiful and powerful, like a fucking phoenix rising from the ashes of her old life.

"You," he breathed, shaking his head. Anger burned in his blood-red eyes, but there was respect there too, along with a desire neither of them could deny.

"Did it work?" he asked, dragging his thumb across his lips, wiping away the last bit of blood. "Did you prove to yourself that your monster could stop the feed before bloody well killing you?"

Charley smiled, reaching out to smooth the grumpy wrinkles between his eyebrows.

"I'm not the one who needed convincing, Mr. Redthorne." She pressed another soft kiss to his lips, then pulled back, gently cupping his face. "So you tell *me*. Did it work?"

His admonishing glare finally faded, replaced with a reluctant acceptance.

And then, at long last, the devilish grin she loved finally appeared.

"You're going to be the death of me, woman," he grumbled.

"Unlikely, considering you're an immortal vampire and I can't even properly wield a stake. But I *do* like bossing you around."

He laughed and captured her in his strong embrace, no longer content not to touch her.

"*That*," he said, nipping playfully at her neck, "was a one-time deal."

Charley giggled in his arms, light and carefree, a few of her old ghosts floating away.

"We'll see, vampire king. We'll see."

When they arrived at Ravenswood, the circular drive was full of fancy cars, with even more vehicles parked on the grounds. In a clearing next to the manor, a black helicopter loomed like a war machine.

Aiden was waiting for Dorian out front, the urgency clear in his eyes.

"What the hell is going on?" Dorian was out of the limo before they'd even come to a full stop, Charley close on his heels.

"If you'd check your phone once in a while," Aiden said, "you might have your answers."

"I was busy!"

Aiden took in their appearance—Dorian, his shirt untucked, his hair tousled. Charley, definitely rocking the freshly-fucked-in-a-car look. She wore it well, but still.

Dead giveaway.

"Malcolm has called a… meeting," Aiden said carefully. "A business… *council*… meeting."

Dorian fumed, every muscle in his body instantly rigid.

In a low, menacing voice, he said, "You're telling me my manor is filled with a dozen ancient bloodsuckers?"

"More like three dozen, and they're not all ancient. He's invited some new blood as well, no pun intended."

A quiet rage rippled through Dorian's body. "I need you to escort Charlotte upstairs at once. Where are Gabriel and Colin?"

"Gabriel is on his way back from the city. Colin is still... working on his research. He asked not to be disturbed."

Dorian nodded, then turned to Charley, his eyes softening.

"I don't want you to worry, love," he said, cupping her face. "But it seems my brother has invited some unsavory guests into our home. I need you to go with Aiden and stay in the bedroom. I'll join you as soon as I can rid us of these... intruders."

Charley nodded. Aiden and Dorian's brothers were intimidating enough; she had zero interest in meeting three dozen more.

"*Your* bedroom?" she asked, just to be sure.

Dorian smiled. "I wouldn't have you stay anywhere else, Ms. D'Amico."

Charley couldn't hide her grin. After last weekend's banishment to the guest bedroom, the invitation felt like an extension of trust—a trust she wouldn't take for granted again.

"I'll be with you shortly," he said.

"Are you sure? It sounds like you've got a lot going on."

"I do. And none of it is as important as you." He leaned

in and brushed a sweet, sexy kiss to her lips. "Will you wait for me tonight, love?"

Charley nodded, her chest filling with a different kind of warmth—one that had nothing to do with his sexy kisses and masterful touch. "I will *always* wait for you, vampire king."

CHAPTER TWENTY-SEVEN

It was worse than Dorian had imagined.

Crammed into the dining room he despised, some camped around the table, others standing shoulder to shoulder behind them, three dozen vampires bickered and speculated and otherwise fouled up all the air in the room.

Dorian's air.

House Connelly, House Pritchard, House Dade. Thompson and Blackburn, Morris, Deegan, Silvestri. A good lot of them Dorian didn't recognize at all—clueless upstarts, doubtlessly eager to make a name for themselves.

Malcolm sat at the head of the table, a smug and self-important host.

When they finally noticed Dorian looming in the doorway, the room fell silent.

Malcolm glanced up at him, his eyes full of challenge and conceit. "Well! Good evening, brother. I'm so glad you could take time out of your busy schedule to join us."

Dorian glared at their guests, each one shrinking beneath his scrutiny with nothing more than a few grumblings of "Good evening, King Redthorne," and "lovely to see you, your excellency."

Bloody cowards. And these were the vampires Malcolm had recruited to help usher in his new world order?

Dorian hated all of it. Hated all of them. Hated his brother most of all.

But oh, his evening was about to get *so* much worse than that.

A wet, wheezing sound drew his attention behind Malcolm's chair, where two vampires from House Connelly stood before the fireplace. They parted before his impatient glare, and there, chained inside a metal dog crate behind them, was a sight that turned Dorian's blood to liquid fire.

A gray.

They'd captured a fucking gray. And they'd put it inside a crate meant for an animal the size of a German Shepherd.

The wretched beast slumped in the corner, rocking back and forth, blood leaking from a wound in its side. Every few seconds, it bashed its head against the bars and opened its mouth as if to scream, but no sound escaped but that terrible wheeze.

Dorian dragged his gaze back to Malcolm, barely containing the fury burning through his veins. "*Explain.*"

"The gray?" Malcolm waved a hand through the air, as if the mere request for an explanation was an epic overreaction. "I discovered the poor creature on a drive through the mountains earlier—nearly ran it over. I thought our

273

brothers and sisters should be made aware of the dangers we're facing now."

"And you thought it wise to bring that danger into our *home*?"

"Relax. This one's harmless." Malcolm rose from his chair and approached the cage, then gave it a swift kick, startling the gray. "It'll be dead by sunrise."

Dorian couldn't help but notice the amulet around the creature's neck. "No, it won't."

He took a deep breath, temporarily stowing his fury. He'd deal with his brother's treachery later. Right now, he needed to regain control of this ridiculous sham of a meeting and usher these sycophants out of his home.

"Friends," he said, turning his attention back to the mob with a cold smile, "thank you all for coming. I want to personally assure you that the members of House Redthorne—along with our trusted associates—are doing everything in our power to track down and eliminate the grays. At this point, we have no reason to believe they won't be contained."

"And what of the murders in the city?" Kate Connelly —a friend of Aiden's who'd first reported the demons' presence at Bloodbath—asked. "What of House Duchanes?"

"Excellent question, Ms. Connelly," Dorian said. "As many of you have undoubtedly heard, Renault Duchanes went into hiding after an unprovoked attack at one of my residences. We're still searching for clues to his where-abouts, as well as proof of his rumored association with demons and their connection to the influx of grays in the area."

A vampire from House Deegan spoke up. Dorian remembered him as one of the relics from the original council his father had disbanded—a former state senator. "While the members of House Duchanes continue to do his bidding in the city," he said, "Renault has allegedly taken refuge with a coven in Paris."

Dorian lifted his brows. This was news to him. "And you have proof of this, Senator Deegan?"

The vampire reddened slightly. "At this point, it is but a rumor, but one worthy of investigation."

"And one I would be more than happy to investigate," Dorian said sharply, "if you'd bothered to share the relevant details."

"My contact in Paris says Renault is building a case against House Redthorne. A case to *legitimately* overthrow your rule."

"He has no claim," Dorian said, "and no cause."

"He *will* find one, highness," Deegan said. "And what then? We should all bow as pliantly to our new rulers as we have to the old?"

"It's funny, Senator Deegan." Dorian narrowed his eyes, making the old bastard squirm. "You speak of pliancy, yet as I recall, you were one of the more... *outspoken* members of my father's council. One who caused him a fair bit of legal trouble over the decades."

Lawrence Deegan was a belligerent drunk and a womanizer whose antics on Capitol Hill had nearly gotten vampires exposed on national news. In the end, Augustus had given him an ultimatum: retire from the human political realm... or die.

The old senator bristled, lowering his eyes. "I fail to see—"

"And that's precisely the problem, Senator," Dorian said. "You fail to see."

"Why should we presume Duchanes' guilt without proof?" a vampire called Regina Olivand asked. "And furthermore, why *shouldn't* we consider a regime change? Perhaps our lives would improve with some new blood at the helm."

"New blood?" Dorian paced the small space that still remained in the overcrowded room, his eyes never leaving hers. "And you believe, Ms. Olivand, that King Duchanes would simply allow you to go about your business unmolested?"

"We all want peace, your highness," she said. "That's all."

"Duchanes wants peace?" Dorian shook his head, disgust churning inside him. "Renault Duchanes is working with a powerful demonic faction to overthrow this city as we speak, and you believe he'll simply smile and wave and wish you well on your journey? Extend the ring for a kiss, and offer you many blessings in return?"

"House Redthorne is not united," one of the upstarts chimed in. "That much is clear. How can you keep our communities safe and at peace when you can't even keep your own house in order?"

Dorian wanted nothing more than to feed the little shit to the gray, but again, he reined in his anger, forcing his smile back in place.

"We're still trying to get a handle on the situation unfolding beyond our walls, but I assure you, we will. As for House Redthorne..." Dorian glared at Malcolm, who sat primly with his hands folded on the table, a smile twitching at his lips. "We are experiencing some personal difficulties following the death of our father and former king. All shall be resolved in time."

"Of course," the upstart said. "And I'm sure I speak for all of us here when I say I'm sorry for your loss. But in the meantime, I think reuniting the council is a good start. We're your allies, Mr. Redthorne. We want to help."

"Is that so, Mr.—Sorry, what did you say your name was?"

He puffed out his chest. "I'm Dominic of House—"

"Stop." Dorian cut him off with a raised hand and a steely glare that instantly drained the blood from the young man's face. "I don't actually care what your name is, blood-sucker. And do you want to know why?"

"I... I..." He stammered like a sodding fool, all of his bravado evaporating. "Yes, sir."

"Because you're a sniveling twat with a bubblehead full of idealistic nonsense. Yesterday you were undoubtedly still trying to give yourself a blowjob in the bath, yet here you are tonight, elbowing your way to a place at the grown-ups' table."

"I'm sorry, Mr. Redthorne, sir. I—"

"Yes, you *are* sorry. And from now on, you'll address me as highness or king, if you address me at all, which I prefer you do not." Then, whirling to face Malcolm again, "And you, brother? What are *you* proposing? Would you like to see us fall at the feet of King Renault Duchanes as well?"

Malcolm rolled his eyes. "Don't be melodramatic, Dorian. I simply want everyone's voice to be heard. That's why I've decided to reconvene the council, along with new delegates representing a diverse cross-section of the community at large."

Dorian made a show of glancing around the room, seeing many of the same old faces of the past. Even the new ones looked the same to him—an endless supply of wealthy, privileged vampires, the sons and daughters of those who'd come before.

"No shifters represented?" Dorian asked. "No witches? No fae? I hardly think this room represents a fair sample of the so-called community at large."

"The other supernaturals need our guidance." Malcolm got to his feet, the facade of cool superiority finally beginning to crumble. "Vampires are the ruling family for a reason."

"You are a prince, Malcolm," Dorian warned. "Not a king. It is not for you to decide how and to whom such guidance is given."

"Yes, I am a prince. But *you*, highness…" He sneered at Dorian, disdain rising in his eyes. "You're a pathetic excuse for a vampire king who lives and dies by the fickle whims of his cock."

Dorian blurred through the crowd, stopping just before his brother and lancing him with another warning glare, but Malcolm was just getting started.

"Your blindness is the only reason House Redthorne even exists," Malcolm spat. "If you'd been a bit more discerning as a human, you might've noticed your whore was a vampire before—"

Malcolm blurred inexplicably from Dorian's view, crashing hard into the adjacent wall.

Gabriel, who'd just arrived, had him pinned by the throat. "Easy, brother. No need to air the Redthorne laundry in front of our distinguished guests."

Before Dorian could even process the fact that Gabriel, of all vampires, was actually *defending* him, Malcolm fired off a few more rounds.

"You killed our witch!" he shouted. "You tore apart our city, slaughtering entire families with no remorse! You *destroyed* us, Dorian. And every day you exist, you continue to consume this family like a cancer!"

Dorian stood there, taking every bullet to the chest, knowing each one was true.

"Even tonight," Malcolm said, his teeth gritted, eyes sharp with rancor, "you've brought a human traitor into your bed. A woman connected to Alexei Rogozin."

A collective gasp spread around the room like wildfire, igniting the gossip as sure as it ignited Dorian's wrath.

Everything else had been fair game. Cruel, perhaps, but fair.

But Malcolm had *no* right to bring Charlotte into this. No right to put her in danger.

Malcolm's vacated chair was close at hand, and Dorian grabbed it without a second thought, smashing it against the table. Gripping a sharp, jagged piece of wood, he turned to the mob and shouted, "Who among you can claim innocence? Who among you hasn't spilled a single drop of blood?"

Dozens of eyes stared back at him, shocked and vacant in their pale faces.

No one uttered a word. Not the assembled guests. Not his brothers. Not Aiden, who'd just joined them.

"Who among you is prepared to deal with our enemies by any means necessary?" Dorian asked, turning to the cage behind him.

Still, no one spoke.

In a blur, he smashed through the cage and hauled the gray out by its throat, lifting it to its feet. Then, with everyone watching in abject horror, he buried the stake in the creature's chest.

It should've killed it—should've killed *any* vampire— but of course, it didn't.

Gabriel released his hold on Malcolm, and the vampires in the vicinity skittered backward, shocked and confused by the ineffectiveness of the stake.

"What about you, brother?" Dorian asked, turning the gray toward Malcolm. "Since you're so keen to lead us into that big, bright future, perhaps you've already got a plan for dealing with this?"

"*Dorian*," Gabriel warned. "Now is not the time for—"

"Oh, for fuck's sake." Dorian rolled his eyes. Keeping one hand secured around the gray's throat, he shoved his fist through its back and tore out the heart.

Again, the gray survived.

"This." Dorian held up the ravaged heart, blood dripping down his arm as the gray moaned and twitched in his grip, broken and bloodied but just as alive as every other vampire in that room. "This is but a preview of what Duchanes is planning. So, I ask… Who among you wishes to challenge your king for a shot at the helm?"

Silence.

"After all your talk of regime changes and peace," he said, "is there no vampire brave enough to take the reins?"

None of them spoke. None of them even breathed. The only sound in that room was the gray's blood splattering on the hardwood floor.

"Ours is *not* a democracy." Dorian pitched the heart onto the table, where it slid and skidded to a halt in front of Lawrence Deegan. "We unite, under *my* rule, or we die. If any of you need a moment to consider your options, feel free to take a stroll outside to clear your minds. Though, I'd advise you to stay within shouting distance, unless you're keen to meet another of our less civilized brethren."

With that, as swiftly as he'd torn out the bloody heart, Dorian ripped the amulet from the gray's neck. Seconds later, the creature—heart and body both—turned to ash.

Dorian pitched the dark amulet into the fire, where it exploded in a burst of black and purple smoke.

Shaken and unsteady, Lawrence Deegan got to his feet, slowly backing away from the pile of ash before him. "Perhaps we should reconvene when things are—"

"We will *reconvene*, Mr. Deegan," Dorian said, "when I decide you can be of use to me. Until then, all of you may carry on with your lavish parties and petty squabbling, conniving and drinking and scheming and fornicating to your heart's content. But when you go to bed each night, I want you to close your eyes, remember this moment, and remind yourself who's *allowing* you to carry on. Because the minute you forget, the minute you let your guard down... Well. Perhaps your king will let his down as well. Do we understand one another now, *friends*?"

Dorian took the time to meet each and every gaze, waiting for their acknowledging nods.

Satisfied he'd made his point, he clasped his bloody hands together and grinned. "Excellent. Meeting adjourned."

Almost at once, every visiting vampire in that room rose to their feet, quickly making their way toward the exit.

The air was so thick with cowardice, Dorian nearly choked on it.

The last simpering imbecile had finally cleared out, leaving only Dorian, Aiden, Gabriel, and Malcolm. The cowardice in the air was immediately replaced with tension, sparking like a live wire.

Dorian stalked toward his pathetic excuse for a brother, looming so close to Malcom's face he could count the man's fucking eyelashes.

"What you've done is tantamount to treason," he said, his voice dark and menacing. "I should kill you where you stand."

Malcom glared at him in silent rebellion, anger and frustration flashing in his eyes.

Dorian didn't want to see anger and frustration.

He wanted to see regret.

He wanted to see *fear*.

Without warning, he shoved his fist through Malcolm's chest, surprising the hell out of them both.

"What the fuck are you *doing*?" Gabriel shouted.

Aiden was there too, desperately trying to calm Dorian's rage.

But that was an exercise in futility.

Malcolm only gasped, his eyes wide, his heart beating frantically in Dorian's unrelenting grip. In his gaze, Dorian found no further trace of anger. Only a debilitating fear that filled Dorian with a deep satisfaction.

Perhaps that should've concerned him.

But it didn't. Not tonight.

"You're so convinced I've got a soft heart, Mac, but let me tell you something." Dorian squeezed harder, fingers digging into the wet muscle. One swift jerk, and he could end this. End *him*. "All hearts are the same on the inside. Remember that next time you're thinking about undermining your king, *prince*."

He held fast another minute, digging in deeper until Malcolm finally nodded, his eyes glazing with pain.

Dorian released the heart and yanked his hand out of

Malcolm's chest, and Malcolm pitched forward, staggering as he attempted to catch his breath, his wounds already closing.

The bastard might've uttered something after that—an apology, a curse, a threat—but Dorian would never know. He was beyond caring. He stalked out of that room, blood running down his hands—the gray's, his brother's, all of it was the same now—leaving a trail on the gleaming hardwood floors.

When Dorian passed by the large mirror in the foyer, the brief glimpse of his reflection sent shockwaves of pain and fear rippling through his heart.

In that reflection, he saw a vampire full of ire and violence.

He saw a man full of hatred, capable of the worst kinds of cruelty.

He saw his father, Augustus Redthorne, smirking at him from the depths of hell.

He saw his own death.

"*Fuck!*" Dorian launched his fist through the glass, shattering it into a thousand deadly shards.

"That's bad luck, Mr. Redthorne," a voice hissed in the darkness.

Dorian spun around as a figure stepped out of the shadows, cloaked and hooded.

He blurred into the man's space, gripping him by the throat. "What part of *meeting adjourned* did you not understand, bloodsucker?"

"I'm no bloodsucker," came the reply.

The hood fell back, revealing the would-be assassin's identity.

He was a *she*. And she was—thankfully—neither vampire nor assassin.

She was a witch.

CHAPTER TWENTY-EIGHT

"Isabelle?" Dorian released her at once and blinked, not trusting his own eyes. He hadn't seen Isabelle Armitage since the disastrous fundraiser, and in the wake of the stalled acquisition talks, he'd feared he'd never see her again. "What are you doing here? Is your father with you?"

"No. We'd heard whispers that Malcolm was reconvening the council tonight. My brothers are concerned vampires are gaining too much power—they wanted to be sure the interests of mages and witches are well represented."

"I'm sorry you've wasted the trip, Isabelle." Dorian sighed, clasping his bloody hands before him. "There is no council. Just a good bit of family drama centuries in the making."

She offered an understanding smile. "I said my brothers were concerned about their interests, but that's not actually why I've come. I need to discuss something with you—their insistence was merely a convenient excuse."

"Is everything all right?"

Isabelle nodded, keeping her voice low. "Am I correct in assuming once your company secured Armitage Holdings, your intention was for House Redthorne to propose a bonded partnership?"

"That was my intention, yes. But with the deal currently in limbo, I'm not sure we should hold out hope for such an alliance."

Isabelle glanced toward the dining room, where the tattered remains of Dorian's family lingered, undoubtedly wondering if their eldest brother had finally lost his bloody mind.

Sensing Isabelle wanted some privacy, he led her into the study and shut the door behind them.

"My father is unwell, Mr. Redthorne," she said. "That's the real reason for the delay with the acquisition."

"Unwell? What's wrong?"

"He's suffering from early onset Alzheimer's. His mind is fracturing, and my brothers are concerned about his ability to make decisions."

"I'm so sorry. I had no idea."

"We've tried to keep it quiet," she said, her eyes filled with sadness. "He has his good days as well as his bad, though lately I'm afraid the latter are eclipsing the former."

"Is there anything I can do?"

"All I'm asking is for your patience. My brothers know Duchanes is a loose cannon at best, but they see my father's illness as a way to secure their own financial futures, and Renault has promised to double FierceConnect's offers at every turn. They're pushing for a quick sale, confusing my father with talk of counteroffers and legalities…" Isabelle sighed. "I'm doing my best to keep them at bay, but it's not easy. Father's health is my priority, and I don't wish to upset him. But I know selling to FierceConnect is what he would've wanted."

Frustration mounted in Dorian's chest, but he understood.

"FierceConnect's interest in Armitage Holdings remains strong, Isabelle. We can wait as long as necessary."

"And your interest in the bonded partnership?"

"It would be an honor to offer you such a proposal," Dorian said. "If and when the time is right for you."

Isabelle nodded. "I can't pledge myself in an official capacity at this time without upsetting the balance at home, but I *will* help you, Mr. Redthorne—in any way that I can—until such time as our partnership can be solidified."

Fresh hope rose in Dorian's heart. A bonded witch, after more than fifty years without one…

It felt like a dream. No more chasing down freelancers. No more fading tattoos, eyes aching in the sunlight, mind clouding with confusion. No more falling victim to his insatiable hunger so soon after a feed.

He could regain his full power. Protect his family. Protect his woman.

It was almost too good to be true.

"You're… certain?" Dorian asked. "I'm not sure how

much of that meeting you overheard, but I feel compelled to warn you my family is not in its strongest position right now. And with Duchanes causing havoc from afar… You're putting yourself at risk, Isabelle."

In response, she gestured for Dorian to hold out his hands, palms up.

"You'll have to excuse the blood," he said. "Malcolm and I—"

"I know." She placed her hands over his, their palms touching. "May I?"

Dorian nodded, and Isabelle closed her eyes, whispering an ancient incantation that warmed his skin, sending waves of heat cascading up both arms.

The magic was following the lines of his tattoos, he realized. Strengthening them as surely as Charlotte's blood had strengthened them. But unlike the spell, the blood was a remedy Dorian couldn't rely on. Not without putting the woman he loved at risk.

He needed the witch. *All* of them needed the witch.

"Better?" she asked, pulling away.

Dorian rolled his shoulders, the magic finally dissipating, but the power still coursed through him like lightning. His vision sharpened, his mind clearing at once.

Without an official witch-vampire bond, the spell wouldn't last long. But it was enough to bolster him for the weeks to come. More than that, it was a show of trust and commitment at a time when Dorian's life was lacking in both.

"Thank you, Isabelle. You've no idea what this means."

A kind smile touched her lips. "I understand all too well the obligations of family, and the often-thin line between duty and imprisonment."

"A line that grows thinner with each passing day, I'm afraid."

Dorian escorted her out of the study and back to the front door. He offered her payment in vampire blood, but she refused, telling him there would be plenty of time for that later.

"In the meantime," she said, "if you need anything, I want you to call me. Oh, and Mr. Redthorne?" She took his hands again, her eyes full of understanding.

This time, it was hard for him not to shy from her touch. Isabelle was an empathic witch; Dorian couldn't hide his emotional state, no matter how vulnerable and weak revealing it made him feel.

"Do not allow the brutality of your past or the grim realities of your present to harden your heart," she said. "In our world, love and kindness are strengths. They should be revered as such."

CHAPTER TWENTY-NINE

Always turned out to be a little longer than Charley had expected.

Waiting for Dorian in the master bedroom, she counted the minutes until she'd be in his arms again, but soon those minutes began to drag.

Anxious to pass the time, she showered and changed into one of Dorian's T-shirts and a pair of leggings she'd left behind last weekend.

She texted with Sasha, who was having a blast with Darcy's family on a fall foliage tour in Vermont for the weekend.

She checked in briefly with Rudy, who'd been oddly distant all week, letting him know she was at Ravenswood on another "fact-finding" mission.

She listened to some music.

Flipped through the Met's online gallery.

Gazed out the window and counted the stars glittering over the Hudson.

And still, her man did not return.

At some point, Charley must've fallen asleep. Because when she opened her eyes again, three hours had passed in a blink, and the manor was as silent as a graveyard.

She couldn't see the driveway from Dorian's bedroom, but when she peeked out the window, the shadow of the helicopter was gone.

Charley wandered the halls of the manor like a ghost, desperately seeking her vampire king. With no sign of him upstairs or on the main level, she decided to wait in the study, where the fire still burned and crackled.

Wrapping herself in the blanket she now thought of as her own, she sat at the desk in the corner of the room and looked out across the study, trying to see it as Dorian might. She wondered how many family meetings had taken place in here—arguments as well as celebrations. She hoped there were more of the latter, but given what she'd observed so far from the Redthorne Royals, she didn't see how that was possible.

Still, she understood why Dorian loved this room so much. It was elegant without being pretentious, offering a rare bit of cozy charm in a home whose vast halls echoed with loneliness.

Glancing down at the desk, Charley noticed what looked like an old scrapbook. She turned over the cover, revealing a collection of newspaper articles dating back to the 1970s.

Each article was more horrifying than the last, detailing a series of gruesome murders attributed to a killer they'd nicknamed the Crimson City Devil. Charley wasn't alive then, but she vaguely remembered her parents talking about it once, after seeing it mentioned on a TV show about serial killers and unsolved crimes.

Tucked into the back of the scrapbook, Charley found a spiral notebook full of names—pages and pages of neat, precise lettering she recognized as Dorian's. Each name was identified as a son, daughter, cousin, or spouse, listed beside another name with a date of death.

For each entry, there were other notes too:

College tuition - Stanford connections?

Daughter needs heart transplant. Contact U. hospital to facilitate.

Mortgage in default. Call First National to make arrangements.

Some of the notes had check marks next to them, while others had question marks and follow-up notes Charley couldn't even begin to decipher.

Were these Dorian's business associates? How did he know these people?

Scanning through the pages, her eyes landed on a familiar name beside a small red checkmark.

Marshall Goldman. Curator, Jewish Historical Society. Son of Landon Goldman, DOD Aug. 10, 1972. Whitfield painting — possible interest?

Charley's heart stalled.

Not associates, she realized. *Victims.*

The names and dates of death in the notebook matched those reported in the newspaper articles.

There were a lot of them. Easily over a hundred victims, each connected to more names than she could count.

Holy shit…

"Can't sleep?" Aiden asked, startling her from the doorway. "If you need some reading material, you might try the library down the hall."

He crossed the room and joined her at the desk, reaching down to close the books.

"Why does Dorian have this stuff?" Charley asked, not bothering to apologize for peeking. It was out on the desk, sitting there for anyone to see. "What is it? Some kind of sick trophy collection?"

A heavy sadness washed over Aiden's face, drawing his mouth into a deep frown. "Not trophies, Ms. D'Amico. Penance."

Penance?

Charley's hands trembled, her mouth dry. "For what?"

It was a stupid question—one she obviously knew the answer to, having read the articles. But she couldn't bring herself to admit it.

When she tried to reconcile the Dorian Redthorne she'd fallen in love with and the so-called Crimson City Devil the papers had described, she couldn't do it. The gulf between the two versions of her vampire was so wide, it damn near swallowed her up.

Aiden opened a desk drawer and placed the books inside, then slid it closed, his eyes shining with pity. "It's not your place to sift through the skeletons of another man's past, nor mine to help you assemble the bones."

"It's mine." Dorian's voice, dark and ominous, echoed across the small room, sending a shiver down Charley's spine. He towered like a vengeful god in the doorway, the firelight reflected in his eyes, blood staining his shirt.

Crimson City Devil strikes again...

Charley gasped at the sight, and Dorian glared at her, his golden eyes blazing.

"Leave us, Aiden," he ordered. "Ms. D'Amico and I have some things to discuss."

CHAPTER THIRTY

Dorian had never wanted to have this conversation with Charlotte.

He'd never even wanted her in this room, in this house, in the dark spaces of his heart.

Yet there she was, invading every part of his life. Every part of his home. Every part of his being.

He could no more avoid his darkest confessions than he could avoid his feelings for her; attempting to do both had only made the bitter pills harder to swallow.

"The night I met you—only an hour earlier, in fact—I'd been reminding myself about the dangers of falling in love." Dorian handed Charlotte a glass of scotch and settled himself in the chair across from her, taking a moment to look at her in the firelight.

To *truly* look at her.

She was radiant and alive, glowing with a deep inner

beauty that never failed to captivate him. Even the darkness inside her was beautiful.

"Have you ever been?" she asked, pulling the blanket tighter over her shoulders and taking a tiny sip of scotch. "In love, I mean. As a vampire. After... after Evie."

"Once. Not counting..." He smiled softly, but didn't fill in the word.

You. Not counting you.

Since that night in Charlotte's bedroom, he hadn't found the courage to say the words to her again, and now, he likely wouldn't get the chance.

"It was a long time ago," he continued, ignoring the ache in his heart. "You weren't born yet. Your parents were, though. I'm sure they remember what happened in this city back then."

Charlotte nodded and closed her eyes, and Dorian glanced at the desk behind her, where he'd stupidly left the scrapbook. He'd only intended to be gone from the study a moment, but then he'd ended up in the crypts with Colin, still theorizing about the origins of the demonic book they'd found. Dorian had all but forgotten the damning evidence on the desk.

"In any case," he said, "yes, I loved a human woman. So much so, I wanted to spend my life with her."

Charlotte nodded again, but didn't open her eyes.

It was probably for the best. Dorian had no interest in watching those gorgeous copper eyes fill with revulsion... or worse.

Fear.

Fear was for his enemies. For his brother. Not for the woman he loved.

"I didn't have a choice in whether I became a vampire," he said. "It's a fate I eventually learned to accept, but I wanted better for Adelle."

At this, Charlotte finally met his gaze, but her thoughts remained guarded. "And you think being human is better?"

"No. I think having a choice is better." He sipped his scotch and shook his head, the old warnings rising to the surface. "I never should've let things progress as far as they had, but our relationship moved so quickly. We had no secrets between us but one. The blackest one."

"She didn't know you were a vampire?" Charlotte guessed.

"She did not. So one night, just days before I'd planned to propose, I sat her down in the rose garden. After sharing a lovely dessert of German chocolate cake and coffee, I confessed. I wanted her to make the choice—*choices*, actually. Whether she wanted to walk away, or remain with me, knowing my true nature. And if she remained, whether or not she wanted to turn. I would've done it for her... I thought she... I..." Now it was Dorian who closed his eyes, the memories rushing at him like wraiths. "I simply wanted to honor her wishes. But it... it didn't go well."

"What happened?" Charlotte whispered.

"She didn't believe me at first. Thought I was playing some terrible prank, or trying to scare her into breaking things off, as if I were too cowardly to do it myself. She called me every name in the book for that. Nothing —*nothing* I said could convince her otherwise. Not even when I showed her the ring I'd already bought for her. Eventually, I had no choice but to play my last card. I grabbed her and blurred her across the garden, and then I transformed, turning from man to monster before her eyes."

The scotch turned over in Dorian's stomach. He'd never forget the terror on Adelle's face, the mix of fear and disgust in her eyes.

Frightening her like that... To this day, it remained one of his greatest shames.

"Our bonded witch was still with us at that time," he continued. "Rosalind. Adelle had always assumed Rosalind was a live-in housekeeper—an assumption I never discouraged. Anyway, Rosalind heard the screaming and rushed outside, only to see Adelle threatening me with the cake knife. She couldn't have hurt me, of course, but Rosalind had always been rather protective. She stepped between us, intending to diffuse the situation. But in Adelle's mind, Rosalind—sweet, playful Rosalind who'd always treated Adelle like a sister—was suddenly a threat. Another vampire, perhaps, or worse. Without thinking it through, Adelle..." Dorian finally opened his eyes, tears blurring his vision. "She attacked Rosalind. She stabbed her, and she..." His voice broke. "It happened so fast, Charlotte. I tried to save her, but she refused. She didn't want to risk turning into a vampire. She... she bled out in my arms. Adelle was so distraught over what she'd done, I had no recourse but to compel her to forget everything that had happened that night."

He could still hear the cries—Rosalind's, as she gasped her final breaths. Adelle's, when her senses had finally returned and she realized what she'd done. In that moment, Dorian knew she'd never forgive herself, and never accept him as a vampire.

In the span of fifteen minutes, he'd completely altered the course of her life.

"Certain she had no memory of the incident after the compulsion, I broke off the relationship, acting as if I'd simply grown bored. I was cruel and terrible to her, but I knew she had a much better chance of surviving a broken heart than surviving the trauma my earlier confession had inflicted upon her."

"Dorian, I... I don't know what to say."

"There are no words, Charlotte. Believe me, I've tried them all, and none of them ever make it any better." He downed the last of his scotch, then headed back to the bar.

The next part of the story was the worst part, and they both needed another drink.

He grabbed the bottle and topped off her glass, then returned to his chair, trading his empty glass for what remained in the bottle.

"It was my fault Rosalind died. I'd allowed her to get involved in something I should've dealt with long before—something I never should've brought to our doorstep in the first place. And then, when it mattered most, I failed to protect her. That is a vampire's sworn oath to his bonded witch, Charlotte. Protection. Other than our blood, it's the most precious gift we offer.

"Rosalind's family had been bonded to our line for generations, but when they learned what had happened, they immediately broke their alliance—and rightfully so. Word travelled fast throughout the witch and mage community, and the once esteemed House Redthorne became overnight pariahs. Almost immediately, the spells and enchantments Rosalind's family had imbued in us— everything that allowed us to walk in the daylight and live essentially as humans—began to fade. My father and brothers found ways to cope, but I... I didn't handle it well. Something inside me broke, and I just..."

Dorian took a long pull from the bottle, welcoming the burn. Across from him, he felt Charlotte shiver and shift in her chair, but he didn't dare look at her again. He couldn't. Not now. Not for this.

"No longer kept in balance by Rosalind's magic," he said, "unwilling or unable to consider alternatives, I began to revert to a vampire's natural state."

"Like the grays?" she asked, and Dorian nodded.

"The bloodlust quickly overwhelmed me. I flew into a murderous rage. Like a rabid animal, I tore my way through the city, slaughtering scores of innocents. I hunted them. I killed them. I didn't feel anything—only blood and death. That was my life. I cared for nothing—no one. Not my family. Not my duty. Not even myself. The more lives I devoured, the worse I felt, yet I couldn't stop. It was like something had taken possession of me, consuming a bit more of my soul with each passing day. The emptiness, Charlotte... It was like... like I died again every day.

"One by one, my father and brothers turned their backs on me and left—all but Aiden. No matter how ruthless and terrible I'd become, he never gave up on me." Dorian took another swig of scotch. "One night, after a particularly barbaric weekend, Aiden tracked me down—bloody hell, he quite literally fished me out of a dumpster, into which I'd stumbled hours earlier after killing four innocent college students out for a pub crawl. I was delirious from the blood overdose, but somehow, he managed to get me back to Ravenswood. I hardly recognized my own home, Charlotte. Hardly recognized my best friend. I was vicious and cruel to him, yet still, he remained by my side through all of it. He brought me back from the brink, and simply refused to let me fall again. To this day, I don't know how the hell he did it."

Dorian shook his head. Those days... The recovery... It was the darkest time in his life. He barely remembered it, each day blurring into the next, a haze of hunger and pain and shame so hot and intense he'd feared it would incinerate him.

"What you found," he said now, his voice thick with that old, familiar shame, "was the record of my rampage." He finally met her eyes, bracing himself for the inevitable fear. The revulsion. The end. "I'm the Crimson City Devil, Charlotte. Never caught, never prosecuted, never punished. But guilty just the same."

"And... and the names in your notebook?" she asked,

her voice a broken whisper, her eyes shining in the firelight. "They're all..."

Dorian tipped back the last of the scotch, then set the empty bottle on the table beside him. "They are the descendants of the one hundred and forty-nine innocent people I slaughtered. Every last one I've managed to track down over the years, hoping to offer some sort of... some..."

Charlotte stared at him in silence, and he trailed off, not quite knowing how to finish the thought.

No amount of penance could ever absolve him of these sins—Dorian had always known as much. But seeing it now, through the eyes of the woman he loved, he realized just how meager and pathetic his efforts had been.

Mortgages, tuition payments, paintings, hospital wings donated in the names of the dead... Dorian nearly scoffed at his own gall.

As if *any* of that could ever make things right.

Absent a time machine, *nothing* could make things right.

"Dorian," Charlotte whispered. "I can't... I don't..."

City streets run red with blood...

A single tear slid down her cheek, and he waited for the terror to register in her eyes. Waited for her to bolt for that door and flee his home for good, taking her chances with the monsters outside.

Crimson City Devil eludes authorities...

But she didn't flee. Didn't look at him as if he were a villain.

Crimson City Devil strikes again...

Instead, she set down her drink, rose from her chair, and dropped the blanket from her shoulders.

No end in sight for grisly crime spree...

"Charlotte..." he whispered, instinctively reaching for her, damn well knowing he shouldn't.

And she came to him. She knelt before him on the floor and took his hands, bringing them to her lips. With a soft, gentle touch, she kissed him—kissed the hands that had slaughtered innocents, that had made the city streets run red with blood. The hands that had nearly killed his own brother tonight.

Deep in Dorian's chest, an ancient pit bubbled and roiled, full of hatred and self-loathing as black and viscous as boiling tar.

"You were right to call me a monster, love," he whispered. "I *am* a monster. More terrible than the *vilest* beasts that haunt your nightmares." Tears of shame slipped down his cheeks, and he jerked his head toward the door, no longer caring if she saw him at his weakest. "So leave me, Charlotte D'Amico. *Please*. Get to your feet, put one foot in front of the other, and walk out of this manor before you live to regret the day the devil crossed your path."

Still, she didn't leave.

She climbed into his lap and took his face between her hands, her thumbs catching his tears, her mouth so close he felt the hot sweetness of her breath on his lips.

Dorian closed his eyes and shook his head, unable to bear the weight of her last goodbye.

All he wanted to do was kiss her.

It was more than he deserved, yet the thought of losing her nearly swallowed him, like some great hole opening up beneath him, plummeting him straight to hell.

"Look at me," she whispered.

Demanded.

Begged.

When he finally opened his eyes again, Charlotte smiled, her eyes filling at once with sadness and longing and hope, and there, beneath all the pain, burning hottest and brightest of all…

Love.

She brushed a soft kiss to his forehead, then whispered the words that finally shattered the chains inside, cracking Dorian's heart wide open, setting the broken pieces aflame.

"I love you, Dorian Redthorne. I *love* you. And if you think for *one* minute I'm walking out that door just because you told me to, you can fuck right off." She pressed a hot kiss to his lips, then smiled again, achingly beautiful, achingly real. "I choose option two."

CHAPTER THIRTY-ONE

Words.

Right ones, wrong ones, broken ones, it didn't matter.

Words had always been the hard part. But now, for Dorian and Charlotte, what came next was easy.

Here before the roaring fire in his favorite room in the manor, there *were* no words. Only Charlotte, the feel of her perfect mouth on Dorian's throat, her lips and tongue sending ripples of pleasure throughout his body.

He sat in his chair, relishing in her sweet explorations until the fire burned down to embers and a chill finally crept into the room.

Silently, he carried her to his bedroom, and after a blissful shower to wash away the last of the evening's brutalities, they slipped between the satin sheets of Dorian's bed, naked and vulnerable, stripped bare of everything but flesh and bone.

And still, neither of them spoke. It was as if they both understood they'd crossed into new territory, vast and unexplored. Neither wanted to shatter its pristine beauty with something as basic and limiting as human language.

Here, in this new world, they relied on pure instinct. Touch. Heat.

Charlotte spent a long, sinfully delicious hour exploring the newly visible network of his daylight tattoos with her mouth, kissing and licking, nipping and teasing, sending spasms of pleasure across nerves Dorian didn't even realize he possessed.

When it was his turn, he skimmed his mouth along her curves, drinking in every inch, unleashing soft moans that made him melt as surely as they made him hard. It was slow and sweet and perfect, a rare evening between them with no commands, no sexy games, no race to the finish line.

All of those things had their place, and Dorian had loved every red-hot experience they'd previously shared. And tomorrow, he was certain, they'd be right back to their old mind-blowing tricks.

But tonight was different.

Everything was different.

I love you, Dorian Redthorne. I love you...

Her voice echoed through his memory as he kissed his way down her throat, savoring the taste, sweeter in the wake of such confessions.

Charlotte slid her fingers into his hair, slowly urging

him toward her breasts. He grazed her nipple with his teeth, and she gasped, arching closer, her hips undulating beneath him.

Heeding her body's seductive call, Dorian shifted between her thighs, teasing her with the tip of his cock. More than anything, he wanted to be inside her again, to fill her, to feel her shatter around him. But first, he needed to taste her.

He pulled away, and she cried out in desperate agony, but he knew how much she enjoyed his relentless teasing. From their first moments at the Salvatore, he'd learned to decipher her body's signals—to know when she needed it hot and hard and fast, or when she wanted to be teased.

Right now, she wanted option two.

Blazing a trail of hot, wet kisses down her stomach, Dorian worked his way lower, his head dipping between her thighs, hands sliding up to spread her wide. He ran his tongue over every delectable curve, slowly taking his fill, inhaling her scent.

Bloody hell, he loved eating that pussy.

He craved it like a drug—one in which she was more than willing to indulge him.

He licked her again, and Charlotte sighed, fisting his hair and pulling him closer as he kissed her hot flesh. Beneath the demanding pressure of his hands, she spread herself even wider, and Dorian blew a soft breath over her clit, stroking her with the tip of his tongue, tracing every inch with slow, delicious precision.

Her muscles began to tremble, and he knew she was getting close—his favorite fucking part. Without warning, he gripped her thighs and crushed his lips against her clit, kissing and sucking, swirling his tongue as she writhed beneath him.

But no matter how badly he wanted to grant her this exquisite release, he couldn't let her come alone. Not tonight. He wanted to see it in her eyes, wanted them to collapse into that wonderful oblivion together.

And he was already so fucking hard, so fucking close.

At the last possible moment, he pulled back, dragging his mouth along her thigh, her belly, kissing his way up toward her lush mouth.

Silently, she reached for him, welcoming him back with a dazzling smile and a deep kiss, filling his mouth with a delicate moan.

She parted her thighs and arched her hips, and he slid inside her with a long, slow thrust, her body clenching around him, drawing him deeper until he filled her completely.

With every thrust, they found their perfect rhythm, Charlotte's gaze fierce and unwavering as their bodies drew together and apart, again and again and again, their skin slick with sweat, mouths hot and eager as they tasted and touched, pushed and pulled.

She ran her hands along his back, down to his ass, and clutched him hard, his fevered thrusts intensifying, everything inside her slippery and hot, driving him wild.

The trembling started in her thighs again, and Dorian knew she was right there—right *fucking* there.

"Dorian," she breathed, finally breaking their intense silence, her eyelids fluttering closed as the orgasm began to pull her under.

He wanted to let her go, to watch her drift off to that perfect place where nothing could hurt her, nothing could break her heart, even just for a moment. But before she let go completely, he cupped her face and whispered against her lips, bringing her back.

"Open your eyes, Charlotte." He brushed the hair from her face, his other hand finding hers beneath the sheets and holding it tight. "Stay with me, love."

She nodded, her heart thudding wildly beneath the press of his muscled chest.

"Stay with me," he whispered again, squeezing her hand like he never wanted to let her go.

Eyes wide open, locked in his intense gaze, Charlotte gasped, her body clenching around him, the wave cresting and breaking over them both as Dorian plunged inside her with a growl that rumbled from his chest, their mouths seeking a last, desperate kiss as they tumbled headlong into that final, bruising moment of pure ecstasy.

Minutes passed. Hours. Lifetimes. And when he finally pulled back and looked into her eyes once more, he knew.

She was his eternity. She was his forever.

Dorian's forever would almost certainly outlast hers, and perhaps that was his true curse—an immortal monster roaming the halls of Ravenswood, endlessly chasing her ghost long after she'd passed on.

Centuries. Eons. Millennia.

And still, in that moment, Dorian *knew*.

He would *never* love another.

"My heart is yours, Charlotte D'Amico," he whispered. "Tonight, and always."

CHAPTER THIRTY-TWO

Charley had no idea how they'd managed to stop time, but somehow, they had.

And for an entire Saturday, she floated on the clouds, suspended in a bubble of happiness that not even Rudy's irritating texts could pop.

Dorian spoiled her with breakfast in bed, followed by a long, languid hike through the woods. The day was bright and beautiful, no grays afoot in the sunshine, no traitor vampires lurking behind the trees.

They talked about the things they'd temporarily set aside last night—things they'd been setting aside for weeks. Dorian's brother's betrayal, the council meeting, the witch who'd come to Dorian's aid. Charley told him more about her father and uncle, the jobs she'd worked, her unconventional childhood. She hadn't yet told him about Rudy cutting her off, or her fears about losing her penthouse, but that was only because she knew he'd try to fix it for her, and she wasn't quite ready for that conversation.

There was still so much she didn't know about her vampire either—about his family, about old rifts, about why Colin was spending all his time in the crypts, about the darkest days of his life he'd only just begun to tell her about in the study last night.

But all of that would come, she trusted, in time—all part of the slow, delicious dive of falling in love, getting to know each other bit by bit, story by story, dream by dream.

Confession by confession.

In every way, it'd been a perfect day. A perfect evening.

But at some point in the middle of the night, the warm, solid weight of Dorian's body vanished from the bed and didn't return.

In his place, she found only a note.

Gone for a midnight snack. Sleep tight—be back soon.

Charley paced the circular drive, waiting for the infuriating vampire to return. She didn't want to text him—didn't want to be that girl, but *really*? A midnight snack? With a full pantry and fridge, Dorian decided to just pop on over to the convenience store for some chips and salsa? No way. He was definitely up to something, and she wouldn't rest until she figured out what.

After nearly an hour of incessant pacing, two sets of tell-tale headlights finally appeared in the drive.

Charley's breath left her in a hot rush—relief, mostly, followed by supreme irritation.

You are so *busted, Redthorne.*

She recognized Dorian's BMW at once. Aiden's Lexus SUV pulled in behind him, carrying an additional conspirator—a man she'd never seen before. When he exited the SUV, she got a better look—big and muscular, handsome in a rugged, outdoorsy sort of way. Despite the rough-around-the-edges exterior, he was dressed in a bespoke three-piece suit and carried some kind of gilded statue under his arm.

What the fuck?

"Charlotte? What are you doing awake?" Dorian stepped out of the BMW, forcing an innocent smile Charley could see right through. She knew that look. She *invented* that look.

"I was about to ask you the same thing," she said.

"You should wait inside, love." He leaned in and kissed her cheek, his mouth warm and soft in the chilly night. "It's not safe out here at night."

"Good evening, Ms. D'Amico," Aiden said, approaching with his mysterious friend. "How is Sasha?"

"She's good—she's in Vermont for the weekend. But she wanted me to tell you she's still holding you to your promise. She *really* wants to learn how to play chess."

Aiden grinned. "Next time you bring her round, it's a date."

"And who's your guest?" Charley asked, smiling at the newcomer.

"You must be Charlotte." The man returned her smile

with a warm, genuine grin that immediately put her at ease. "Feel like I already know you, considering Red here can't shut the fuck up about you for more than five seconds, pardon my French." He reached out to shake her hand. "Cole Diamante. *Charmed*. That's what you're supposed to say when you're wearing a monkey suit like this, right Red? *Charmed*?"

Dorian grumbled something indecipherable, but Charley was too captivated to ask him to repeat it.

"*Cole Diamante*," she breathed, her smile stretching so wide it hurt her cheeks. "Oh my God. I'm a *huge* fan of your work. Not just your landscapes, but your portraits and still life—all of it. I'm… Wow. It's an honor to meet you, sir. I'm… I don't even know what to say."

Cole laughed. "Oh, I like her already, Red."

"Yes, and apparently she likes you too." Dorian wrapped a possessive arm around her shoulder. "Perhaps you can ask for his autograph, love. Better yet, a studio tour."

"I'd rather see his lioness, *Red*," she said, finally realizing what Cole had been cradling in his arm.

Why the hell is he carrying around an ancient Egyptian artifact as if it were a case of beer?

Fangirl moment aside, the whole night had taken a *very* strange turn, and despite all the friendly banter, Charley couldn't shake the feeling these three co-conspirators were up to something big.

"All right boys." She popped her hands on her hips. "Spill it."

The three of them looked at her with sheepish, guilt-ridden faces.

Charley held out her arms for the statue, and Cole handed it over without protest.

She inspected it carefully—the head of a lioness, the body of a woman. The base was carved with hieroglyphs—spells to aid the royal deceased through his underworld journey.

Charley was shocked. Even in the darkness, she could tell it was the real deal.

"Where did you get this?" she demanded. But then, before any of them could respond, the pieces clicked into place. "*Shit*. You made contact with Vincent Estas."

Wisely, Dorian didn't deny it.

"How much?" she asked.

"Five hundred thousand," Dorian said. "Cash."

Charley let out a low whistle. "Personally, I wouldn't have paid a *quarter* of that, but to each his own."

"Do you recognize it?" he asked.

"Sure. It's Sekhmet." Despite the circumstances, she couldn't help but be awed by the beautiful carving, the gold overlay shimmering in the darkness as if it had its own life force. "Part of the vast Egyptian pantheon—a powerful goddess whose breath was said to cause the desert winds. I don't know much about the cult, but her bloodlust was legendary."

"I told you," Aiden said to Dorian. "She was practically the first vampire."

"Authentic?" Dorian asked.

"One hundred percent," Charley said. "This piece was discovered in the tomb of King Tut and was reported missing from the museum at Cairo in the seventies. Authorities believed one of the workers stole it, but they could never prove it."

"Cairo?" Dorian's brow furrowed. "I was hoping it was from the One Night Stand cache."

"Sorry to rain on your secret-mission parade, boys."

"But you said there were several statues of Sekhmet in that cache. Bronze, faience, gilded—"

"Do you know how many Egyptian antiquities are floating around on the black market?" Charley returned the statue to Cole, her frustration growing. "Hell, Dorian. You can buy a royal mummy if you know the right people. They used to eat them."

"Is that true?" Aiden asked.

Dorian scoffed. "Forgive me for not knowing the quote unquote *right people* in your vast underground network of criminals and thieves."

"You can really buy a mummy?" Aiden asked. "How much do they—"

Charley cut him off with a look that could shrivel his balls.

Dorian sighed. "Fine. It was a long shot, granted."

"You spent a half-million dollars on a long shot?" she asked. "I'm selling a bridge in Brooklyn if you're interested."

"I might be," he snapped, "if I thought for one *moment* it would help us nail the bastard who likely wants you and your sister dead, and—lest we forget—is working for the bloody demons, who likely want *all* of us dead."

Dorian's words found their target, piercing Charley's heart with stunning accuracy.

What could she say to that? He was right, and despite wracking her brain all week for information on Rudy, she hadn't been able to come up with anything particularly useful.

It wasn't surprising Dorian had made a move.

She just wished he'd trusted her enough to tell her about it first.

Now, fully taking in the sight of her for the first time since he'd pulled in the driveway—messy bun, leggings, a baggy sweatshirt she'd pilfered from his closet—Dorian said, "What are you doing out here, anyway? Did something happen?"

Silence fell between them, an eerie hush marred only by the crickets and the whisper of dried leaves. Suddenly, all of Charley's frustration faded, replaced by a deep sense of foreboding.

"I woke up, and you were gone," she said, the admission leaving her raw. "We said no more secrets, and you snuck out anyway."

Aiden coughed, a gentle reminder they still had an audience, but Charley no longer cared.

"We arranged the meeting days ago," Dorian said. "I thought if we could get a foot in the door with Estas, we might be able to track down some relevant intel about your uncle's involvement with Rogozin. We're running out of time, love. I'm not sure what else to do."

He was right. They *were* running out of time. And his instincts to go through Estas were good; Charley just wasn't sure making clandestine art deals was the right approach.

She took a deep breath, steadying her frayed nerves.

Her feelings about Dorian, the complications, the what-ifs... All of that had to take a backseat to the urgent reality confronting her.

For whatever reason, fate had seen fit to bring her and Dorian together. And now, it seemed their dark paths were converging as well—Rudy, the planned heist, the demon connection, Duchanes, all of it.

She and Dorian were in this together—along with Aiden, Cole, and Dorian's brothers—and they needed a solid plan.

"You can buy up all the art you want," Charley said. "The whole seventy-million-dollar cache—or what's left of it. But that's not going to help us, Dorian. It's only going to make you go broke, and—"

"Seventy million? Not likely."

"*And,*" she said, "you're putting your life at risk. All of you. I can't let you do that. Not for me."

"We've made our choices," Dorian said, and Cole and Aiden nodded.

"Dorian." Charley shook her head, grateful for the anger rising up again. She needed it to fuel her, to make her strong in the presence of the man whose touch had the power to melt her every defense. "This is *ridiculous*. You guys are sneaking out in the middle of the night with a suitcase full of money like it's all some epic caper you can laugh about over drinks later. If your theories about my uncle are on point, then these are *demons* we're talking about. Demons who can very easily kill you."

"You should've considered that before you asked for my help," Dorian said.

"I never meant for you to go behind my back and make contact. We're supposed to be in this together. And now you're—"

"Oh, for fuck's sake." Aiden's voice shattered the calm night. "You *are* in this together. He's bloody well in love with you. And you obviously think he's the dog's bollocks, so let's say we cut short this little quarrel, I'll take Cole home, you two can run along upstairs and have a good shag, and we'll all meet up for brunch tomorrow in the kitchen."

Dorian pinched the bridge of his nose, sighing into his hand. "Thank you, Aiden. You've got us all sorted now."

Heat rushed to Charley's face in the wake of Aiden's blunt assessment and Cole's quiet snicker, but she pressed on.

"Estas *is* the right call," she said. "But if we want a real shot at finding dirt on Rudy, we need to know where Estas lives. There might be something there—pictures, account numbers, computer files, some kind of paper trail." Charley thumbed toward Cole, who was still cradling the $500,000 mistake. "Sekhmet here will make a fine addition to your collection, but I'm afraid she can't help us. We need an address."

"Smashing!" Aiden said, beaming at them. "I've got the address. Shall we go, then?"

Charley and Dorian both gaped at him.

Aiden laughed. "Do you honestly think I'd agree to this —what did you call it? Epic caper?—without running a thorough background check on the man? Demon or not, he's got human records. Let's see... Primary residence just across the river. Owns a commercial space on Fifth Avenue that's currently being renovated. Where do we start?"

"Aiden, you're a genius," Dorian said.

"Yes. I am. And remember, nothing says 'thank you' like a raise."

"Take the lioness," Dorian said. Then, to Charley, "Okay, we've got the address. So how do we get the evidence?"

"That's the easy part." Charley arched an eyebrow, her smile turning mischievous. "We break in, and we steal it."

But Dorian didn't share her sudden enthusiasm. His jaw clenched, his eyes turning cold and resolute. "You're talking about breaking and entering into the home of a demon. Absolutely not."

"Why not?" she asked. "Does he live in hell?"

"Woodstock, actually," Aiden said.

"Is his house some kind of crazy supernatural lair that turns mere humans into dust?"

"*Charlotte,*" Dorian warned. "You—"

"Don't you *Charlotte* me, Dorian Redthorne." She jabbed a finger into his chest. "You may know your way around the supernatural realm, but when it comes to a good ol' fashioned smash-and-grab? That's *my* area of expertise."

"Quite a little spitfire you got there," Cole said to Dorian. "This woman's gonna get you into trouble. The good kind."

"You don't say." Dorian swept her into his arms, a spark of humor glinting in his eyes as he backed her up against his BMW.

Aiden mumbled something about reconvening tomorrow morning to make a plan for the break-in, but Charley was barely listening, already losing herself in the pleasure of Dorian's kiss.

The other men headed back toward Aiden's SUV, and Dorian shifted his mouth to Charley's ear, whispering a hot warning against her skin. "I should bend you over this car right now and have my way with you. *That* will teach you not to leave the manor after dark."

Charley laughed. "You're a naughty vampire, Mr. Redthorne."

"Don't tell me you're suddenly taking issue with fucking in public places." He lifted her, setting her on top of the hood and guiding her thighs around his hips. "As I recall, that's precisely how we met."

"Your driveway isn't exactly public, but... Fair point." She cocked her head and tapped her lips. "What are you proposing, vampire?"

"Shall I draw you a sketch, then?"

"I'm much better with hands-on learning." She tightened her thighs around his hips and pulled him close, eager for another kiss—for whatever filthy, exquisite fun he had in mind.

But just as his lips brushed her mouth again, the phone buzzed in her pocket.

"I'm vibrating," she said.

"Me too, love," he whispered.

"No—my phone. Someone's texting me."

"Leave it," he said, kissing a path to her neck. Between her thighs, he was already growing hard for her.

But Charley's gut tightened with worry. Aside from Dorian, there were only two people who regularly texted her—Sasha and Rudy. She couldn't risk missing a text from either of them, especially at this hour.

"Just... one sec." She put a hand on Dorian's chest and reached down to retrieve her phone.

It wasn't Rudy.

A shot of raw adrenaline flooded her veins, and Charley hopped off the car, heart leaping into her throat.

"Charlotte?" Dorian asked.

"My sister's in trouble."

"I thought she was in Vermont?"

"So did I." With a trembling hand, she held up the phone to show Dorian the text.

Emergency. In trouble. Meet @ Perk ASAP. Back entrance. Come alone no matter what, Charlotte!

"Bloody hell. *Aiden!*" Dorian flagged him down just as Aiden was pulling out. The SUV came to an abrupt stop, and Dorian wrenched open the back door, waving Charley inside.

"What's wrong?" Aiden asked.

"Sasha's in trouble." Dorian climbed in after Charley and slammed the door. "We need to get to Manhattan —now."

Without another word, Aiden shot out of the driveway, hit the main road, and floored it.

CHAPTER THIRTY-THREE

Aiden sped toward the city, but the clunky SUV was not Dorian's Ferrari, no matter how hard he pushed.

Charlotte was silent in the backseat beside him, chewing her thumbnail, her knee bouncing as she frantically tried to call her sister. Dorian reached over to give her a reassuring squeeze, but he couldn't stop her fretting.

"Everything will be okay," he said softly.

He believed it. He needed Charlotte to believe it too.

Sasha was smart and resourceful—just as tough as her big sister. They'd get to her soon enough, figure this out, and then he'd bring both women back to Ravenswood permanently. No more free rein in the city, no more unplanned road trips. He didn't care what Charlotte needed to tell her uncle to keep up the ruse. He only cared that she and her sister were safe.

"Everything will be okay," he said again.

"How can you say that?" Charlotte snapped. She had

her phone in a death grip, but Sasha hadn't responded to any of her calls or texts. "I have no idea what's going on. Sasha's probably freaking out. Aiden, can't you go any faster?"

"I'm trying," he said, but there was nothing he could do. Eighty was about the limit on this beast, and FDR Drive was always a crapshoot. Aiden finally made it to the exit, but the moment they hit Ninety-Sixth Street in Manhattan, a wall of brake lights appeared ahead.

"For fuck's sake." Aiden eased them into a stop. "What now?"

Dorian opened his window and leaned out to see what was going on.

His stomach dropped.

Several NYPD cars blocked the intersection ahead, attempting to redirect traffic. On the sidewalk, they were just starting to set up barricades, clearing away a rapidly gathering crowd of onlookers.

"What's happening?" Charlotte asked, opening the window and craning her neck to get a better view.

A fire engine roared past them, followed by two ambulances and a fire chief's SUV.

"Looks like a fire," Dorian said.

Two military vehicles came next, followed by a S.W.A.T. van.

"Or... not," Aiden said. "Sometimes I *really* hate this city."

"Shit." Charlotte pounded her fist against her thigh. "Shit, shit, shit!"

They were at a complete standstill, boxed in from all sides, nowhere to drive. Up ahead, two cops walked down from the main intersection with police dogs. Two more followed behind them, holding poles with mirrors attached to the ends. It looked like they were stopping at each car, checking out the undercarriages, talking to the drivers.

"They're looking for someone," Dorian said. "Or something."

"I can't stay here." Charlotte unbuckled her seat belt. "They want those dogs to sniff everyone's ass for drugs or bombs? Fine. But I need to get to my sister."

"Charlotte," Dorian said. "Try to relax. We'll get through this snag and—"

"*You* relax. My sister needs me. Now."

"We'll get to her as soon as we possibly can," Dorian said. His insides churned with worry and frustration, but he kept his voice calm. "Let's just—"

"I'm going on foot." Charlotte pushed open the door, but Dorian caught her arm.

"Wait," he pleaded. "We'll cut across town as soon as we reach the next block."

"Do you see this mess?" Charlotte gestured out the windshield, the cars in front of them deadlocked, police presence rapidly increasing. Construction on the other side of the street wasn't helping matters, either. "We're going nowhere in this."

"She's right, mate," Aiden said. "You two need to go. Now. Cole and I will meet you at Perk once we get through this shit."

Dorian clapped him on the shoulder, then climbed out of the car with Charlotte. They hadn't even taken a step when one of the cops jogged over, hand on his gun.

"Hey, hey, *hey!*" He shouted at them. "Back in the car."

"What's going on?" Dorian asked.

"Just another day in fuckin' paradise," the cop dead-panned. "You can read all about it in the morning papers. Now, get back in the car."

"Actually, we're going to leave, and you're going to turn around and forget you ever saw us." Dorian smiled at the cop, hitting him with a deep wave of compulsion until the man could no longer remember why he'd harassed them in the first place.

Then, without a second to lose, he wrapped Charlotte in his arms and blurred them down Park Avenue, leaving fuckin' paradise behind.

Dorian stopped on Park and Eighty-Third Street, just a couple of blocks from the coffee shop. Now that they'd passed the police mess, this part of the street was desolate, the high-end shops and restaurants closed for the night, the foot traffic almost non-existent at this late hour.

"What are we doing?" Charlotte asked, breathless after the blur. "It's… it's this way!"

She turned to bolt, but Dorian grabbed her arm.

"Charlotte, wait. Listen to me. Whatever's going on, it's almost certainly a trap. Sasha said for you to come alone."

"Of course it's a trap, but we can't just leave her there."

"No. But we also can't just charge in without—"

"Dorian!" Charlotte's eyes widened. "Behind you!"

He spun around just in time to catch two vampires blurring into view, trailed by a demon.

Two members of House Duchanes and a Rogozin half-wit.

Bloody fucking hell.

"Charlotte?" Dorian glanced at her over his shoulder. *"Run."*

"But you—"

"Get to your sister," he ordered. "I'll be right behind you." Then, as the dark hunger swept over him and the fangs sliced through his gums, he shot her one last wicked grin. "Just as soon as I finish my snack."

CHAPTER THIRTY-FOUR

The night was black and sinister as Charley approached the wide alley that led to Perk's delivery entrance, her nerves raw, her eyes alert.

The vampires and demon had paid her no mind as she'd made her quick escape. Those assholes only had eyes for Dorian, and those assholes didn't stand a chance. Two sickly looking vampires and a raggedy-ass demon against the Redthorne King? Yeah, good luck.

At least, that's what she told herself as she crept toward the café.

Dorian could take care of himself. He *had* to.

Right now, she had to get to Sasha.

In the distance, a clunky street-sweeping truck whooshed along the avenue like a damn freight train. But back here, long before the morning deliveries were set to arrive, the alley was quiet, dark, and deserted.

Charley's instincts were screaming at her to get out of

there. Dorian was right—the whole setup *screamed* trap, but what choice did she have? Two hours had already passed since Sasha's text. There was no time for fear or second-guessing.

Cell phone in hand, she moved further into the darkness.

Up ahead she saw the delivery doorway, dim and abandoned. Just outside the door, someone had knocked over a big plastic trashcan, its contents spilling all over the pavement.

Fighting to keep her voice steady, she called out for her sister. "Sasha? You out here? Sash?"

Bad idea, bad idea, bad idea…

A skittering noise behind the trashcan made her jump, but in the dim light of the alley she saw only shadows.

Probably just a rat.

Charley thumbed back to her sister's text, wondering if she'd missed something.

Emergency. In trouble. Meet @ Perk ASAP. Back entrance. Come alone no matter what, Charlotte!

Charley had sent a dozen urgent texts in response, but Sasha never replied.

But wait…

Holy. Shit.

Charley's heart nearly stopped. Only now did she see what she'd missed before.

Come alone no matter what, Charlotte!

Sasha *never* called Charley by her full name. Which meant someone else had sent the text.

Charley's body went rigid, her muscles tensing as she slowly turned around, scanning her surroundings.

Something crunched in the darkness, like wheels rolling over crushed glass.

Charley crouched down low.

Too late, she noticed the limo, black and sleek, no headlights.

Too late, she felt the hand clamp roughly over her mouth.

Too late, she felt the impossibly strong arms hauling her up and sweeping her feet out from under her.

Too late, her phone clattered to the ground.

Too late, she remembered Dorian's Midnight Marauder lessons—*a direct hit to the knee, a stomp to the foot, take the most effective shot.*

She was paralyzed with fear, unable to hit any of those targets as the man dragged her toward the limo and tossed her into the backseat. He climbed in behind her and slammed the door shut, trapping her on the bench seat between his own bulky form and that of another man, faceless in the dark shadows.

Oh, hell no.

Survival instinct finally took over, and she thrashed and kicked for all she was worth. The shadowed man put his hands up to protect his face. Instead of gouging out an eye, she snagged his watch, popping the clasp. It fell from his wrist just as the other man yanked her backward by the hair.

The shadowed man leaned in close, his features coming

into sharp relief. "Good evening, Charlotte. Feeling feisty tonight, I see."

"Uncle... Rudy?" Charley gasped. It *was* Rudy... but it wasn't. Same hair, same suit, same threatening grin. But his eyes, cold and calculating on the best of days, were nothing more than black pits in a twisted face.

Charley's throat closed up, her legs thrashing again as she tried to get away from him.

But the other man tightened his grip on her hair, making her eyes water. "Stop fighting, bitch."

Rudy bent down to retrieve his watch. The moment he fastened it back in place, his eyes returned to normal.

"Jesus *fuck*," Charley breathed. She had no idea what that watch magic was all about, but one thing had just become painfully clear.

Her uncle wasn't just *working* for the demons. He *was* a fucking demon.

"Language, Charlotte. Honestly." Rudy rolled his now-human eyes. Then, nodding at the other man, "Do it."

Before Charley had time to wonder what "it" meant, the dude released her hair and gripped her shoulders.

"You didn't see anything strange," he said smoothly, staring deep into her eyes. "Just your uncle Rudy and his associate, here for a little chat."

An uncomfortable pressure built up inside her head, as if some invisible force was trying to push its way in.

Vampire, her intuition whispered. *He's trying to compel you, girl.*

"Everything is fine," the man said. "You're going to calm down, and you're going to answer our questions."

Charley forced herself to relax beneath his touch. She knew, thanks to Dorian, she couldn't be compelled. He'd said it was one of her many mysteries.

Right now, trapped in a limo with her demonic uncle and his crazy vampire sidekick, it was also her only advantage.

"I saw my uncle Rudy," she said, keeping her voice calm and steady. She looked at him with wide, dreamy eyes, willing her heart rate to slow down.

Answers, she told herself. *They only want answers.*

"Who is Dorian Redthorne?" the man asked her.

"He's our mark," she said evenly. "The CEO of Fierce-Connect. Owner of Ravenswood Manor in Annandale-on-Hudson."

"Is Dorian aware of your uncle's plans?"

"No. He thinks I'm in love with him. He's taking me to Hawaii. The heist can proceed as planned."

"Ask her about the sculpture," Rudy said, seemingly satisfied with her bullshit answers. "Ask her why it wasn't on the list."

Charley's chest tightened. A sculpture not on the list?

Had they found out she'd lied about the Hermes?

"Have you ever seen a sculpture at Ravenswood called Mother of Lost Souls?" the vampire asked. "It's a fertility goddess statue."

Charley wanted to cry with relief. At last—a question she didn't have to lie about. "I'm familiar with the piece, but I've never seen it there, and Dorian has never mentioned it."

"Fuck." Rudy tensed beside her. "Ask her again, Silas."

Silas. Charley made a mental note of the name. She wondered if he was from House Duchanes, or some other despicable family Dorian would be burning to the ground later.

Dorian. Where *was* he? He should've been done with those other vamps by now.

A new worry worked its way into her chest, but Charley pushed it aside, forcing herself to stay focused. She couldn't lose her shit now. She needed these assholes to believe they had the upper hand.

The vampire tightened his grip on her shoulders. "Think very carefully, Charlotte. Mother of Lost Souls. It's a statue of a pregnant woman with the head of a demon."

Charley shook her head. "It's not there. Like I said, I know the piece. I would've remembered seeing it."

Finally, the asshole released her.

Charley wasn't sure how long compulsion was supposed to last, so as she turned back toward her uncle, she did her best to appear a little dazed.

"Rudy?" she asked, blinking fast. "What's... Why are you here? Little late for a cappuccino, don't you think?"

Rudy laughed, his whole body shaking with exaggerated effort. Metal glinted in his hands.

That fucking gun.

This time, Charley was pretty sure it was loaded.

335

She swallowed hard, and her uncle—the demon —grinned.

As if the vampire weren't enough of a threat, the dickless demon needed a gun too. Charley didn't know a lot about demonic powers, but she was pretty sure they didn't need guns to defend themselves.

Which meant Rudy was either torturing her for fun... or he was the demonic equivalent of impotent.

"Do... do you know where my sister is?" she asked, trying to sound properly cowed. "I was supposed to meet her here, but she didn't show."

Rudy narrowed his eyes, laughter and malice dancing behind his gaze, but he didn't respond.

She'd never wished so hard for his death.

Seconds ticked by like hours.

Finally, he frowned and said, "Do you know the most heartbreaking thing about the One Night Stand job?"

The One Night Stand job? Now *he was bringing that up?*

Charley shuddered. Whatever her cruel fate tonight, she wished Rudy would get to the point, not drag her down memory lane.

For *months* after her father's death, she'd wanted nothing more than to talk about this, but Rudy forbade it. Now, five years later, she was no longer interested in his thoughts—not unless he was ready to confess to murdering her father.

"No," she said. "But I really need to find Sasha, so..." She turned to reach for the door handle, but the vampire beside her wouldn't budge.

"It was supposed to be his last job," Rudy continued. "None of us wanted that—he was far too talented a thief for an early retirement. But there was his precious little girl to consider, wasn't there?" Rudy reached for her face, but Charley flinched away. "He wanted you to have a normal life."

Rudy was probably lying, but even so, the idea filled her with regret.

Had her father really intended to leave the game?

"After the job," Rudy said, "he was planning to take his share and get you out of the country. Start over somewhere new. Of course, I had no idea he was planning to double-cross us. In the end, I suppose it didn't turn out well for either of you."

"Please," Charley said, keeping her tone meek. Rudy needed to believe he had a lot more power over her than he did—that she'd never do anything to betray him. Every second that passed was another second Sasha—and now possibly Dorian—was in more danger. She needed to get the fuck out of there. "I... I need to leave. I'm supposed to meet my sister."

"Sorry," Silas said. "She can't make it tonight."

Without thinking, Charley swung at him, but he dodged her easily. In a blur, he dragged her across the small space to the bench seat that faced them and shoved her up against the door, pressing his forearm across her throat.

"I say we end this bitch right here," Silas said.

"Easy, Silas," Rudy warned. "She's not ours to end. Remember?"

Not theirs to end? What the fuck does that *mean?*

Charley struggled against the vampire's impossible hold. Silas removed his arm from her throat, but as soon as she sucked in her next breath, he hit her again, shoving her face into the window. "Sasha's tied up at the moment. Sorry you didn't get the message."

Charley tasted blood. She forced herself to take a deep breath.

Stay focused. He's lying. Play it cool, and eventually Rudy will tire of the games and let you go. Sasha is fine. She's fine. And so is Dorian. And Aiden and Cole. Everyone is fucking fine...

Silas finally backed off.

"Do you know what they say about apples falling from trees, Charlotte?" Rudy asked.

Charley nodded, unable to take her eyes off the gun, the glint of it in the moonlight.

"It's just that I worry," he said. "What if you have the same plans for Sasha, whisking her off into the sunset and betraying us in the process?"

Charley's mouth hurt to form words, her lip split and bleeding, but she forced herself to speak. "Sasha doesn't even know about this. She has a life here. School, work, friends. I wouldn't take her away from—"

"Still, I don't think I'd be where I am today if I didn't consider all of the possibilities and take the necessary..." He raised the gun, aiming it at her head. "...precautions."

"Please, Rudy," she whispered, fear leaking into her voice. "Where's my sister? Is she in trouble?"

Silas laughed.

"Trouble?" Rudy asked. The ice in his tone chilled Charley to the core. "I suppose that depends on you, Charlotte."

Rudy nodded at Silas, who pulled a cell phone from his shirt pocket.

A cell phone with a pink-and-white striped cover that most certainly did *not* belong to the vampire goon.

He thumbed over the screen and read, in a high and mocking voice, "Come alone no matter what, Charlotte!"

Charley's whole body went limp, her heart sputtering to a stop.

They had Sasha's phone.

They had Sasha.

A demon and a vampire, and who knew what other monsters... They'd taken her sister.

Charley stuck a fist in her mouth, biting down to keep from vomiting. Tears stung her eyes, but she didn't feel the pain in her hand, even when she drew blood.

"She'll be well taken care of." Rudy finally lowered his gun. "Three meals a day, a shower, some books to keep her occupied. As long as you cooperate, and our Ravenswood job goes off without a hitch, you'll be reunited soon enough."

The interior of the limo spun before Charley's eyes. The whole world was tipping on its side, leaving her scrambling for purchase on a slippery slope, nothing beneath her but a bottomless pit.

"Don't... don't kill her, Rudy," she whispered. "She's just a kid."

"Kill her? Aww." Rudy's voice was mocking, his eyes dancing with pure hatred. Reaching across to pat Charley's knee, he said, "I suppose we *could* kill her, but I don't think you'll let it come to that, will you?"

"What… what do you want?" Charley's voice was trembling and weak, but at that point, she didn't care. She wasn't acting. She wasn't manipulating them. This was real. Rudy had taken Sasha, and Charley would do whatever it took to get her back.

"Simple," Rudy said. "As long as the job goes off as expected, and we recover *all* the artwork we're looking for, I will personally deliver Sasha to your door the following weekend."

Charley swallowed her panic. "Rudy, please. Please! She's still just a kid. You can't keep her hostage and—"

"Relax, Charlotte. Enjoy your time in Hawaii with your billionaire boyfriend. When you and your sister are reunited, you can swap vacation stories."

"But I—"

Rudy cut her off with the wave of his hand, a signal that Silas interpreted as permission to hit her again. He shoved her against the window, fingers digging hard into her shoulder.

Charley was hot and dizzy, sweat trickling down her back, her mouth filling with the salt-and-copper taste of more blood.

"No more questions," Rudy said. "No more talking. We all have roles to play, just like your father had a role to play.

Just like Dorian Redthorne has a role to play. Even Sasha. I suggest you learn yours, Charlotte."

Rudy nodded at Silas.

"Time for a nap, bitch," the vampire said, wrapping an arm around her midsection like a vise. He opened the door and hauled her out into the alley.

"I'll be sure to give Sasha a goodnight kiss for you," Rudy called out, then closed the door. The limo didn't peel out of the alley—not like she expected it to. It simply rolled away, taillights glowing like vampire eyes as it drove off into the night.

Without warning, Silas grabbed her and blurred. When the world finally came back into focus, she was in a different alley, dark and unfamiliar and terrifying.

Before she could ask what the hell was going on, Silas lifted her over his head and threw her down into a dumpster. There wasn't much trash inside to cushion the blow, and she hit the bottom hard, the impact sending a sharp, lancing pain all the way up her arms and into her shoulders. Broken glass sliced her palms. Pinpricks of light swam before her eyes.

"Goodnight, bitch." Silas slammed the metal lid closed.

She hoped he was fucking gone.

She tried to sit up, but the world was spinning again, the darkness creeping in, blackening the edges of her vision.

In the distance, she heard another street-sweeper, a police siren, a group of drunk people laughing around the corner. Something skittered across the alley, and Charley tried not to think of a swarm of rats.

She didn't even know where she was.

Okay, girl. Step one—stop freaking out. Step two—get your ass out of this dumpster.

Mustering the last of her energy, she scrambled to her feet, popped open the heavy metal lid, and peered out through the gap.

Oh, fuck me.

Filling the alley, appearing so suddenly Charley knew it *had* to be a setup, a writhing mass of inhuman monsters stalked toward her.

She saw the outstretched hands, fingertips dripping with blood.

She saw the hungry mouths, the glassy eyes, the jagged fangs.

And in that brutal, terrible moment, Charley recognized her foes.

Fucking grays.

And they were heading straight for her.

She dropped the dumpster lid. Crouched back down in the corner. And grabbed the biggest shard of glass she could find, hoping like hell she wouldn't have to use it.

CHAPTER THIRTY-FIVE

"Where is she?!"

Dorian's furious roar echoed down Park Avenue, scaring the rats and the squatters alike out of their dark holes.

He was bloody *beside* himself. Those fucking vampires and their demon *stain* had waylaid him for far too long, and though he'd slaughtered them in the end, the victory had come at too great a cost.

He'd lost Charlotte.

All that remained of her was a cell phone, shattered on the ground in the alley behind Perk. There was no sign of Sasha, either.

"Find her!" he bellowed. "Find her, or I will demolish this *entire* city, brick by fucking brick until—"

"We *will*," Aiden said, placing a hand on Dorian's shoulder. Cole was several paces ahead of them on the sidewalk, frantically trying to pick up her scent. "But you need to calm down and focus, or you'll—"

"*Don't...*" He jerked free of Aiden's grip and whirled on him, intending to let loose another endless rant, but the moment he saw the concern in Aiden's eyes, all the breath rushed from his lungs.

"I'm sorry," Dorian said, his voice cracking. His heart shattering. His mind splintering into tiny fragments. "I'm falling apart, Aiden. The thought of losing her... I can't... Where *is* she?"

"Breathe, Dori. Please."

Dorian closed his eyes and took a deep breath, but it was no use. The fury boiled up again. He felt like he was going to explode.

He wanted to blur out of there, to kill someone, to find a nest of demons and eviscerate every last one. But he couldn't leave the city. He needed to walk, block by fucking block, inch by fucking inch, until he found his woman. His fucking heart.

"*Charlotte!*" he shouted into the night.

"Got her," Cole said suddenly. "This way."

They followed him down Seventy-Second, stopping at the mouth of a narrow service alley.

"She's right down..." Cole sucked in a sharp breath. "Oh, fuck your *mother.*"

Dorian followed his gaze, his heart damn near ready to pound out of his chest.

"And your mother's mother," Aiden added.

The alley was full of grays. Dozens upon dozens—more

than he could count at a quick scan. But they seemed subdued, or possibly sick. They milled around the alley like zombies, some of them scratching at the walls, some of them feeding on each other, others standing still as if they'd just run out of batteries.

But there, in the back of the alley, something had drawn their attention.

"Something in that dumpster's got 'em riled up." Cole shook his head as the grays shoved against the dumpster, looking for a way in. Some of them had climbed on top, but they couldn't open the lid. "I got a shit feeling about this."

"Are you sure she's here?" Aiden asked, unable to hide the worry in his voice.

"If she ain't here now," Cole said, "she was. Scent's still fresh."

"Charlotte!" Dorian called out, desperation and hope colliding with the fear and fury in his heart. The grays closest to them turned to look, but he didn't care. If she was here, he needed to get to her. Now.

If she's even alive...

"Charlotte!" he called again, forcing the thought from his mind. There was no room for it.

Bloody hell, woman. Where are you?

"Charlotte!" he repeated.

A small, muffled voice finally broke through, echoing across the sea of writhing grays. "Dorian?"

Dorian nearly fell to his knees. His name on her lips was a sonnet, a symphony.

"Charlotte," he breathed, the sound of her voice—however faint—giving him new life. "Where are you?"

"Trapped in the dumpster!" she called back.

"Stay put," Dorian said, scanning the mob of grays again. "We're coming for you."

Fucking hell, there were a lot of them. Too many to blur through.

They were going to have to fight.

Cole's words from that first night in the cabin echoed.

Blood and death, brother. Blood and death.

Dorian turned to his friends. "If anyone wants out, now is the—"

"See you on the other side, brothers." Cole shifted into his wolf form and charged ahead, taking down two grays in quick succession.

Aiden and Dorian exchanged a glance.

"Yes, and about that raise..." Aiden said.

"Fuck yourself, mate."

"Let's hope we live long enough for that."

And with that, Dorian and his best mate charged into the shit show.

As Dorian knew it would, the unprovoked assault put the beasts on the defense. It was as if someone had flipped the switch; all at once, they attacked.

Side by side with his friends, in a desperate bid to reach his woman, Dorian fought them off, dodging their vicious but uncoordinated attacks, ripping heads from bodies as if he were pulling weeds from the garden. More than half of them had the demon amulets, their bodies rising again almost as soon as they hit the ground.

How the fuck had so many managed to reach the city? And why were they all in a single location?

The question prodded the back of his mind, but Dorian didn't have time to ponder it. Right now, there was only the fight. Another head, another bloody heart, another amulet ripped from its cord, another pile of ash at his feet. The stench of so much rotten blood and gore nearly overwhelmed him. Yet all the while, the sight of that grimy black dumpster in the shadows was a lighthouse in the storm, keeping him on course.

Charlotte was in there.

She was alive.

Getting to her was *all* that mattered.

The fight had drawn the grays away from her, and Dorian didn't let up. Hours? Days? Time lost all meaning. He had a job to do, and he fucking did it—his arms burning, his body soaked with their foul blood, his eyes blurry—until the last gray in his sights turned to ash.

"Will you please fuck *off!*" Aiden shouted, and Dorian spun around just in time to watch him shove a metal pole through another gray's throat, then rip off its head.

That one wore no amulet, his body turning to ash before its head even hit the ground.

Certain that was the last one, Aiden dropped his weapon, the clang of the metal pole ringing out across the now quiet alley.

"Tell you one thing," Aiden said, leaning back against

the brick exterior to catch his breath. "These assholes are even more relentless than the pigeons in Times Square."

"And they taste a lot worse too," Cole said, dragging an arm across his bloody mouth. He'd just shifted back into his human form, naked and covered in gore, but unhurt.

A river of blood washed down the alley, mixing with the ashes of the dead into a bright red paste. Dorian tried not to slip on it as he picked his way toward the dumpster, heart thudding against his ribs.

Why was she so quiet?

"Charlotte?" he called softly.

No response.

A pulse of fear shot through his heart.

"Charlotte, love?"

Nothing.

The world tilted on its axis, nearly dumping him off.

No. She can't be...

Behind him, Cole and Aiden fell silent.

Terror shook him to his core, but Dorian forced himself to continue that long, agonizing march to the dumpster.

A familiar scent rose above the stench of the alley, sharp and sweet. Unique. His.

It was Charlotte's blood.

Fucking hell...

When he finally reached the dumpster, the scent of her blood nearly overpowered him. He wrapped his hands around the edge of the lid, closed his eyes, and made a wish. One fucking wish in his entire immortal life. This was all he wanted—all he'd ever ask for again.

Please, please let her be alive.

He shoved open the lid. And then, without looking, he hauled himself over the edge and dropped down inside.

The dumpster was mostly empty, but for a few bits of trash and broken bottles. And there, huddled in the corner, a small, dark lump.

Hot tears welled in his eyes, and he fell to his knees, afraid to call to her again. Afraid she wouldn't respond.

But he had to know.

He reached out and touched her shoulder.

The lump twitched, and she lifted her head, turning to meet his eyes in the darkness.

"Dorian?" She smiled faintly, a flower blooming in the trash.

"Bloody hell, woman." The breath rushed from his lungs, kickstarting that slab of meat in his chest. Ignoring the blood covering his body, he scooped her into his arms and got to his feet, drawing her close. "I've got you now, love. And I'm not letting you go."

CHAPTER THIRTY-SIX

Charley should have felt the needle.

She should've winced at the pain, but instead she was numb, sitting on a stool in the overly bright Ravenswood kitchen while Colin stitched up the cut inside her lower lip.

All of them had offered to heal her with vampire blood, but she was too afraid to try it, certain she was close enough to death that vampire blood would turn her.

Both of her hands were bandaged, and someone had stripped off her clothes and put her in one of Dorian's oversized white T-shirts, but she didn't remember it happening. Vaguely, she was aware of Dorian standing behind her, his strong hands gently rubbing her back as Colin finished his work.

There was a woman too. Isabelle—the witch who'd helped Dorian. He must've called her, but Charley didn't remember that either. She'd been trying to do a tracking spell to locate Sasha, but without one of Sasha's possessions on hand, she wasn't having much luck.

Dorian's touch was warm, but despite his calm demeanor, he was nervous; Charley could feel the slight tremble in his fingers. Somehow, he'd gotten to her in time. He'd dragged her out of that dumpster and carried her away from the clutches of something dark and evil—something she'd felt so certain was coming for her.

If those grays had been able to get into the dumpster...

She closed her eyes, willing away the images of their bloody fingertips shoving through the gap, the sounds of their hoarse moans echoing across the alley.

She'd been saved. That's what mattered.

The thought should've brought her a measure of relief.

But every kind word, every gentle touch, every concerned look... It only made her feel worse.

Charley glanced down at her hands. The white bandages around her palms were stark against her red, raw skin. She wanted to scream.

These were the hands that couldn't save my sister.

At her fresh tears, Colin assured her he was almost finished. But like Dorian's gentle touch, his brother's words couldn't comfort her. They couldn't bring Sasha back from the monsters who'd taken her.

"All set," he finally said, packing up his medical supplies. He turned to Dorian and rattled off instructions for caring for Charley's wounds—something about checking on her every hour at night. She should've been listening more attentively, but she couldn't focus.

And then Colin was gone, leaving her alone in the kitchen with Dorian. Her vampire. The man who saved her. The man she loved.

The man she didn't deserve.

"How do you feel?" Dorian asked.

Charley ran her tongue along the inside of her lip, wincing when she hit the stitches. Her head throbbed, and beneath the bandages, her palms stung. She vaguely remembered Colin flushing out her cuts with something that smelled like a hospital and burned like hell.

Her own uncle had done this to her. He'd kidnapped her sister. He was...

Oh, God.

"Rudy's a demon," she whispered.

"I know, love. You told me. We're going to figure this out. Gabriel's working on it—Cole and Aiden too. All of us. We won't rest until Sasha's safe and your uncle is..."

Charley nodded, the rest of the words unnecessary.

Dead. On fire. Tortured. Banished to hell.

Whatever got the job done.

Fear reached into Charley's chest again, squeezing her heart as Rudy's threats echoed through her mind.

She'll be well taken care of... As long as you cooperate... you'll be reunited...

He'd promised to return Sasha to Charley after the heist, but she knew better than to believe him.

He was a fucking *demon*.

A shudder wracked her limbs.

I have to find my sister. Now.

She hopped up from the kitchen stool, but the sudden movement made her swoon.

"Easy," Dorian said, steadying her.

She lowered herself back to the stool and closed her eyes.

"Sasha," she whispered. "They took her. Did you see them drive off?"

"No." Dorian stroked her cheek. "We found you in a different alley altogether."

He told her the story, but she suspected it wasn't the first time she'd heard it. Her mind was so hazy. Her uncle, the demon eyes, the grays...

All of it was blurring together.

"Silas," she blurted out. "That was the vampire with Rudy. He tried to compel me."

Dorian pressed a kiss to her forehead, his lips lingering for an eternity.

Charley grabbed his hand and held it to her cheek, slowly shaking her head. "I don't remember everything. Why don't I remember?"

"Shock, most likely," Dorian said. "But Isabelle and Colin have both assured me you're going to be okay. Just a little banged up is all. We need to watch you for any symptoms of concussion."

Concussion? It seemed so minor, so insignificant compared to what Sasha was going through.

"But my sister—"

"We'll get her back, Charlotte." Dorian pressed his lips to her forehead again, his kiss as gentle as his voice. "You

353

need to rest tonight. Can you do that for me? Let me work on this while you—"

"No. No way." Charley tried to stand again, but Dorian put his hands on her shoulders, holding her in place. She looked up at him through watery eyes, every muscle screaming in protest. The pain didn't matter, though. Charley felt like a mother bear, overcome with a fierce need to find her sister. "I have to go to Rudy's place. I have to get to him and—"

"And do what?" Dorian asked. The gentleness evaporated from his voice, anger taking its place. "He's a violent psychopath and a demon, for fuck's sake. And right now, he's holding all the cards. He's using your sister as bait. He wants you out of the way, Charlotte, and if you think he won't finish the job he started tonight…"

Dorian's voice broke at the end, and when Charley met his eyes again, she saw her own fear reflected right back at her.

She pressed her bandaged palms to her temples. "I have to try. I can't just stay here and… and do nothing while she… and I'm… and the heist is… and…" Charley tasted blood in her mouth again, another cut that wasn't deep enough for stitches but still stung like a bitch.

Fuck.

She was being ridiculous. She couldn't even stand up, let alone face off with the demon who'd done this to her. She had no fight left—not tonight. She could barely breathe.

Charley felt like a child stuck in a nightmare, crying out for a mother who would never come.

"I thought I'd lost you," Dorian whispered. He bent down and gathered her in his arms, pulling her to his chest in a suffocating embrace. "Nothing else matters but you and Sasha."

"But—"

"*Nothing*, Charlotte." He pulled back and met her eyes, the intensity of his gaze leaving no room for argument. "When I tell you we're going to figure this out, I mean it. We're going to get your sister back, and we're going to make sure that bastard never hurts either of you—or anyone else—again. Do you trust me?"

Do you trust me?

They were only four little words—words Charley should've been asking Dorian, not the other way around. But now she was locked in his unrelenting gaze, his honey-brown eyes seeing right through her, stripping her down to the core.

She was vulnerable and scared, ashamed of everything she'd done to bring this situation to his doorstep, but when he looked at her like that—like he believed in her, like he had total faith in her ability to get through this or anything else, like he loved her—she felt strong, somehow. Capable. Wanted. Cared for. Unstoppable.

Forgiven.

Charley's heart expanded in her chest, and the moment felt suddenly huge and all-encompassing.

The question...

Dorian's intense eyes...

Those four little words...

They weren't just talking about getting her sister back.

Charley blew out a breath.

She'd never, ever trusted a man before—not like this. She'd learned that lesson early on, and though she'd regretfully and stupidly allowed her life to be dictated and controlled by men for decades, she'd never *trusted* them.

But Dorian wasn't those men. He was a vampire. He was a king. He was strong and honest. Sincere. Protective. Even after everything she'd put him through—all the lies, the trickery, the games—Dorian Redthorne hadn't run away. He hadn't turned her in to the police, or threatened her, or twisted her weaknesses into something he could use against her for his own gain.

Whatever had happened between them, whatever she'd done to betray him, Dorian Redthorne had come back for her. He loved her. He was *here*. Now. Right by her side. And one look into his eyes told her that he wasn't going anywhere—no matter what.

"I trust you," she whispered, and those three little words from the bottom of her heart paved the way for the next ones. "You have my heart, Dorian Redthorne. Tonight, and always."

They were the same words he'd said to her last night, but only now did she truly understand the depth of their meaning.

Loving someone... That was easy by comparison. But giving someone your heart? Freely, without strings, without expectations? It was exhilarating and terrifying, like jumping off a cliff and having no idea what awaited you at the bottom. No idea if there even *was* a bottom.

But you took the risk anyway, because you knew—you *knew* it was worth it.

Charley smiled, and then closed her eyes, her body slumping forward with exhaustion.

Dorian caught her against his chest, resting his chin on the top of her head.

"Ah, love," he said, so softly Charley wasn't sure she was meant to hear it. "What have you done to me?"

And then, for the second time that night, Dorian's strong arms encircled her, lifted her up, and carried her away to a better place.

CHAPTER THIRTY-SEVEN

"Isabelle? Is something wrong?"

Dorian had just gotten Charlotte to bed, and now he returned to the study to retrieve a much-needed bottle of his favorite scotch. But instead, he found the witch pacing before the fireplace, her shoulders bent with the weight of bad news.

"I need to speak with you," she said urgently.

"Were you able to trace Sasha's location?"

"I'm still working on it, but this isn't about Sasha."

"Charlotte?" His chest squeezed tight. "But you and Colin said… She's fine, Isabelle. I've just gotten her settled. She's already feeling much better, and—"

"*Dorian.*"

Her sharp tone, the uncharacteristic use of his first name…

Dorian's blood turned to ice.

"May I speak plainly?" she asked.

"I'd prefer it."

Isabelle let out a deep sigh, then shook her head, as if she herself didn't want to believe whatever came next. "Charlotte... She's demon-touched."

"Demon... *what*?" He blinked at her, trying to follow. "What does that even mean?"

"It's a claim, essentially. I can sense it in her energy field."

"I still don't understand. Does this have something to do with your empathic gifts?"

"Yes. I read emotional energy, which comes through your heart, your mind, and your soul. Feelings, intentions, thought forms... I don't get specifics, as a mind reader might. Just general impressions. And with Charlotte, the energy of her soul is..." Isabelle frowned.

"Isabelle, you're mistaken."

Again, she shook her head. "There's no mistaking the mark of the demon-touched, Dorian. It's almost like a dark shadow—a mark on her soul. I'm sorry."

"What the bloody hell does that mean?"

"It means that at some point in her life Charlotte was promised to a demon lord. And judging from the strength of the mark, the end of her term is nearing. It won't be long now before he comes to collect."

Promised to a demon lord? It won't be long before he comes to collect?

Dorian shook with rage, his fangs descending, the familiar hunger rushing into his veins.

I'd like to see him try...

He glared at Isabelle, outrage turning his vision red.

"Why are you standing here blathering on about this?" he shouted. "Get rid of the bloody thing!"

"The mark is bound to her soul. If I so much as *attempt* to manipulate it, magically or otherwise, it will kill her. If she dies, her soul goes to hell, and her body becomes a demonic vessel. If she lives, her contract comes due, and the demon comes to claim her, to do with as he sees fit. There is *no* way out of this."

She took a step closer and placed a hand on Dorian's arm, her eyes full of a compassion he did *not* want to see. There was no need for such sentiments. Not in regard to Charlotte. This story about the demon mark... *No.* Dorian had never heard of such a thing.

He said all of this out loud, again and again, his mind spinning, searching for a way to tear the bloody heart out of this fucking nightmare.

Yet still, the witch looked at him, her eyes glassy in the firelight, unwavering in her relentless concern.

"This is her fate, Dorian. There's not a damn thing you or I or anyone else can do to save her." Isabelle reached up and touched his chest, a tear glittering on her cheek. "Charlotte D'Amico belongs to hell. I suggest you make peace with that and say your goodbyes."

It's not over yet! Dorian and Charley's story continues in Dark Obsession!

Charley and Dorian have found their way back to love, and there's nothing the vampire king won't do to protect his woman. But with enemies closing in on all sides and a demonic claim on Charley's soul, is their happily ever after even possible? Find out what happens next in **Dark Obsession, book three of the Vampire Royals of New York series!**

Vampire lovers! If you loved reading this story as much as I loved writing it, please help a girl out and **leave a review on Amazon!** Even a quick sentence or two about your favorite part can help other readers discover the book, and that makes me super happy!

If you really, *really* loved it, come hang out at our Facebook group, Sarah Piper's Sassy Witches. I'd love to see you there.

XOXO
Sarah

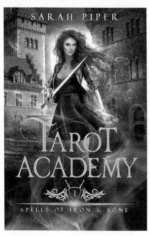

ABOUT SARAH PIPER

Sarah Piper is a Kindle All-Star winning urban fantasy and paranormal romance author. Through her signature brew of dark magic, heart-pounding suspense, and steamy romance, Sarah promises a sexy, supernatural escape into a world where the magic is real, the monsters are sinfully hot, and the witches always get their magically-ever-afters.

Her works include the newly released Vampire Royals of New York series, the Tarot Academy series, and The Witch's Rebels, a fan-favorite reverse harem urban fantasy series readers have dubbed "super sexy," "imaginative and original," "off-the-walls good," and "delightfully wicked in the best ways," a quote Sarah hopes will appear on her tombstone.

Originally from New York, Sarah now makes her home in northern Colorado with her husband (though that changes frequently) (the location, not the husband), where she spends her days sleeping like a vampire and her nights writing books, casting spells, gazing at the moon, playing with her ever-expanding collection of Tarot cards, binge-watching Supernatural (Team Dean!), and obsessing over the best way to brew a cup of tea.

You can find her online at SarahPiperBooks.com and in her Facebook readers group, Sarah Piper's Sassy Witches! If you're sassy, or if you need a little *more* sass in your life, or if you need more Dean Winchester gifs in your life (who doesn't?), come hang out!

Made in the USA
Middletown, DE
13 November 2020

23881340R00220